OFF DUTY

also by Andrew Coburn
The Trespassers
The Babysitter

OFF DUTY

By Andrew Coburn

W·W·NORTON & COMPANY
London · New York

Library of Congress Cataloging in Publication Data

Coburn, Andrew.
  Off duty.

  I. Title.
PZ4.C65840f [PS3553.O23]   813'.5'4   79–24670
ISBN 0–393–01369–3

1 2 3 4 5 6 7 8 9 0

For my wife,
Bernadine Casey Coburn,
and our friends, Bob and Mary Mascola.

CONTENTS

ACKNOWLEDGMENTS

Nicki Thiras, Atha Tehon, Joseph V. Mahoney, Bill Heath, Betsy Wise, Daphne Abeel, Chuck Townsend, Peter Skolnik and Starling Lawrence, for help past and present.

OFF DUTY

1.

BOSTON

Back in the endless winter of '78, Rupert Goetz said to Frank Chase, "You're doing the smart thing."

"You think so," Chase said, lifting a lean face.

"You look amused, Frank."

"Believe me, I'm not."

Goetz manipulated a knife and fork into the red remains of a tenderloin, while Chase slouched back, leaving most of his untouched. They had a window table in Newbury's steakhouse on Massachusetts Avenue. The window presented a fuzzy picture of floating snow and a brisk sidewalk crowd. It was midday and dark.

"A man leaves that much on his plate, Frank, means he's not worried about his next meal. Must make you feel good."

Cigarette smoke curled from Chase's immobile hand.

"You've got nothing to worry about," Goetz said, chewing vigorously.

"If we're talking only about Ida, I agree."

"The other thing too."

"Then I've got everything to worry about."

"No, you don't. You're making all the right moves. I'd tell you if you weren't. You're cool, Frank. The way a cop should be."

Chase shifted his gaze to the window and felt a chill from within. The chill came frequently, sometimes from a mild sense of shock when he thought about leaving the force and other times from hidden guilt when he considered the money, a hundred thousand dollars crushed into a green oversized shoe box. He refocused his gaze, glimpsing a blur of passersby.

Goetz said, "Lots of people watch the world go by. Not me. Not you either. That should make you feel good."

Chase shifted his position, sat straight, and felt a tingle in his back, the source of another chill. It was a puckered scar from an old knife wound that could have been fatal, the result of poor police procedure, Goetz's fault as much as his, though promotions had followed, not reprimands. And the wound had brought him weeks of tender loving care: Ida's.

Goetz leaned forward. "Frankie, nothing's going to go wrong for you."

"So let's not talk about it."

"Don't be touchy." Goetz pushed aside his empty plate. His dark suit, tailored to his muscular body, made him look more like an entrepreneur than a ranking police official. His graying blond hair was skull-tight, like a dried spill of paint, and his pale eyes were barely blue. His smile increased. "I understand you're moving to a swell town. A fancy prep school there. Maybe David could go to it, he gets old enough. I'd like that."

"Nothing's definite."

"Come on, Frank. You and Ida have already picked out a house. She told me."

"She told you too much."

"See! You are touchy."

Chase stared at a man and woman edging their way to the salad bar, the woman leading the man by the hand as if onto a dance floor. Goetz flung a hand up to catch a busy waitress's eye. A signal for two coffees.

"A question you could easily ask yourself, Rupert, is whether *you* are doing the smart thing."

Goetz grinned. "That, Frankie, is off limits."

"Why should it be?"

"Seniority and rank, simple as that."

"They don't hold any more."

"Sure they do. Things like that stick forever, you have my word on it."

Goetz took his coffee black, and Chase creamed and sugared his and then lit another cigarette. He looked younger than he was, no gray, no hard lines, a genetic gift. Slowly he went on the alert, feeling eyes on the back of his head, somebody near enough to touch him, and he spent several seconds studying Goetz's blank face for a clue. Finally Goetz laughed.

"You know something? You're good. Be a while before you lose that instinct. But you will, you know. No doubt about it. Will that bother you?"

Chase didn't answer. Turning deliberately in his chair, he regarded a young woman he had glimpsed many times in Goetz's presence but had met face to face only once before, their secret, though she may have forgotten it. Chase suspected otherwise. He nodded as she removed smoke-colored glasses and folded them away. Her smile was generous.

"My teenybopper. Help her off with her coat, Frank."

The smile turned indulgent. She was probably twenty-two now. Chase rose to help her out of a fur-collared storm coat he had seen before, when it was new, probably right out of the box. She had on a sleek cream-white shirt and jeans rolled to the top of her leather boots. Traces of snow glistened in her hair, which cascaded over her shoulders and down her back. Chase dropped the coat over an extra chair, and she slid into a chair between him and Goetz. Goetz gazed at her proudly.

"I can't remember. You two ever been introduced?"

Her smile was direct. "It would seem so," she said easily and for a calculating moment stared into Chase's eyes, challenging him. "Rupert says you're marrying Ida."

He flushed and was immediately angry at himself.

"It's not a secret, is it?"

"No." He studied her face for underlying expressions. The

face seemed at once exquisite and silly, a gorgeous blend, movie-star looks, with a body made for a short chemise. Chase felt detached, as if he belonged at another table, and silently cursed Goetz for not telling him that she was coming. Goetz, sipping coffee, gave out a tight smile.

"Frank's the serious sort."

"I can see that."

"He didn't eat his steak. How about you? Let me order you something."

"I've eaten."

"How about a drink?"

"Nothing." Her eyes, hazel a moment ago, were now green. They darted back to Chase. "So you're free?"

He did not understand at first. Then, instead of the chill, a small wave of depression touched over him. "Yes, as of next week."

"Will you miss it?"

"Hard to say."

"What will you do?"

Goetz winked, perhaps at Chase, perhaps at her. "I told him to go into real estate. Get a broker's license and hawk houses. Lot of money there, prices sky-high where this fellow's going."

"Where are you going?" she asked.

"Nothing's definite."

"Come on, Frank. You can tell her. He's moving twenty miles away to green grass and swimming pools. Nice, huh?"

Chase glanced away, one too many voices detonating in his ear. The young woman—her name was Sherry—peeled open a pack of Tareyton Lights and slowly tapped one loose. Goetz lit it for her.

She said, "Rupert and I are leaving for a long weekend, getting an early start."

She did not say where they were going, but her tone was lightly insinuating, as though certain adventures, both ordinary and extraordinary, were due her, part of a deal, the words written into a contract. Goetz gave her a private smile that seemed to seal it. Chase easily pictured her lying with bare breasts on a beach a few hundred air miles away, Goetz beside her in Tarzan tights. He felt vaguely like their travel agent.

"Maybe you should thank me."

Goetz gave him a guarded look. "Thank you? Sure, we'll thank you if you think we should."

Sherry said, "Thank you for what, Frank?"

"I was joking." He glanced at his watch, though no demands were on his time.

Goetz said, "You have to leave?"

"Yes."

He reached for money, but Goetz clamped a hand over the check. He rose with a parting nod at Sherry, who propped her chin and smiled, her cigarette smoke drifting up.

"Wait a minute."

Goetz was on his feet, for a last word, his lap shedding a soiled napkin that sailed into the aisle. They stood near a table of businessmen who were telling a few hard jokes, the punch lines private, the laughter ferocious. Goetz tilted his head toward Chase's.

"You ticked off about something?"

"I have no reason."

"That's right. None in the world."

Chase was silent. Goetz nudged him.

"You're getting a great woman. Think about that."

Chase's voice had an edge. "I don't have to think about it."

"So what's the matter?"

"Nothing, except the nagging suspicion it was too easy."

Goetz's blue eyes took on a cool antiseptic quality. "Some people don't like to be winners. You're not one of those guys, are you, Frank?"

Chase shrugged off the question as foolish.

"Good," Goetz said and slapped him on the shoulder. Then he dropped back into his chair. "Give my best to Ida."

Sherry, with a straight face, said, "Give her mine too."

Goetz drew the waitress's attention. Sitting back, he said, "We feel like cognac. We're celebrating." The waitress nodded and left. Goetz, cocking his head, watched her. "Who does she remind you of?" he said.

"The waitress?"

"Yuh."

"I don't know. Who?"

"Ida. I mean, just a little."

Sherry shook her head. "No, not at all." Then she lighted a fresh cigarette. She seemed quietly amused and somewhat adrift. Goetz watched her lips form words, but he failed to hear any. He pulled himself forward.

"What did you say?"

"I said it's almost incestuous, isn't it? You, me, him, her."

"Bother you?"

She leaned toward him as their cognacs arrived. "Kiss me," she said.

Frank Chase, hatless, felt the snow accumulating in his hair, large flakes, the intense start of a storm that was already bogging traffic on Massachusetts Avenue. The sidewalk was slippery, and people came at him in bursts, their heads lowered. He held his head high, a hand warming one ear, and searched for a public booth. The one he found was broken, the glass reflecting a debased copy of himself, but the phone worked. He called Ida.

"Do you still want to?"

She was silent for a second, disturbed. "Frank, that's a strange question."

"What are you doing?" he asked, suddenly wanting to change the subject.

"Is anything wrong?"

"No. What are you doing?"

"I was lying down," she said, and immediately the figure in the forefront of Picasso's "Three Bathers" came into his mind.

A reproduction left by the previous tenant hung in his apartment. "Frank, where are you calling from?"

"The cold. Meet me at my place. Can you?"

"Tell me what's wrong."

"Nothing. I love you."

"Something is the matter."

"No, nothing," he said. "I just want to hold you."

2.

ANDOVER

David stood still like a post among creeping shadows in right field. A bit heavier and softer than his mates, he was a forgotten figure in crimson cap and matching jersey, pale pants, striped socks, scuffed sneakers—the Little League version of a Red Sox uniform, the sneakers purchased last April from the Adidas outlet in North Andover. The opponents were the Dodgers, league leaders costumed in blue and raising their score prodigiously through opponent errors, none by David yet. No balls had been hit to him. He took a few steps backward, deeper into the shadows, while smacking a fist into a cumbersome glove he'd brought from Boston a good year ago, a big move in his young life. He was forgotten in the field except by Frank Chase, who silently cheered him.

Chase stood alone, by choice, near a chain-link fence and failed to notice a woman approaching him from the stands. She followed his intent gaze and said, "Poor David. He looks lost out there."

Chase reacted slowly to the angular face, which was sharply defined and oddly attractive. She stood quite still beside him, but her manner was restless. Her loose blouse, spread at the top, revealed collarbones and breastplate. She wore slim shorts and had the striking legs of a heron. Her name was Lee Gunderman.

Chase said, "Where's Karl?"

She jerked a thumb. "Back there, a few rows up."

Chase didn't look. He said, "I've lost track. What's the score?"

"Don't ask." Her son Brian was pitching, heaving his heart out with an erratic right arm. He walked the batter to load the bases. "The umpire has cataracts," Lee said. "Give me a cigarette."

Chase gave her one and lit it from a bright book of matches advertising Gunderman Realty. He watched her blow out a swift line of smoke.

She said, "I hear you might be handling the old Kimball house on School Street."

"Darling Associates got hold of it," he said, suspecting she had known that. He sensed something was coming.

"You must be all adjusted to the town by now."

"I'm getting there."

"Want some advice?"

He smiled and waited, watching her curb her impatience as her son verged on walking another batter. He stole a look to right field at David.

"You could use more suburban smarts. In a town like this it's a matter of style, quiet but subtle. The house you live in, and the neighborhood—you're right on base there. What I'm talking about is personal style, the way you present yourself. You're *too* quiet, Frank. *Too* subtle. At parties—brag a little, hint at things. After all, you weren't just an ordinary cop. You were a detective. Homicide. What else? Karl said drugs. Sure. Talk knowledgeably about drugs and kids. People here are scared about that. Are you laughing at me?"

"No. Go on."

"You went to Northeastern, right? No degree. Mention you have one. Who's going to know the difference? You can even make it a master's." She paused. "And flirt a little, I mean just to be sociable. It doesn't mean anything."

"You're serious?"

"Sure. Parties are always sexual, beginning with the conversations. But that doesn't mean they end in orgies. Flirt just enough to please the women and flatter their husbands. They'll remember you when it comes time to sell their houses."

"Did Karl put you up to this?"

"I swear he didn't."

"Then why are you telling me this?"

"I like you. God, you're suspicious." She looked away. There was noise from the stands, confusion on the field. "What's happening?"

"Runs are scoring."

"Oh, God."

"I still think Karl's behind this."

"All he said was that you're not aggressive."

"He has never said that to me."

"He's a little afraid of you. Don't ask me why."

"And you're not."

"I'm not afraid of anybody."

There was more confusion on the field, this time involving David. A ball that sailed his way bounced off the heel of his glove, and another run was scoring. Chase closed his eyes.

"You ought to get him a different glove," Lee said. "That one's too big."

"It was a gift from his father," Chase said quietly.

"Then teach him to use it. Practice with him in the yard. That's what Karl does with Brian."

Chase opened his eyes.

"Did you hear me, Frank?"

"Yes, but I don't think I'd be much help. I was never good at the game."

"You're kidding. You're built like a ballplayer." She gave his belly a quick tap. "Unless you're just sucking that in all the time. What did you play—basketball? Nothing?" She laughed. "I won't tell anybody."

He looked away. Lee's eyes stayed on him. They were very intense.

"You and Ida are happy. I can tell."

Chase lifted his eyes. A few clouds were threatening. He looked at Lee. "Aren't you happy?"

"Sure, I guess so. But not like you two."

"You're a romantic."

"Maybe. But I think you're more of one." She slipped an arm under his. "That's why I like you."

Chase looked toward the stands. Karl Gunderman's face, large and mobile, was easy to spot. The eyes looked back at Chase from the distance as Lee leaned against him. She kissed his cheek and then broke away.

"See you."

The game, with its lopsided score, was called in the sixth inning because of sprinkles. Chase and David shambled to the ranch wagon and drove to Friendly's for ice cream, a ritual. Friendly's was situated next to the police station, their small brick buildings of similar colonial design and their parking lots converging at a ridge of concrete. The sky had darkened considerably. As Chase maneuvered the wagon into the lot, the headlights illuminated a young couple in a small car. They did not break their clinch. David, who had been very quiet, said, "They're making out, aren't they?"

"I guess you could say that. At any rate, they're kissing."

Chase parked the wagon deeper down in the lot, facing the police station, which was lighted, a cozy scene, a pipe-smoking desk sergeant reading the newspaper, with a younger officer looking over his shoulder. Chase, reaching for money, felt a small sense of dislocation. David slipped out of the wagon.

He returned with two chocolate cones, their rigid favorites. The boy, more quiet than before, seemed to be brooding. He had his father's fair complexion, but the rest of him was his mother, particularly the dark eyes and large soft mouth. Chase, watching him lick the cone, said, "It was only a game."

The boy wiped his chin.

"And you didn't do so badly."

"I made four errors."

"I saw only one."

"You weren't watching."

"Yes, I was. The others looked like hits."

"You say that because you're my . . . stepfather."

"No, that's how I'd have scored them."

The rain began to fall in earnest as a cruiser pulled into the station lot. A young officer climbed out gingerly. He had spent money on his uniform, which was tailored and tight, and he didn't want to get it wet. He sprinted into the station. Chase, holding his cone to one side, started up the wagon. He glanced at David.

"OK?"

"Sure."

Chase drove slowly up Main Street, wipers working, and still made the lights through Andover Square, all the stores closed except for CVS and Barcelos Supermarket.

"We need anything?" Chase asked.

The boy shrugged. He could not finish his ice cream, and he cranked down the window and threw it out.

"That's not nice."

"Mom says the birds eat it."

"She's right. In Boston the rats do."

"Mom says there aren't any rats in Andover."

"There are, but a different kind. They live in the woods."

"I've never seen any."

"You probably won't."

They were cruising toward South Main Street, the lighted landscaped campus of Phillips Academy on each side, the buildings nestled in, the rain sparkling on the ivy. Chase pointed to his left, the major part of the campus.

"That's where your mother and I would like you to go when you're ready."

David didn't answer. He snatched up his outsized glove and

pounded a fist in it. His silence hardened and didn't break until Chase reached Colby Lane and pulled into the drive, barely missing Ida's three-speed bike left out in the rain. As soon as Chase switched off the ignition, David said, "I saw you talking to Brian's mother."

The question sounded casual, but Chase knew it wasn't. "Right," he said.

David squinted. "I guess you have to talk to her because you work for Mr. Gunderman."

"No," said Chase. "I'd talk to her, anyway."

"You like her, don't you?"

"Sure I like her. She's a nice lady."

"But you like Mom better," the boy said almost in a burst. His eyes were hot. Chase kept his cool.

Chase said slowly, "I like Mrs. Gunderman. I like a lot of people, but I love your mother, the same as I love you."

The boy's eyes had filled, and he looked quickly away. Then he yanked at the door. "I'll take care of the bike," he said.

Chase watched him run to it.

"Rupert phoned," Ida said.

"What?" Chase said, though she had spoken with keen clarity.

"Rupert phoned. He wanted to know if everything was all right."

"You mean with David?"

"No, I don't think so."

"You mean with us? That's none of his business."

"No, I don't think it was that either."

"Then what was it?"

Ida was tense, her shoulders stiff. She stood near a potted geranium in bloom, the effect of its colors doubled because it was placed in front of a tall mirror. "Maybe you ought to call him back, talk to him yourself."

"What specifically did he say?"

"Frank, I told you. He asked if everything was all right, and I said fine."

"Then what's the problem?"

"His tone, Frank. Something about it. As if he thought something had happened to us."

"What?"

"Frank, I don't know. And maybe I'm imagining things."

"No, you read him well. Too well."

Her shoulders stiffened even more. "Was that a dig?"

"Maybe. I'm sorry." He went to her. He slipped a hand under her hair and rubbed the back of her neck, as if erasing something.

"Not so hard."

He dropped his hand.

"Are you going to call him?"

"No. The hell with him."

3.

THE MESSAGE

"Where's Donovan?"

"Over there, chief."

Rupert Goetz, head of Homicide, left his chauffeured car and strode past a hot held-back crowd in a pocket of Roxbury where police were seldom seen. The temperature was in the nineties, the humidity oppressive. The massed black faces watched his every step in near silence, the only noise coming from children, a couple of them jeering the barrier of uniformed officers. When the eye of a shoulder-held camera angled in on him, he imperceptively flexed shoulders already as straight as they could be. He moved briskly, ignoring the shout of a *Herald American* reporter but making a mental note to get in touch with the man later. Donovan, a gray figure poised near a cruiser, lowered a walkie-talkie and pointed.

"They're about to bring him down."

"No trouble?"

"Coming like a baby."

They focused attention on the front door of a broken brick building, home for maybe a hundred blacks, with screens sliding off windows and graffiti sprayed onto the brick high up where only daredevils could have done it. Goetz rubbed his chin.

"How'd you pick up on this guy?"

"A bit of luck. One of Frank Chase's old snitches must've figured I was OK. We owe Frank."

"I see him, I'll tell him."

"See him much?"

"No."

The crowd stirred, and members of the media tried to press past boundaries. Four detectives emerged from the building, one with a shotgun. In their midst was a manacled man, black and barefoot, shirtless, boy-sized, with a contorted miniature face that reminded Goetz of a chihuahua.

"No question he's our baby?"

Donovan shook his head. "He's good for all four killings."

"And we've got a good case?"

"Airtight on one."

"One's enough."

The detectives hustled the little man toward the cruiser. Donovan opened a rear door and stepped aside. Goetz positioned himself. He wanted a close look at the man and a word with the detectives, who pulled up like cowboys on horses, their man thrust forward, his head hanging. Goetz stood stock still with the smallest possible smile. He spoke to the tallest detective.

"You guys didn't bat him around, did you?"

"No, sir."

"What about the cuffs? Didn't put them on too tight, did you?"

"No, sir."

"Good," said Goetz, sensing the distant aim of more television cameras. Increasing his smile, as though his function was to soothe, he passed a hand in front of the man's half-hidden face. "Just want to make sure you're alive."

The man looked up expectantly, as if he thought Goetz might help him. Goetz patted him.

"Busy little bastard, weren't you?" Then Goetz turned away, slapping Donovan on the shoulder. "Who says you're not going to make Lieutenant?"

Goetz's face flashed onto the screen during the six o'clock

news, channels 4, 5, and 7, and his image reappeared in the morning papers. In the *Herald American* he shared picture space with Donovan. In the *Globe* Donovan was cropped out, Goetz being younger and more photogenic, dapper in a lightweight three-piece suit from Newbury Street. Later he was invited to an impromptu wine-and-cheese at City Hall, with key newspeople in attendance. They sought him out, and for a while, sipping expensive wine out of a plastic cup, he held court. Then a soft-looking freckled hand with surprising strength tugged at him. A bland face under faded hair smiled at him as they glided to one side. The police commissioner was a medium-sized fat man, but his step was nimble, as if his weight were irrelevant. His voice was low.

"Don't upstage anybody."

Goetz, smoothing his sleeve, winked. "Meaning the mayor? I'd never do that, sir."

"I know you wouldn't, but I mention it anyway, to be safe. The mayor's grateful to us. This is election year, and the Roxbury thing was hurting him, people there saying he didn't give a good shit about them or care how many little black girls got raped and ripped apart. Yesterday's arrest takes us all off the hook."

"So we're OK, sir."

"We're never OK. That's advice I gave you a long time ago."

"Yes, sir," Goetz said, staring into the commissioner's bland eyes, which told him nothing. "Want me to get you some more wine?"

"Get some for the mayor."

"I don't think he even knows me."

"He does now."

The mayor, who was the host, was not even in the room, but he appeared presently, a staged entrance, which agitated his awaiting workers, who already had been milling about. Goetz edged away from the wine table with two cups in hand, his arms raised to the elbows, a smile filling his face. "Excuse me," he said, gingerly pushing forward until a young wild-eyed aide of the mayor's stepped in front of him and reached for the wine.

"I'll take those."

"The fuck you will."

The aide glared. "What are you, a diamond in the rough?"

"You guessed it, kid."

"I see now how you came up so fast through the ranks."

"You don't see anything, junior." Goetz brushed away from him. With the delicate use of both elbows he wended his way to where he wanted to be and offered up one of the wines in a husky voice. "Sir." The mayor's long face turned toward him. The deep-socketed eyes assessed him suspiciously and then acknowledged him slowly but in a way that made things happen. A photographer on the public payroll went into a quick crouch. The mayor, gripping the cup of wine in one hand and reaching for Goetz with the other, addressed the gathering.

"A toast," he said. "From one public servant to another."

Goetz was blinded by the flash of the camera.

The sign greeting the brutal commuter traffic on Storrow Drive said: *If you lived here, you'd be home now.* Goetz lived there: Charles River Park Apartments. He was home early and lounging in his underpants, sipping his third bourbon to rid himself of the taste of wine and to curb his impatience over Sherry's absence. When the phone rang he thought it was she to tell him where the hell she was. He took his time answering. A man was on the line.

"Hello, hero."

Goetz did not recognize the voice and did not like the tone of it. "Who is this?"

"Up your ass."

Goetz took a shallow breath and said, "I wish we were face to face."

"Why, what would you do, big shot?" The man laughed, and Goetz made a helpless fist, the knuckles squeezed white. The man said, "You ain't dealing with niggers now to get your picture in the paper. This is big league."

Goetz was about to hang up. "You fuck!" he said instead, using the obscenity as a fierce noun. "Who are you?"

"That ain't polite."

"And how did you get this number? It's unlisted."

"People I work for can get anything. They told me to call you, friendly-like."

Desperately Goetz tried to dredge up a face for the voice but came up with nothing. "They must be assholes too."

"They wouldn't like to hear you say that."

"Who are they?"

"They figure you know."

Goetz let a couple of seconds go by. "It so happens I don't, but I've got a trace on this call."

"Hey, I'll help you out. I'm at a pay phone on D Street, your old neighborhood. Right?"

"You're cute."

"You too, big shot. But also stupid! That's what I was told to tell you."

Goetz did not speak. His mind was moving too fast.

"You still there, hero?"

Goetz forced a voice. "You sure you got the right number, creep?"

The man laughed. "People I mentioned don't make mistakes, but you sure as shit did."

Goetz hung up.

He had dressed, a new tie to go with another new suit, three-piece like all of them, and was sipping a fresh bourbon when Sherry came home, her eyes hidden behind those smoke-colored glasses, her luxuriant hair flowing over her shoulders, and her blouse opened too many buttons down. He viewed her coldly.

"Where the hell have you been?"

She removed the glasses with deliberate casualness. "I had

lunch with Betty."

"Who the hell is Betty?"

"I told you before. Maybe you should listen."

"Tell me again."

"A friend from Cambridge."

"That so? Lunch was at least six hours ago."

"It was nice seeing her again. We talked. Then I went to Barnes and Noble. That all right with you?"

"I don't see any books."

"You know how I am. I browsed."

"Then what?"

"I'm here." She sighed. "Go easy, huh, Rupert?"

He finished off his bourbon and put the glass down, next to the phone. "What if I don't want to go easy?"

"What the hell's the matter with you?" Her color rose. "And what are you laying on me. We have agreements, remember?"

He squinted at her, as if he had one eye to a keyhole, and his manner softened slightly. "That doesn't mean I'm supposed to go without supper."

"You have two hands, Rupert, and you cook a hell of a lot better than I do. Besides, I thought we were eating out. Change your mind?"

He closed his eyes for a moment. "I forgot."

"No, you didn't." Her green eyes swept over him. "You're dressed for it. You look gorgeous in that suit. I like it."

The suit was dark, with a barely visible pinstripe, the blue cuffs of his shirt showing. He moved toward her.

She said, with a smile, "You dress better than Kojak."

His large fingers pressed into her arms through the flimsy material of her blouse. She stood her ground. He said, "I love you. You understand?"

"I love you too, but you're hurting me."

"You can get away with a lot, but don't take advantage."

"It's tough convincing you I don't."

He released her, and she massaged her arms, viewing him

with concern. "Something's the matter, I can tell. What is it?"

He was silent, observing.

"I asked you something."

"Nothing's the matter," he said, the coldness creeping back. "Unless you tell me something is."

"OK, we'll play it your way. Are we going out?"

"Maybe."

"What's that supposed to mean?"

"Means *probably.*"

"It might rain. Will that make a difference?"

"No."

"Then I'll shower."

"Do that."

He poured himself another bourbon and stood sipping it until he heard the rush of water in the bathroom, a fast needle spray. He picked up the phone. He wanted Frank but got Ida.

4.

THE BODY

In the dark of their bedroom Frank and Ida Chase broke their embrace and lay as they fell, without covers, their arms at their sides, hearts thumping, a moist breeze blowing over their bodies. The rain had stopped, but the night air was muggy. Ida got her breath back and murmured, "Towel." Chase reached over the side, feeling for one. Two were on the floor. They vigorously shared the one.

"You love me, Frank?"

His eyes were used to the dark, and he could almost see her face. She was sitting with a raised knee, her chin resting on it. He tossed the towel away and shifted toward her, pressing his cheek against a cool part of her leg.

"Yes."

They lay together under a sheet, listening to sudden and furtive footsteps, David's. The boy was returning from a quiet trip to the bathroom, no flush, hardly any sound at all until he closed the door to his room.

"I thought he was asleep," Chase whispered into Ida's hair, and she snuggled closer.

"Don't you know what he was doing? Listening through the door."

Chase was upset. "How do you know?"

"I know. When he hears what we're doing, it reassures him we still love each other and are going to stay together."

"How do you know *that?*"

"A very educated guess."

Chase freed an arm and wedged his hand under his head. "All this has been catastropic to him, hasn't it?"

She paused for a number of seconds, then said, "I think he really loves you, Frank."

Chase's pause was longer than hers had been, and when he spoke his throat sounded sore. "I think he needs to feel secure. I think that's most important to him."

"That goes without saying, Frank. But what I said still holds."

He closed his eyes. She fell asleep well before he did, with a large leg thrown over both of his and with her head tucked against his naked shoulder, her hair tickling it. She snored lightly and a couple of times moaned. In time her weight grew uncomfortable, and as he was slowly extricating himself he heard David make another quiet trip to the bathroom, this time legitimately.

The flush broke the silence.

Goetz was oblivious to the late-night commotion on Storrow Drive, a car with a blown-out muffler, a noise like ten trucks. Sherry was under him, her hands rearranging her mass of hair so he could better see her face in the tiny light, a mere spark over the bed. He was propped on strong arms and gently laying into her. Conscious of the biting odors between them, he paused to savor the moment. His pleasure was deep and showed up like pain on his face.

"You've got a big face, Rupert," she whispered, raising an affectionate hand. "Sometimes it looks like it weighs a ton."

His response was a shudder, then a jitter in his tense tough arms, which seemed on the point of buckling, especially when he felt the coil of her legs. He spent a number of seconds staring into the shadows of her eyes. She smiled.

"You're teasing me, you know. It's OK. I like it." Her fingers slid over his high forehead and scraped into his flat hair. "If you had a forelock, you'd look like Joe Palooka."

Then she pulled hard at him, as if wanting more than he could give. He wanted to give more, everything, and struggled to do so with a frantic clumsy strength. His arms collapsed, and he worked from his elbows. When he was on the verge of satisfaction, he felt her quiver and knew she was coming too. Her sounds left him with no doubts.

He rose with a jolt, spent a number of minutes in the bathroom, and came back clean. She lay as he had left her.

"Why do you always do that, Rupert?"

"What?"

"Wash, the split-second after."

"Why not?" he said, moving to his side of the bed and stopping. Never bothered you before."

"Doesn't bother me now. I'm just curious." Her smile was almost cruel. "After all, I'm your wife now, not something off the street. Did you do that with Ida too?"

"Knock it off."

"Don't be mad, baby. I knew a black guy like that, back when. He—"

Goetz, standing only a few feet from a wall, drove a fist into it, smashing paint and plaster. "I don't want to hear!"

Ida woke with a start, as if someone had laid a hand on her, not Chase. Chase was well into the sheets and deep in sleep, his back to her, his breathing heavy and a little troubled. She wondered what the dream was. She rose quietly. It was dawn, and she could hear the cool twitter of birds.

She used the big bathroom rather than the one in their bedroom. The big one had ample space and a soft rug for what she wanted to do. Bending abruptly at the waist, she easily touched her toes and awkwardly glanced at herself in the large mirror. She was evenly brown from the sun except for her livid backside. She kept her belly flat through morning exercises, daily swims, and a bit of biking.

After her exercises and an indulgently long shower, she ran a brush through her hair, which was black and beginning to gray just enough to notice, as if she had stepped out for a moment in a mist. She rather liked the effect, but Chase had suggested she rinse it away, as if he wanted to keep her fresh. Goetz would have insisted upon it.

She slipped on bright culottes and one of Chase's shirts. With a cup of quickly brewed coffee in one hand and a cigarette in the other, she stepped barefoot out the front door and sat on the damp bottom step. The early sunlight seemed watery. A robin was perched in the driveway, its breast reflected in a puddle. This was her favorite hour, this tender time with its slow invasion of life. Only as she was taking her second sip of coffee did she notice what she should have seen immediately. A man lay neatly on the lawn, near a tree, his head tucked away, as if he were hiding it.

She knew without moving an inch that he was not alive.

She didn't scream. She rose with her back arched, her coffee cup held high, and marched rigidly into the house to wake Chase.

5.

NIGHTSTICK

It was the summer of '67, with a basket on a blanket, a private part of a public beach seven miles from Boston, the sun glaring. The three of them sat eating fruit. Ida Goetz, less than a year married, wore a toweling jacket over her bikini bottom, which was a string thing, a snatch cloth, nothing more. She picked at shrimplike sections of a tangerine. Rupert Goetz went from the wet flesh of a peach to the blood-veined muscle of a plum and then dramatically dropped a green grape into his mouth. Frank Chase murmured, "Pig." A quiet double entendre that produced smiles. A knife glinted. Chase halfed a pear—two miniature violins with seeds instead of strings. He passed one over to Ida, keeping the other for himself. Goetz, watching, wiped his mouth.

"They'll be calling you a pig too."

Chase shook his head. "I'm still undecided about that."

"You worried about passing the exam? I can get you a copy of it. Fifty bucks under the counter to a Civil Service twerp."

"Rupert!" Ida was not certain he was joking. "Frank could probably pass it with his eyes closed."

A wink at Chase. "Never hurts to have an edge."

"Just because you're a cop doesn't mean he wants to be one. Besides, he almost has his degree."

Goetz consumed more grapes, plundering a stem. "You think a degree's going to help him that much. If it was Harvard, some place like that, OK. But it's not. Right, Frank?"

Chase made no reply. He was an evening student at Northeastern University. It seemed, at times, that he'd been going
there forever. It was where Goetz had gone. It was how they
had met. Goetz was winking again. Ida leaned toward the
basket.

"There's still a sandwich left. Anybody want it?"

No takers. She put it back. Goetz got to his feet. He had on
slick rubbery trunks with a jungle design, Tarzan-type, muscles
showing in his thighs, knots in his calves. His blunt blond head
beamed.

"A cop is something special, Frank. Don't let nobody kid
you."

Chase was staring off at the chop of the sea and at two gulls
perched on a distant boulder. They looked like man and wife.
A good distance away, to his left, two adolescent girls, raced
toward the surf to taste the water. Quick silent splashes. They
were up to their heads, awash in the waves. Ida lighted a
cigarette.

"The only thing special about a cop," she said, "is he has too
many deadly weapons at his disposal."

Goetz scoffed. "She's talking about my nightstick."

"He was called down for being too quick with it."

"You have to be." He stood with his hands on his hips, as
if he were not in near-nakedness but in uniform, his mouth
curving toward a smile. A remark was coming. Chase could
sense it, had heard it before. A bad bedroom joke about the
nightstick.

Goetz told it, personalizing it.

Ida flinched. "For God's sake, Rupert."

Goetz showed his teeth. "Frank's embarrassed."

"So am I."

"Frank is going for a walk." Chase's third-person voice. He
was on his feet, brushing sand from the seat of his blue trunks,
a lanky figure with the sharp edges of his face burnt by the sun.

Goetz, with a wink, said, "How long will you be?"

Ida snuffed out her cigarette in the sand and watched him

make the hike down to the surf. Goetz squatted beside her. They both watched him. He stood against the ocean in a vast drift of air, a lonesome figure. The two girls who had crashed into the waves were now flopped on the sand far to his right. They looked like beached fish, but they raised their heads to watch him as he moved off to his left, well away from them.

Ida said, "A handsome guy, but he's so quiet."

"Frank's the bashful sort. Makes women want to flirt with him."

She let her head sag forward as Goetz put a broad hand into her strong black hair and massaged the back of her neck. She said, "Doesn't he have a girl?"

"I think he pays for it. I might be wrong."

"You're joking, guessing, or what—because that's a lousy thing to say."

Goetz laughed. "He's all wrapped up in himself trying to put himself through school. Actually he doesn't know what he wants to do."

"Then you shouldn't push him about becoming a cop."

"Honey, I take a liking to somebody, I do what I can for him. Besides, he'd make a good cop. He knows the street. A different part of Boston maybe, but same background as me."

She lifted her head. "And me."

"That's right." Goetz kissed her lingeringly. "Who do you love?"

She gazed toward the surf. Chase was gone. She allowed herself to be drawn backwards on the blanket.

"I asked you a question."

"I love you, Rupert. I love you more than anything." It was what she had told him when she was sixteen, this same beach, maybe even the same spot. She was now twenty-three. He opened her toweling jacket. A big cleavage in a bit of a bra. His thumb almost broke the strap."

"You know, I can have you anytime, much as I want, and I still can't keep my hands off. That must tell you something."

"Tells me you'd better take a fast swim."

"Afraid?"

"Why should we embarrass ourselves and Frank?"

"We've got time. I gave him the sign."

"There are two girls on the beach."

"No way they can see us."

"Let's wait."

"Let's not." He tugged at the jacket. "You haven't had this off all day. You haven't even had a foot in the water."

"I had no intention of parading in front of Frank in this damn suit. I should've worn my other one instead of listening to you."

Goetz's smile was devilish. "Honey, I bought this one for you. A lot of thought went into it. Ask the girl at Filene's."

"Then you must have had her in mind. Next time get the right size."

"It's perfect."

"I'm naked in it, and you know it."

"We'll ask Frank."

"Damn you."

"He likes you."

"No kidding."

"Don't be touchy." His mouth was against her ear, and her jacket was tossed in the sand. His slow hand wiped away the bra and slid down to the bottom cloth. "Frank don't get to do this, ever."

She looked up into his face. Her dark eyes were tender. He struggled with his trunks as she smiled nervously. "The sun's still strong. You'll burn your bum."

"Line of duty."

"I'm not wearing that little thing."

"We'll take the chance."

She closed her eyes. "Make it fast."

"No problem."

With a wistful stride, Frank Chase followed wet footsteps planted delicately in the sand, but they soon dried out, with no smooth figure in sight, only a dead and distended crab that he nearly stepped on. He rounded a bend of boulders to a craggy part of the beach and, squatting, handled washed-up kelp, long and floppy, almost alive, a magnet for horseflies, which drove him away from it much too fast. A crusted rock got in his way and instantly stitched one of his ankles with threads of blood, a fancy design strikingly like a Chinese ideogram. He soaked the foot in a tidal pool until he noticed what was in it: wasted tissues and a smashed beer bottle. He was not in a proper frame of mind but did not want to dwell upon the reasons, and he shuffled forward, the sun glinting directly into his eyes.

"Look out!"

He stopped short in front of a bucket of bait. Beyond it, a white-haired man stood with a sleek and shivering pole held high in the breeze. The man took two or three casual steps forward to cast, and the snap and whistle of the line was like a gun fired at a living target. The man showed no emotion, as if he were truly professional, like an assassin. Chase on the other hand, reacted sharply to the sudden slap of a wave, like a laugh.

"You OK, kid?"

Kid. Christ, he was twenty-six, nearly a year older than Goetz, and he was a navy veteran, an enlistee at eighteen and, at nineteen, a member of the Shore Patrol, with a nightstick as hefty as the one Goetz wielded with unbridled force, except he had never used his that way. Love taps, nothing more.

"You fish?"

The voice sounded like the remains of a cough, and Chase shook his head, with a glance into the bucket, a moving mess of something.

"Don't stick your hand in there." The man ridded himself of phlegm. "You know what those things are?"

Chase didn't.

"Those there are sandworms, except they ain't worms at all. They got teeth. You've got to grab behind the head so you don't get your fingers bit." There was a fierce crinkling of skin as the man smiled. "Like you would a woman."

Chase knew exactly why he was out of sorts.

He made his way to the popular part of the beach, where a woman in a bonnet, pleasantly old, smiled politely at him from the shade of an umbrella. To his left, down in a sunken chair, a pair of lips coated with zinc oxide seemed to blow him a kiss, though he knew he was mistaken. A lifeguard stood with folded arms and the top of his shorts unhooked, displaying belly hair to a blanket of girls. Children swilled by in a race to the water. Chase waded well beyond them and confronted a wave that curved at him like a slice of steel. He half expected it to knock him senseless, but he rode it well and then swam with his face down. His stroke was swift and strong, and he swam parallel with the beach until he was breathless.

Goetz came upon him an hour later. He was sitting a distance from the surf, face dazzled from too much sun, idle eyes watching a heavy woman's struggle to move through the hot sand. Goetz said, "Ida was worried. She thought you might've got lost."

"I'm a big boy."

"That's what I told her."

Omnipresent gulls, nasty-eyed, paraded a few yards away. A breeze wafted off the ocean, a small refreshment, which both men appreciated. Chase forced himself to his feet, brushing at sandy edges and legs scaled with salt. The heavy woman paused in her journey, her bathing suit a blood-orange flash, a strap hanging, a tit showing. Goetz snapped at his Tarzan tights.

"I told Ida she can never get fat."

"What about yourself?"

Goetz patted his belly. "That's muscle, man."

They began the hike back with awkward strides over the shingled sand, their heads and shoulders pitched forward. For a while Goetz whistled his way along. Chase was silent. Goetz smiled at him.

"Ida says I shouldn't push you. Kinda gave me hell about it."

"You're not pushing me."

"But let me tell you, Frankie. There's worse things than being a cop."

"I know that."

"In fact, there's a lot going for it. If you become a cop, you at least get a little clout. And if you've got the brains, you don't have to stay in uniform forever. Detectives have got it made, and don't let anybody tell you they don't."

"From what I hear, it's not always brains that gets you into detectives."

"That's true in anything. So what you do is make friends, the right ones, in and out of the department."

Chase shook his head slowly. "I wouldn't ever want to kiss ass."

"Just the opposite, Frankie. You work it right, they'll soon be kissing your ass. Guaranteed."

"You make it sound easy."

"It's as easy or hard as you make it. When you get sworn into the department, right away you've got security—signed, sealed and stamped."

"Like being back in the navy."

"Less chickenshit. And if you want something more than security, you've got a chance for that too. Whatever you want to make of it. Do you understand what I'm saying."

"I'm not dumb."

"That's why I didn't spell it out."

They were close to the surf now, where the walking was easier, except where rocks cropped up. The man who had been fishing was gone, no trace of him, though gulls were scavenging about where he had been. Chase said, "Why don't we let it rest for a while?"

"Whatever you say, Frankie. But just let me add one last thing. If you decide to do it, you already got me in your corner. Probably the only friend you'll need."

Near the bend of boulders they came face to face with the two adolescent girls, who, flushing, immediately turned their heads to the sea. There was a gurgle from one of them, possibly laughter, the snickering sort. Goetz grinned as they passed.

"I think they got an eyeful a while back."

"Ida must've loved that," Chase said tonelessly.

"She didn't know. I didn't want to spoil it for her."

Chase looked away. The sun, sinking, was a blinding white circle with no give to its glare.

"Here, take this," Goetz said, stripping off his watch and passing it to Chase. He charged into the water for his last dip of the day.

Chase approached Ida alone. She lay asleep on the blanket with her hair unloosed and her arms entwined behind her head. Her jacket in a ball beside her, she was wearing only the scant bathing suit. Her legs were stretched out, with one foot dug into the sand. A long large body, all of it tanned, except for the shaved armpits, which, to Chase, looked terribly tender. His stare was intense, as if he were willing her to open her eyes to see what was in his.

Hers stayed shut.

He stared at the sleek line of her neck. He tried to think of her as somebody different, as a whore with too much weight on her, too much traffic. Holding his breath, he no longer wanted her to open her eyes.

She did.

Neither spoke. Finally she did. "Rupert found you OK?"

"Yes," he said after a hesitation. He felt like a character in a movie, the soundtrack out of sync. She sat up.

"I told him not to push you. Did he tell you that?"

"Yes."

"He means well."

"I know."

She sneaked a hand toward her jacket. "But you mustn't take him too seriously.

"The problem is I take myself too seriously." He was no longer looking at her. Goetz was coming up behind him.

Goetz, with a laugh, said, "Caught ya!"

6.

COPS

Dearborns had been in Andover longer than anybody could remember. Early ones were farm hands in West Andover, mill workers in Shawsheen, and grave diggers in Spring Grove Cemetery. Though none ever became a doctor or a lawyer, got into Phillips Academy, or made a killing in real estate, most survived nicely and prospered to a degree. Of the current crop, a good number worked for Gillette and Raytheon, and several worked for the town. A few were public works laborers, one was a fireman, and another a policeman—a detective-sergeant. That was Lionel Dearborn, the most ambitious of the lot. When he viewed the body on the Chases' front lawn, he experienced a rich charge of excitement, though his face showed nothing except a little color.

"Jesus Christ," said Dix, a patrolman in civilian clothes. "Hornets are going for his face."

"What face?" said Dearborn, stooping over the body. The face was unrecognizable, shredded, flayed by something that had removed flesh, big bits and pieces, and dislodged an eye. Dearborn patted the clothes for identification and found nothing except money, maybe a hundred dollars. He straightened.

"Keep everybody away," he said. I don't want people seeing this, especially kids."

"How'd he get here?" Dix was agitated and appeared ill.

"He's an import," Dearborn said, as though he could see

everything, maybe even the murderer. "He's got it written all over him, Boston, Revere, Chelsea, one of those places. He was dumped."

"But why here? Why didn't they just throw him in Harold Parker State Forest. Would've been easier."

Dearborn said nothing. He was staring up at two small clouds floating side by side, like fish. Dix could not take his eyes off the dead man's face.

"That's a dirty way to kill somebody."

The sun, starting to show strength, was narcotically warm, and Dearborn hated to leave it. He also didn't want to abandon the body, his prize. With a sudden tenseness of expression, he said, "Stay here. When the photographer comes, tell him don't spare the film, but don't take his time either. And find out what's holding up the medical examiner."

Dix nodded, and Dearborn headed toward the house.

Chase opened the door immediately, as if he'd been waiting behind it. He took Dearborn through the dining room to the sun porch, and they sat in white wicker chairs Ida had bought in a flea market in Ipswich. The sun was flashing through jalousie windows.

"To save time," said Dearborn. "I know who you are."

"I'm not trying to hide it," Chase said evenly.

"But you're not broadcasting it either."

"Why should I?"

For a moment Dearborn said nothing. He sat with his blue socks showing. His suit was a summer lightweight and seemed to be gray. "What I'm trying to tell you, Frank, is I'll help you if I can."

"You're jumping to conclusions."

"That's bad. I don't want to do that." Dearborn pursed his lips for a smile that didn't come. Chase changed chairs to get the sun out of his eyes. Dearborn said, "But I've got a job to do, you know that."

"We're not buddies. You don't owe me anything."

"Right, but I want to be fair."

"Then we don't have a problem."

Dearborn took out a pocket notebook encased in vinyl. The pen in his hand was a gold Parker bearing his initials, a birthday gift from his wife. The birthday was his thirty-ninth, which he figured was approximately Chase's age. "I know you already talked to someone, but maybe you could give it to me."

Chase took no more than thirty seconds, for he had nothing much to tell, but Dearborn's pen moved as if he had said a great deal. Then Dearborn appeared to contemplate what he had written.

"Off the top of my head, Frank, I'd say the body was out there most of the night. What's your guess?"

"I wouldn't know. As I said, my wife and I went to bed about eleven."

"And you heard nothing at all."

"We're both sound sleepers."

"But your wife got up early."

"Yes."

"She in the habit of doing that?"

"Yes."

"Where is she, Frank?"

Chase understood too well the procedural and ironic use of his first name, but it annoyed him all the same. "She's trying to keep our son occupied. I was hoping you could hold up on your questions to her."

"Sure, I understand." Dearborn turned a page in his notebook and began writing again. The words were illegible. It was no kind of shorthand. It was nothing. "Did you touch the body, Frank?"

"Yes. I thought he might be alive."

"You saw the condition of the face."

"Yes."

"Make you a little sick?"

"I've seen worse."

"Yeah, I guess you have. What do you think was used,

Frank? I've been trying to figure that out."

Chase shook his head.

"And you have no idea who he was?"

"No."

"Maybe a guess?"

"No."

Again Dearborn pursed his lips, and this time the smile arrived. "Frank, we're on the same side, aren't we?"

"I'd say so, in a manner of speaking."

"Could you be clearer?"

"No hidden meaning there," Chase said.

Dearborn sat back. "I don't have to tell you others will be nosing around. Everybody's got to be represented, and I wouldn't be surprised we eventually get a visit from Narcotics. I'm talking Federal, Frank, depending on how things go."

"Why Narcotics?"

"You tell me."

"Wish I could."

Dearborn dropped his smile. "You trust me, Frank?"

"Sure."

"Say it like you mean it."

Chase sighed, as if bored.

"OK," said Dearborn. "I'm not going to try to bullshit you. I'm at this point ninety-percent guessing about everything, which you know. So you could help me a lot if you wanted to. What I'm saying is you could do me a favor. Hell, and do yourself one too."

Chase glanced away, as if keeping track of the sun. Dearborn sat forward.

"Frank, look at me. You want a partner? You got one."

Chase smiled. "A partner in what?"

"That's up to you." Dearborn tucked away his notebook and held his pen like a cigarette. "This is a nice town, and I know you like living in it. That's why it'd be good to have me in your corner."

"What would you do, come out fighting for me?"

"Who knows?"

Chase, shifting his weight, glanced at his watch. "Are we done sparring?"

"Let me lay it out for you." Dearborn lowered his voice. "I've got a wife, five kids, a big mortgage on a little house, bills you wouldn't believe, and a job that can go either way because of a physical I got to take sooner or later. Man, I'm locked in. I breathe, but I don't move. OK, that give you enough to trust me?"

"You're trying to cut yourself in on something that doesn't exist. Either that or you're testing me. There's nothing to test."

"OK, Frank, play it close if you want. But that thing out there with no face, I find out who he is, that takes away the guesswork." Chase said nothing, and Dearborn rose with effort, smiling. "Know what I think? I think whoever left that thing was trying to tell you something. Just like I am. I guess in time you got to listen to one of us, huh?"

Neighbors stood in the street trying to glimpse the body, which was still on the grass, with the medical examiner down on one knee and leaning over it, the fire department ambulance waiting to take it away. The photographer, his job apparently done, lounged to one side, as if he liked being part of the set. Dix stood like a grim soldier as Dearborn approached. Together they watched the medical examiner, an old man, snap his bag shut and struggle to his feet.

"I'd say he's been dead since late yesterday afternoon. I get him on the table I might find a bullet buried somewhere, but he could've died from the beating, the shock of it. Pretty brutal."

"Ever see anything like it?" Dearborn asked.

"Not quite," said the medical examiner. "That's not a face anymore."

"To me, looks like an animal ate it," Dix interjected with a grimace.

"Any ideas about the weapon?" Dearborn asked.

"Something that shreds," the medical examiner said. "That's all I can say."

As the medical examiner left, one of the ambulance attendants stirred, but Dix stayed him with a gesture. Dearborn said, "Anybody from the DA's office show up?"

"Not yet," Dix said.

"Well, I'm not going to let that body just lie there. Release it."

Dix snapped his fingers and then stepped back with Dearborn to watch the attendants deftly package the body and slip it onto a stretcher. People on the street murmured. After the ambulance sped away, they reluctantly dispersed toward their houses. All would have to be questioned, a chore Dearborn figured would be fruitless and had already decided to have Dix do it. Dix was watching the bright descent of a jay on the lawn. Dearborn tilted his head toward the Chases' house.

"Know what we're dealing with in there?"

"What?"

Dearborn smiled. "An ex-cop."

Chase stood in the kitchen, and Ida appeared presently, her heavy hair pulled back and her eyes fixed intently on him. His face was drained of expression. He took her into his arms and kissed her as if he were taking a needed mouthful of cool water. Her head dipped to his shoulder, and he murmured, "How's David doing?"

"Reading one of those baseball books you bought him."

"He's all right, then."

"I think so."

They parted and sat across from each other at the table. Chase stared off into space, as if his senses were dulled. He appeared to be looking toward the window, where the tops of sunflowers were visible. One had a visitor, a goldfinch. Ida placed an elbow on the table.

"What did you tell the officer?"

"Nothing."

"Did he give you trouble?"

"A little."

"Is he dangerous?"

"I don't know," Chase said, watching the finch fly away. "I used to be able to size up people fast. Now I need more time."

"Frank." Ida's voice was strained. "That body out there. You knew the man, didn't you?"

Chase took the question in slowly and then nodded ever so slightly. Ida drew a breath.

"Was he a friend?"

"No, but I liked him."

"They'll identify him eventually."

"I need the time to think."

The muscles in Ida's face went tight. "I got you into this, didn't I?"

"No, you didn't." He looked at her and smiled. "I wish I could blame you, but I can't."

"You don't mean that, do you?"

"No."

Her hand slid across the table to his. "But I had an idea what you were doing. I could have said something."

"I made the decision, not you, and I could've backed out anytime. I didn't."

Ida studied him. "Frank. Can you give the money back?"

"That's a thought, isn't it?" he said, his tone faintly ironic.

"Is it possible?"

"I don't know. I'm not even sure now who I was dealing with. Something about this isn't right."

"What?"

"I don't know."

She squeezed his hand hard. "We're together in this, as in everything."

He stared at her in a way that put her on guard. She let their hands fall apart, and he said, "It's funny, but sometimes I still think of you as Rupert's wife, not mine."

"I love you," she said, once again feeling her face tighten. "How many times do I have to prove it?"

"You don't. I'm sorry." He rose, went to the window, and gazed beyond the sunflowers. "Whose cat is that?"

She joined him. "I don't know. It's always around."

He kissed her, and she kneaded the back of his neck. His stare out the window turned vacant.

"Now what are you thinking about?"

"I wish I were still a cop."

7.

MEETINGS

Frank Chase married Ida in the spring of '78. Rupert Goetz gave them his calculated blessing more than a year before the ceremony, working it out first with Ida, lunching with her at the Maison Robert, the setting gracious, the prices fancy. He tapped her wrist and nodded over the crowd toward a distant table near the wall, at present occupied by a clutch of ornate-haired women, some of them eating mussels.

"That's where the mayor and his gang sit when they come here."

Ida stared at him. "What do I care where he sits?"

Her mood was not good, which he tried to ignore. Her face was flushed, her lips darkly colored, and her black hair yanked back severely, making her look somewhat exotic, like a gypsy, which displeased him. She was wearing a tailored flannel pant-suit that was stylish, but he preferred her in a dress that clung and revealed her impressive breasts, drawing attention to her and to him. She took a quick swallow of Dubonnet and scowled at the menu.

"You'd better order for me, since I can't read this thing, unless maybe I have it upside down."

"You can order in English."

"I'd rather fake it, wouldn't you?" she said in a voice too loud for his liking, and he gave her a warning look.

"I know what you're doing," he said, scarcely moving his

mouth. "So cut it out."

"What am I doing, Rupert? Tell me." Her dark eyes were fierce, and he glanced away, his shoulders stiffening into his familiar policeman's pose. She said, "Why don't you undo your jacket so your holster shows?"

"I'm not wearing a weapon," he said quietly.

"Isn't that against regulations?"

"I consider myself off duty."

"Still making up your own rules, I see." She slapped her menu shut. "I'll have a soufflé. That's all I want."

"Fine," he murmured. "I might try the chicken in red wine."

"Say it in French, Rupert. *Coq au vin.* Sounds snappier. Practice it before the waiter comes."

"On the other hand," he said, studying his menu as though she hadn't spoken, "the beef burgundy sounds good."

"I wouldn't advise it. It usually makes you fart."

He stared at her coldly. "Do you want to leave?"

She was rigid, as if bracing herself against the inevitable sadness of the situation. Half closing her eyes, she said, "Ten years of marriage down the drain. No, Rupert. Let's get it over with."

They ordered.

He said, "I know you're seeing Frank."

"That's no secret," she said. "You have what you want. Shouldn't I have something?"

"You don't understand. I think it's great."

"I'm sure you do. You think you've arranged it all. You're an intriguer, Rupert, and you always have been. I wouldn't mind if you were dangerous only to yourself, but you're dangerous to me too. And maybe to Frank."

He sought her hand, and she pulled it away. "Ida, I only want what's best for you."

"You want what's best for yourself."

He showed chagrin, and he pointed a finger at her. "I'm being twice as fair as I have to be, and your lawyer knows it. Plus you're getting full custody of David."

"You don't give a damn about David."

He appeared hurt and finished the remains of a bourbon he'd been nursing. "I know Frank would be good to him. And to you too, Ida."

When the waiter served their lunch, she closed her eyes, as if everything were real and unreal at the same time. When she heard the waiter move away, she let her arms sag, a pleasant feeling. "Eat," he said. She couldn't. She did not even want to look at the food. When she opened her eyes she saw that he was not eating either. His attention was riveted far to his left, on a man's lurid smile produced by square teeth in an old face, which was long and gaunt, every bone showing in it. The eyes were penetrating.

"Christ," Goetz murmured, more to himself than to Ida. "How did I miss *him.*"

Ida blinked. "Who is that old man?"

"He's not as old as he looks." Goetz slightly tilted his hand at the wrist, a respectful gesture to the man, an acknowledgment of him. "I'm surprised to see him here. He has trouble walking, arthritis or something. That's a bodyguard sitting with him."

"You're telling me he's important."

"Let's put it this way," Goetz said, shifting his shoulders, as if to ease out of the man's range. "He's one big wop."

"Why don't you just say he's Italian."

"Italian doesn't describe him. Wop does."

"Why is he smiling at me?"

"Smile back. He's paying you respect. He knows you're my wife."

Ida, whose vulgarity was infrequent, said, "Fuck him."

Goetz, who had never struck her in his life, wanted to.

She said, "What's the matter? Don't tell me your little girl friend doesn't talk that way."

"Not in front of me."

"How sweet. But I don't believe it."

Goetz looked again toward the man and lowered his head. "Don't embarrass me."

"Are you afraid of him?"

"Why should I be afraid of him."

"You act it."

Ida studied him. "The smile, Rupert. Is it that important to you?"

He gave a bare nod.

Ida's smile was there all at once, big and broad, stunning in a wide display of teeth and gums. Her face was set. The smile stuck.

Goetz in a low voice said, "That's enough."

"You're sure?"

He thrust an abrupt hand past her and called for the check.

Going back several years, a balmy evening in August, festival time in the North End, the man's face was not cadaverous but simply razor-sharp, and his posture at that time was only partly sclerotic. His teeth were not square but natural, and his hair, though thinning rapidly, was his own. He stood with a companion in the doorway of a furniture store, apart from the noise and swarm, the carnival atmosphere of Hanover Street, the feast of St. Agrippina. Somewhere a band was playing. His companion said, "You want I should get you something to eat?"

"Later," he said, observing the milling crowds, his eye on young women and girls, disfavoring the many in miniskirts, though the fashion was fading. His companion nudged him gently.

"You see him?"

He looked. "I see him."

"He wants to meet you, though he's pretending different."

"Go get him. Tell him I want to meet him."

It didn't take long. The companion made the introductions and then slipped out of earshot but not out of sight as the man in the doorway adjusted his posture. He raised a hand, the long fingers like pieces of white lead, and gestured at the teeming street. "You like our celebrations?"

Rupert Goetz shrugged. "It's festive."

"You should bring your family. You a family man?"

"Yes."

"My wife, she's here somewhere with my sister and nephew. Pretty soon there's a parade carrying a statue of a saint. Maybe you know the custom. You stuff the saint, but you do it from the outside, with money. You pin it on. No dollars. Fives and tens. I write my name on a fifty and do it, a trick my father taught me. Let the priest know whose money he's putting in his pocket."

Goetz nodded. "That way he can tell God."

They exchanged a thin smile, their faces in shadows, the band playing louder, the smell of food rising up. "Goetz. That's a German name. You a Jew?"

"I might have a little in me, who knows?"

"Smartest Jew I ever met, Meyer Lansky. Jesus Christ was no smarter, believe me." There was another adjustment of posture, this one more strenuous, but the voice did not show the strain. "I hear you did a good turn for somebody over there in Dorchester, when was it, last winter?"

Goetz played a part. "I don't remember, unless you mean maybe that business at the hardware store."

"I think that's what I mean. The man could have lost his inventory and worse. Nice that it didn't happen. He's a cousin of mine. Family."

"I didn't know that."

"Is that so?" The smile was there and then not there. "What about your partner that got hurt?"

"He's all right now."

"Chase. His name I read in the paper. Yours I knew. Maybe I should thank him too."

Goetz hesitated a second or two. "I don't think he would understand."

"Ah, I see." He breathed in, the charcoal smell of sausages nearby. "I hear you're in detectives now and already in for another promotion. Maybe I could help."

Goetz glanced away, as if he hadn't heard. He looked toward the vendor selling sausages.

"I know a few people. I could put a word in, might help, might not. Let me know."

Goetz did not say yes, and he did not say no. He said, "I'm a fair guy."

"That's all we want."

Goetz touched his tie, which did not need straightening, and said, "How's the food here?"

"They tell me it's good."

Goetz stepped back into the crowd.

Less than an hour after parting from Ida outside the Maison Robert, he was relaxed behind his desk, feet up, the door closed, Frank Chase standing before him. "For Christ's sake, Frank. No need to be formal. Sit down." Chase did, warily. The pupils in Goetz's blue eyes seemed diamond-shaped. Goetz said, "Did I ever tell you about my father?"

Chase said, "I feel a story coming."

"He was victim of the worst kind of grinding routine. He worked the assembly line in a cat-food factory. He helped can the stinking stuff. He took me there once, I must've been five or six. One whiff and I lost my breakfast. That's why I never blamed him for taking off on us, parts unknown."

"I had the impression your father was dead."

"That's what I tell people. What did your father do, Frank?"

"I think I told you once. He drove an oil truck."

Goetz smiled. I bet you can still smell the stuff."

"Funny, but I always liked the odor."

"I bet *he* didn't."

"I don't know. It's too late to ask him."

Goetz dropped his feet. He sat forward, placing his elbows on his desk, which was clear except for a pen and a pad and two telephones. He spoke quietly. "You and me, Frank, how different are we from our fathers? I mean, if you stop to think about it. We've got ourselves a routine, and it grinds. We throw crumbs in the can, Walpole if we're lucky, Bridgewater if the judge says the guy's crazy. Hell, we're all crazy, especially you and me, Frank, putting our lives on the line in one way, our careers in another. If we don't make an arrest fast when something's politically hot, you've got me on your ass, and I've got the commissioner on mine. And who's he got on his—the mayor. We could make a cartoon of that. I oughta tell Szep at the *Globe.*"

Chase was uncomfortable and on guard, not at all sure what Goetz was leading up to. He lit a cigarette. No ashtray. Goetz provided one from a bottom drawer.

"Our problem, Frank, is we're not Irish. In this tightass city you can't breathe unless it's in some harp's face. Hurley, Curley, Harrington, Farrington, *Jesus Christ!* They control the state, the city, and the police. They've got both hands on the public tit, and they won't let you near the nipple."

"You've done all right, Rupert."

"That's because I'm smart. But what if I wasn't? What if I didn't know what asses to kiss? You and I would still be in uniform banging heads in Roxbury."

"I never banged heads."

"But I did, didn't I? You were the good guy, I was the bad guy. And it worked. I remember those days. I used to tell Ida about it, and she'd have a fit. Then I'd tell her I was only teasing her."

Chase was silent, and the silence grew. Goetz seemed to enjoy it, but finally he broke it.

"Frank, she's who I really want to talk about. That's why I called you in."

Chase colored.

"No need to be embarrassed," Goetz said lightly. "I have a lot of respect for the both of you, and all that matters to me is

Ida's happy, the kid too."

Chase sat perfectly still.

"Frank, I'm not blind. I know you see her, and I'm glad you two are hitting it off. I hope it becomes permanent."

"Nothing's definite."

"Come on, Frank. I know Ida's got her heart set on you, and I have a damned good ida how you feel about her. And what really clinches it is David's no problem. I know you get a kick out of him. Am I right? He's a hell of a kid, isn't he? Ida's looks, thank God."

Chase shifted his eyes to the window and tuned an ear to the muffled noise of street traffic, piercing only when a horn sounded.

"What's the matter, Frank? Don't want to confide in me?" He winked. "You want to make Ida an honest woman, don't you?"

Chase had difficulty controlling his face. "Knock it off, Rupert."

"What's the matter, then? Is it the responsibility? OK, let's talk about that. Boils down to money. There's certainly none in Homicide, we both know that. I mean, without even ever discussing it."

Chase interrupted, softly. "Before we got into Homicide, you did all right in things I never knew about."

"They were things you didn't want to know about, Frank. But I'll tell you something. All I ever took was what the politicians call legitimate graft, chickenfeed you're expected to accept, part of the salary, figured in, though not for tax purposes." Goetz paused to smile and to watch Chase crush out his cigarette. "Of course there's bigger money floating around. I know cops with a lot less rank than me who go home at night to silk sheets. Want me to name a few? No, that's their business, right?"

Chase said nothing.

"Don't be afraid to talk, Frank. Every so often I have every inch of this office gone over." ·

Chase said, "Why are we going round and round?"

Goetz laughed. "You're good, Frank. You sit there like you're only half alert when I know you're wide awake. OK, I'll make it short. It's about your future, what you want to do with the rest of your life, and of course it's about Ida too. Are you serious about her? Come on, yes or no?"

"Yes."

"That's what I thought. OK, it's best you don't work for me. Could be embarrassing for both of us. I'll arrange a transfer. You make out the request. What's the matter?"

Chase had narrowed his eyes.

"Have I ever steered you wrong?"

"Only once."

Goetz sat back. "You talking about Dorchester? You know how to hurt a guy, don't you?"

"You asked."

"You really blame me for that?"

Chase looked away. "No." He looked back. "What kind of transfer are you talking about?"

"Narcotics."

Chase straightened in his chair. "I'm not a kid any more. I could get my head blown off."

"Right," said Goetz in an easy tone. "If you're dumb."

"And if I'm smart?"

Goetz was slow to answer, slow to smile. "Frank, you could make a bundle."

Goetz, using his own car instead of the chauffeured one, fought four-o'clock traffic to Charles River Park and almost would have made better time had he walked. The winter day was ending queerly, with smashes of lightning in a slightly intoxicated sky that seemed like summer. He electrically lowered the window when a new security guard failed to recognize the car and gave him a speculative glance. "Abbott," he said, using Sherry's name as if it were his own, and the guard marked a clipboard and waved him on.

He had a key to the downstairs inner door and another to the apartment, which he entered quietly, tossing his overcoat on a chair. Sherry was lying on the rug, toasting herself in the glare of a large lamp that looked as if it belonged on a movie set. He knelt beside her.

"You've got the nicest shaped ass I've ever seen in my life."

She twisted around and stretched back on her elbows. "See anything else that attracts you?" His hand descended the hot curve of her shoulder. Balancing herself on one elbow, she reached for the knot of his tie. "Get loose and join me," she said.

He pulled back a bit. "I don't think that big bulb is all that great for the skin."

She dropped down and lay flat, rearranging her mass of hair so that he could better see her face. "Kiss me," she said. He did, under the bright light, which made him nervous. She whispered, "Did things go well?"

"Who's to say?" he said, pulling back again. "With Ida it was nasty. The woman knows how to cut."

"You expected that."

"But in ways she surprised me."

"What ways?"

"I don't know," he said, his voice trailing off.

"You still have feelings for her."

He hesitated. "Yeah, sure I do."

"I'm glad you said that. I'd be disappointed if you hadn't. Now tell me about Chase."

Goetz allowed himself a smile. "I think we might have something there. But it's too soon to say."

"Did he agree to the transfer?"

Goetz gave a half nod, a hand moving to her ankle.

"What else?"

"Let's say I laid it out for him, a little."

"Ida might argue him out of it."

"He'd never tell her, and she'd never ask. That's the way I trained her."

"You could never train me, Rupert."

"No need."

"Right." Then she drew her arms back and squeezed her hands under her head. "Get loose."

He did, ignoring the light.

"You're an exciting man, Rupert. Did you ever read Ibsen?"

"I might've. Why?"

"*The Master Builder.* Well, you're the master mover. Rupert, you're terrific."

He slid over her and into her as she lifted herself, a solid uniting. He heard the click.

"What a way for you to get a tan," she said.

"Or burn my ass," he said in a distant voice, as if Ida were under him.

8.

CONNECTIONS

Ida took the phone off the hook. Too many curious people in town had been calling. She was making a sandwich to take to David when Chase reentered the kitchen after sitting alone for an hour near the pool. "Let me make you one," she said. He shook his head and started to replace the phone. "Frank, don't. It'll only ring again."

He let the phone dangle. "Who's been calling?"

"Everybody, including Karl to ask if there was anything he could do and then, more to the point, to see if you had any appointments he should give to somebody else. I told him I didn't want to disturb you, and he got a little huffy."

"The hell with him."

"My sentiments exactly."

"All he had to do was look at my calendar. He was double-checking."

"That's Karl.

"Look, do you mind?" Chase replaced the phone, and it rang. Ida smiled at him ruefully.

"I told you."

Chase snatched the phone, held it to his ear, and said nothing.

"The line clean?" The voice belonged to Rupert Goetz.

"How do I know?" said Chase.

"I heard somebody shit on your grass. That true?"

"You hear fast."

"Hell, it was on WEEI. Been talking to reporters?"

"No, though a couple of them called."

"Any ideas?"

Chase hesitated. "It's not hard to come up with theories."

Goetz cleared his throat. "Wish you had returned my call last night."

"Why, would it have kept my grass clean?"

"No, but you should've called anyway. How's Ida taking it?"

"OK."

"The kid?"

"OK."

"What about you?"

"Don't worry about me," Chase said brusquely.

Goetz sighed. "I think this line's dirty."

"I doubt it. Not yet."

"You said before you didn't know."

"I don't."

Goetz sighed again. "Sit tight. I'm going to come see you, but it might be late. Give me directions."

"That wise?"

"Don't worry. It'll be like I'm coming to see the kid."

Chase gave him the directions and hung up. Ida placed the sandwich she had made on a plate. Without looking up, she said, "I gather he's coming."

"Yes," Chase said.

"That's what I was afraid of," she said, pouring milk into a glass, which had David's name on it.

"Give me that stuff," Chase said. "I'll take it to him."

"No," she said. "We'll both do it."

Colby Lane was a sloping cul-de-sac. The Chase's house was among those at the bottom semicircling an island of grass, which neighbors took turns mowing. The Gundermans' house was at the top and the last that Dix visited. Other neighbors were visibly shaken, but Lee Gunderman seemed pleased. "Exciting," she said. Dix spoke rapidly and tried to keep his questions brief. "No, damn it," she said. "I wish I could help you."

"Maybe your husband heard something, some car, and didn't think anything of it, went right back to sleep."

She shook her head. "Nothing wakes Karl. But talk to him yourself if you want. Gunderman Realty."

"That's where Mr. Chase works."

"Yes. A good man. My husband doesn't hire just anybody."

Dix stuffed away his notebook. "Thank you."

"That's all?" she said, disappointed.

He nodded and rose to leave.

"Just a minute," she said. "As long as you're here, there's another matter you might be interested in. I've been getting obscene calls all summer. Actually they started in the spring."

Dix hid his impatience. "Have you reported it to the telephone company?"

"I'm reporting it to you."

"I'll have somebody get in touch with you." He started to turn away.

"Hold on. Let me finish. I've got an idea who it is."

Dix looked at her more carefully. Her sharp cheekbones reminded him of Katherine Hepburn's. She was wearing a man's shirt and tight shorts, and her legs were thin shapely shoots. He was uncertain what to make of her. "Who?" he asked and watched her expression change.

"Well, let's wait a bit. I don't want to get anybody in trouble, but I'll give you a clue. I always get one after Little League."

Dix lifted his chin a little.

"My son, Brian, plays for the Red Sox. Does that tell you anything?"

"One of his teammates is doing it?"

"Forget it. You've got bigger things on your mind."

She walked him to the door, opened it for him, and then followed him out, as if to make sure no corpse had been left on her lawn. An unmarked police car pulled into the drive, and Lee peered at the face behind the wheel, the face in some odd way familiar to her.

"Who is that?" she asked Dix.

"Sergeant Dearborn. He's in charge of the investigation."

Shielding her eyes, she squinted hard at the face, which stared back at her. It was deadpan and appeared slightly pitted. "Dearborn. Does he have a brother?"

Dix stifled a laugh but let out a smile. "He's got brothers and cousins and everything else." Dix gave her a small salute. "Thanks for your time."

"By the way," she said, holding him with her eyes. "There's a makeup game tonight. Sox versus the Cards."

"Yes, ma'am. When you decide what's best, you let us know."

Dix stepped smartly around the car to the driver's side, and Dearborn shifted over. Lee waved goodby. The wave was partly to Dearborn, who said out of the side of his mouth, "Who the hell is that?"

They took the window table in Finn's, which gave Dearborn a look at traffic passing through the square. When Dix continued talking about Lee Gunderman, Dearborn said, "Enough of her." When the waitress came, he ordered a hamburger, Dix a BLT. The orders didn't take long. For a while, they ate in silence. Dix took time out to wipe his chin.

"Don't you think we ought to talk to her husband?"

"Yeah, we will," Dearborn said, chewing. "No rush."

"He's right here in the square."

"I know where he is."

The waitress returned. "More coffee?"

"Yeah, fill 'em both."

She poured from a carafe and said, "Everybody's talking about it."

"Yeah, what are they saying?" Dearborn asked with a frown. She was married to one of his brothers.

"You know, like who's this fella Chase."

Dearborn ran a hand up her leg. "Let them talk about that."

"Don't be smart," she said with a blank face, backing off and drifting away.

Dix shifted forward. "I still can't get over what you told me about him. How long have you known?"

"How long's he been in town? More than a year?" I recognized his name. He used to get his picture in the paper. He made some pretty good busts."

"Homicide."

"Right. Except he got himself transferred into Narcotics. From what I heard, he stayed there maybe a year and then all of a sudden resigned. Get the picture?"

Dix made a rude noise with his lips.

"There's more." Dearborn sipped his coffee. "The kid they got isn't his."

Dix waited, then said, "OK, tell me."

"Chief of Homicide, Boston. Who is it?"

Dix didn't know.

"A guy named Goetz. That's who Chase's wife used to be married to. That's the kid's father. I got that from Chuckie coaches Little League."

"That means Chase walked off with the boss's wife."

"Interesting, huh?"

Dix appeared puzzled. "But what does it mean?"

"I'm just feeding you information. Make what you want of it."

"What do you make of it?"

Dearborn merely shrugged and drank more coffee. His sister-in-law breezed by the table, but he did not look up. Dix did, secretly. He had seen her in a bathing suit once, Pomp's Pond, two of her youngest kids splashing near her in the water. Dearborn said, "How'd you like some overtime tonight?"

Dix dropped his gaze. "You mean the kind I don't get paid for?"

"Exactly."

Dix stared at his coffee as if he no longer wanted it. "Yuh, OK," he said.

"Don't do me any favors."

"I said OK."

"Attitude, Dix. That's what counts."

Dix flushed, as if suddenly reliving a schoolboy episode, a teacher talking to him.

Dearborn said, "We don't want Chase thinking we're a couple of hick cops. Instead we stay two steps ahead of him."

Dix nodded a small smile, some excitement growing. "Was Chase a tough cop?"

"What's tough? You tell me." Dearborn's voice was unpleasant, along with his look. "Don't let the fact he was a city cop intimidate you. I'm as much of a professional as he ever was."

Dix finished his coffee in two swallows and balled up his napkin. Dearborn's sister-in-law was at another table, clearing it, and Dix again had a vision of the pond, the bathing suit, of thighs long, white and wide, maybe a little too wide. Then he noticed she was glancing toward them, not at him, but wearily at Dearborn. Dearborn looked back at her, for a moment.

Dix whispered, "Chuckie still giving her grief?"

"That's none of your business," Dearborn said, throwing him a dirty look and gathering himself to leave. Dix rose with him.

Dix said, "Shouldn't we leave her a tip?"

"It's enough we eat here. Everybody else goes to Friendly's."

Outside, Dearborn paused to pick his teeth and watch traffic. Dix touched the fender of a parked car, which was baking in the sun, and then quickly drew his hand away. He said, "Tonight, should I wear anything special?"

"Yeah," said Dearborn. "Your shoes."

9.

CALLS

The Red Sox raced onto the field against the Cardinals, and Lee Gunderman peered toward the outfield because the figure galloping toward the shadows in right wasn't familiar. She sat on the first rung of the stands, alone because her husband was showing houses, including two that were Chase's responsibility. Rising, flipping away a cigarette and brushing the seat of her scant shorts, she headed toward the bench, where her son, hunched forward with a few other spare players, was resting his pitching arm for another evening. He made a small face at her approach. The manager, well aware of her presence even before she had left the stands, stood with his big arms crossed high on his chest and stared sourly at the field, pretending not to see her but glimpsing her from the corner of his eye.

"You're not supposed to be here, Ma." Brian held his scowl.

"I don't see any signs." She thrust fingertips into back pockets too tight to accommodate whole hands. Her sunglasses reflected her son and another boy peering up at her. "Where's David?" she asked.

"Didn't show." Brian increased his scowl and readjusted his cap. "Didn't even call Chuckie."

The manager stiffened at hearing his name but didn't turn. He was heavy in the shoulders and thick-legged and wore a crimson cap like the boys and a warmup jacket with his name stitched on it. Lee strolled toward him.

"I'm Brian's mother," she said, which she didn't need to tell him. He knew exactly who she was and did not bother to nod. She stood with her sandled feet together and her fingers still wedged in her rear pockets. "I see you're a Dearborn."

He grunted. He did not want to speak or even acknowledge her presence, but she stood planted, viewing him with darting eye movements, as if she were getting him down cold, which angered him and in a deep way unnerved him. When he finally looked at her straight on, it was with one eye, the sun in his face.

"I thought so," she said. "There's a resemblance. Your brother, I mean. Are you a policeman too?"

"Fire," he mumbled and tugged at his cap. "I can't talk now. I'm coaching a game."

"But the score's always the same," she said and smiled with an open mouth. "It must be frustrating for you."

"I play with what I have."

"I'm sure."

He was unsure of her meaning and felt his face heat. It seemed to squeeze to one side, and again he fiddled with his cap, with an urge to strike her and do worse things. He pictured his hand pressing over her mouth and flattening the tip of her nose.

She said, "I guess you know why your regular right fielder isn't here."

"I heard," he said, switching his gaze to something distant.

"I can't hear you, Mr. Dearborn."

She was trying to trick him, catch him. He could feel it.

She said, "It's not every day somebody leaves a body on the lawn. The poor kid, I hope he didn't see it."

"He should've called just the same. That's the rule."

"Your rule, Mr. Dearborn?"

"League's." He looked at her coldly. "My name's Chuckie. My father was Mr. Dearborn."

"Of course."

He put a hand to his mouth and hollered to his pint-sized pitcher. "Keep the ball down! Down!"

She said, "I don't suppose you can guess what time the game

will be over. My husband and I are going to a party."

His back was to her now, and he didn't answer. He merely shook his head. When he did look at her again, she was moving away, her thumbs extending from her pockets to the sharp edges of her hips, her buttocks no bigger than a boy's. He let his breath out.

"Fucking flake," he muttered, forgetting her son was there.

Chase took the call, picking up the phone on the sun porch. The voice said, "I was told to call you. About your present. Did you get it?" Chase silently seated himself, with a cup of coffee in his hand. Ida had just made it. It came from a small expensive can and was good: rich, strong, aromatic. He took a slow sip, burning his lips. The voice went on, "It got damaged, but maybe you can understand how it happened."

Chase said, "Who is this?"

"A guy who gives things."

"You give too much."

"Those things happen. I'm too good at what I do." He half-laughed. "Now it's your turn to *give back.* Get it?"

Chase put his coffee down. The cup had become too heavy.

The man's voice quickened. "They figure you should add on interest, maybe what your house is worth. Nice house. I described it to them."

Chase said something under his breath.

"You got no call to bitch, pal, so don't make them wait. They might get mad."

"Who are they?"

"Jesus," the man said. "If you don't know, you're in worse trouble than you think."

He disconnected.

For a number of seconds, sitting forward, Chase stared at his shoes. Then he slipped them off, Florsheims on their third set of heels. He had bought them while still on the force. He sat back when he saw Ida in the doorway.

"What was that, Frank?"

"I don't know. A crank."

She came toward him, knelt in front of him, and offered him her hands. "Frank, don't."

"Don't what?"

"Don't do what Rupert did to me."

"I'm not Rupert."

"Good. Then don't keep me in the dark."

"I never should've hired him," said Karl Gunderman, carefully combing his thinning hair after a fast shower and change of clothes. "I should have my head examined."

"You're over-reacting," Lee said, putting finishing touches to her face and smiling at herself through her lipstick. She blotted her mouth on toilet tissue.

"The hell I am. You think people investing a hundred thousand and more for a house will want to deal with a guy like that? Think again. Word gets around fast." He took time to click a couple of throat lozenges around in his mouth.

"Why are you sucking those?"

"I'm hoarse from talking to people. *His* clients."

"Did you sell anything?"

"Yes," he said, fussing with his necktie. "But he's not getting a commission on it."

She went to him, and he lifted his scented chin. His face was soft and sharply shaved, boyish in a large clumsy way and smarting from strong dosages of Old Spice. She reknotted his tie, disliking the feel of it, polyester. Tugging it tight, she said, "Don't be unfair. It's not his fault what happened."

Gunderman pulled away. "Are you kidding? He's mixed up in something. I know it, and you'd better." He pointed a blunt finger at her. "That's something else I shouldn't have done—sold him a house on *our* street."

"You act as if I had something to do with it."

"No, that was another mistake of mine."

She stood tall. "You haven't told me. Do you like this dress?"

"I don't like the slit."

"It's fashionable."

"The front's too low. Lean forward. Christ I can see what you've got. Good thing it's not much."

She gazed at him without a smile. "Hurry up, Karl. It's past nine."

Brian was still in his baseball suit. He and his younger brother, snacking in front of a television, scarcely glanced up when she looked in on them with instructions to phone the Dowells in the event of an emergency. Gunderman peered over her shoulder. "We won't be late," she said.

"Yes, you will," said Brian.

"What's the matter with him?" Gunderman said as they descended the stairs.

"They lost."

"Not his fault. He didn't pitch."

Lee shrugged and took a last look at herself in the hall mirror, with Gunderman again peering over her. They were nearly out the door when the phone rang. "I knew it!" Lee said with a shrewd look and hurried to the nearest phone, in the kitchen. Gunderman followed. It was another obscene call, and she stared hard at her husband, rolling her eyes to let him know.

"Hang up!" he said when she continued to listen while playing with the cord. Reluctantly she replaced the receiver.

"I was trying to catch something telling in his voice. He disguises it, you know."

"I don't want you listening to that garbage. What'd he say this time?"

"Do you really want to know?"

"No."

They reached the door.

"Tell me."

"He said he wanted to stick it to me."

Gunderman cursed, then roughly escorted her out the door.

Rupert Goetz arrived in Andover after dark and then, despite Chase's detailed directions, had trouble finding Colby Lane. Houses blinked at him from behind trees. Staying too long on Wildwood Road, which took him to Route 28, he veered fast onto Hidden Road, thinking it might be an extension of Wildwood, but it meandered back to the highway. Gradually Phillips Academy loomed on each side, and he realized he was heading into the center of town. He made a U-turn and cruised back toward Wildwood, dimming his lights for an approaching car, probably Chase and David on their way to Friendly's.

Ida answered his ring. The outside light harshly illuminated his face, and she watched him swat away a moth. She stepped silently aside and let him come in, closing the door after him. His stare was intense. "You look good," he said.

"Rupert, what's happening?"

"What did Frank tell you?"

"Not enough."

"I don't know any more than he does."

"Somehow I don't believe that."

He gazed beyond her. "Where is he? He knew I was coming."

"He took David for an ice-cream, just to get him out of the house for a while."

"The kid is scared?"

"Pretending hard not to be."

"He's tough."

"Not as tough as you think."

"Frank treating him OK?"

"I don't think you even have to ask."

"I know I don't, but I have the right." He was staring intensely at her again and seemed on the verge of reaching for her. She turned away and led him into the living room, where most of the furniture was familiar to him. He made a small sigh of sadness, which she ignored.

"Do you want coffee?"

"A drink, if you don't mind." He settled in a chair that had been a favorite.

"Bourbon's all we have."

"You and I always had a little cognac on hand."

She ignored that too. She stood with her back to him at the liquor cabinet and poured raw bourbon into a glass, no ice, no water, which wasn't the way he liked it. He took it and said nothing. She said, "I don't want Frank hurt."

"I don't want any of you hurt. I'm here to help."

She started to reply harshly but stopped herself. She sat away from him, her face in a shadow, her hands united in her lap. "I think Frank should give the money back."

For a long moment Goetz studied his drink. "So you know about that?"

"Not the details."

"I don't know them either."

She spoke coldly. "I doubt that."

Goetz spoke patiently. "When Frank went into Narcotics, he was on his own."

"That's what he told me."

"Then you got it from the horse's mouth."

"I want him to give the money back, do you understand?"

Goetz's face turned severe. "That's the worst thing he could do."

"I don't see how. Would you care to explain?"

"Frank and I will discuss it."

Her dark eyes burned. "You can't exclude me any more."

He was no longer listening to her but slowly sipping the warm bourbon, his face grimly set. She remembered the expression well. He was deep in very private thought, and he came out of it slowly, his gaze going to a wall that held a framed picture of David, done in black and white by a local photographer who had caught shades of sadness in the boy. She knew he had seen it the moment he had entered the room. Now, warm drink in hand, he pointed to it.

"The kid's growing up without me. I miss him, Ida." His eyes reached for her. "Same as I miss you."

She did not speak.

"You must know I have certain regrets."

"Rupert. Drop it."

She rose with a jolt, strode to the liquor cabinet, splashed bourbon into a glass, a little too much, and turned toward him with the glass raised.

"This is to Frank and me."

"Yes, Ida. I'll drink to that."

"You bet your life you will."

She took a deep swallow that instantly showed in her eyes. Nothing showed in his, though he tipped his head back and finished what was in his glass. She remained standing.

"I repeat, Rupert. I don't want him hurt."

"We've agreed on that."

"I'd get back at you somehow."

Goetz reacted slowly, as if he hadn't heard right. "Have we really come to this?"

"You'd better believe it."

He gave his head a rueful shake. "I don't understand you. I gave you everything in the divorce."

She nodded. "Yes, you did, but I have an idea you got a good return on it. You see, Rupert, more than ever I don't trust you."

Outside a car door slammed. Goetz rose from his chair slowly, almost like a door being edged off its hinges.

"Is that Frank?"

"Yes," she said.

10.

KEYS

Driving home at two-fifteen in the morning with a tight grip on the wheel, Karl Gunderman said in an ill-tempered voice. "I don't get it. You don't even like Ted Dowell."

Lee Gunderman was slouched beside him with her head tipped languidly back and her eyes shut. Except for a smile, she seemed asleep. Then her head moved, her hair damp, her hand touching him. "Don't make too much of it. I certainly didn't lead him on."

"Maybe you did it without realizing it."

"Oh, no, Karl. A woman always realizes it."

He clenched the wheel harder, stomping the headlights to high beams. "You're treating it as a joke. Did he tear your dress?"

"No," she said and snuggled against him.

"A wonder. He had his hands all over you."

"You're exaggerating."

"I'm not blind."

"But you're cute. Didn't you have a good time?"

"Too many people there."

"Chases weren't."

"Don't talk to me about the Chases. That's all I heard all night."

"You have to learn to loosen up, Karl." Her hand slipped down on him.

"Don't! I'm driving."

"Driving where? Want to go to a motel?"

"Are you crazy?" He made a rough turn onto Wildwood, feeling her foot brush him. The shoe was off. Approaching Colby Lane, he started to brake for the drift into their driveway.

"Make the loop," she said with a rasp. "See if the Chases have a light on."

"Do you know what time it is?"

"Do it, please." She lifted her head. "Maybe there's another body on the lawn."

"Not funny." But he let the car coast down the street, with the moonlight flinging the shadows of big trees at them. A line of shrubs resembled crouching men. The headlights caught the jewel-eyes of a cat near an unfamiliar car in the Chases's drive, and a leafy branch blowing in front of a lighted window made the light look like a flame.

"Whose car is that?" Lee whispered.

"I don't want to know," he said and accelerated around the rotary of grass, a tree swaying in the middle of it, as if falling toward them. He parked deep in his own driveway but didn't move because Lee was still leaning against him. He nudged her.

"What's the matter?" she said.

"You're the matter. You drank too damn much."

She slowly moved her head back and forth. "No. Just enough. I feel good." Then she reached under her dress, freeing skin. He saw the naked gleam of a leg. "Let's be wanton," she said.

"What?"

"What, *hell,*" she said and showed him.

Darkly dressed, Sergeant Lionel Dearborn crouched behind shrubs and watched the car make a slow pass and then accelerate. Half-rising, he watched where it went and saw that it didn't go far, only into the driveway at the top of the street. He continued watching, two minutes passing, and then he whistled softly, which brought a bent figure to his side.

"Did you see where that car went?"

Dix nodded.

"Did you see anybody get out of it?"

Dix shook his head.

"I didn't either."

Dix scratched a bite. The shrubbery was full of mosquitoes. Dix was also dressed in dark clothing, but his face was bright.

"Do you think they saw us?"

"Doubt it." Dearborn scratched one of his own bites, already a welt. "Sneak up there and see what they hell they're doing. But don't get spotted."

Dix slipped away in the moonlit stillness, and Dearborn resumed his crouch near the sun porch, returning his attention to the vague sounds of two voices, a conversation that seemed to have been going on forever, with occasional dead time when the silences were stunning. He had gradually distinguished Frank Chase's voice and soon after learned who the other man was, for Dix earlier had checked the conspicuous car in Chase's drive and returned with a name out of the glove compartment. Rupert Goetz. The name didn't surprise Dearborn until he began thinking about it.

Listening with his eyes shut, he occasionally caught a couple of words, but nothing that told him anything. Another mosquito bit him, and he savagely scratched the back of his neck, which, like his face, was scarred from adolescent acne. His back was stiff and his legs cramped. Then he heard a laugh, distorted and rough, and he was uncertain whose it was.

He guessed Goetz.

The hours slipped by, with Rupert Goetz putting away most of the bourbon and exhibiting no effects, except when he laughed. The laugh was ugly, derisive and incongruous, as if his mind ocassionally strayed to bizarre things unrelated to the conversation. Ida, who had left them alone from the start, had long since gone to bed. So had David, against his will. The boy, after moments of awkwardness, had clung to his father, who, sentimentally and in earshot of Ida, had said to Chase, "You're living like I used to."

Their eyes trained on each other, he and Chased talked at absurd lengths about nothing of note, as though performing a ritual, much of the talk nostalgically initiated by Goetz, seemingly obsessed by past days in the department, the camaraderie, the easier living from relaxed procedures and uncomplicated busts. He brought Chase up to date on men promoted, reassigned, reprimanded, put to pasture. Chase nodded in the right places. The bottle was next to Goetz. He poured.

"I appreciate everything you're doing with David."

"My pleasure." Chase sounded partly anesthetized, but his eyes were alert.

"The baseball bit. I like that." Goetz raised his glass and took a slow swallow. "Were you a player, Frank?"

"No."

"Guys I played with, we had a taped-up ball looked like a glob of iron. Lucky we didn't break our arms throwing it and our hands catching it. We fell, we cut ourselves."

Chase lit a cigarette, crumbling the empty pack. Goetz mismanaged a smile.

"I'm not a bad guy, Frank."

"I never said you were."

"Ida seems to think so. What about David?"

"You know better."

"Yes, I guess I do." He put his glass down and got to his feet. He was quite steady on them. "Excuse me."

The first time he had used the bathroom, Chase had shown him the way. This time he found it on his own, and Chase visualized him poking into the privacy of the medicine cabinet and glimpsing things of Ida's no longer for his eyes. When he returned to the sun porch and resettled in a wicker chair with his drink, Chase rested his gaze on him and said, "Do you want to know who it was?"

"I've got a feeling I don't want to know, Frank."

"But you can guess."

"Yes, I can guess."

"Johnny Kale," Chase said, as if the unspoken name had to be uttered. "He was easy to like."

"Yes, he was," Goetz said, his eyes smaller than Chase had ever seen them.

"Of course you knew him long before I did."

Goetz rubbed his nose. "He was one of those kids could've broken a hand on that ball I told you about. He didn't have a father and nothing you could call a mother. She was an alkie who used to sleep it off bare-assed on the couch, which is how he'd find her when he came home from school. I know because I was with him once, both of us pretending we didn't see her. He kept me in the kitchen, but you could see right into the other room. I remember that like it was yesterday."

Chase brought his hands together and interlaced the fingers. "I looked at him quick, but I didn't see any bullet wounds, only the business with the face."

"That doesn't mean there wasn't a bullet, but tell me about the face."

"Cut, chopped, like the flesh flew out of it."

Goetz suddenly laughed, a sinister sound, as if it had come from somebody else. His eyes were blue chinks. He shrugged, sipped bourbon, and sobered. "You know the weapon, Frank?"

"No."

"Keys. Big old heavy ones, antique, like they came from a castle, a whole big bunch on a ring wide enough for a guy to grip and swing."

Chase let his hands slide apart. "Then you know who did it."

"I'm guessing, Frank, but guessing pretty good. He's basically a beat-up guy. Smashes heads. Somebody you probably don't know because he's only been around these parts for a year. Name is Dance."

"Dance? Who the hell is Dance?"

"Dancewicz is his real name. He used that set of keys on somebody else once. He was hired by persons unknown to do a job on a greedy dope dealer from Roxbury. Marked the guy up for life."

"But left him alive."

"If you want to call it that."

"He could've dumped Kale alive on my lawn, and I'd have got the message. What I'm saying is maybe he didn't mean to kill Kale, but it happened."

"Possible," Goetz said, and for a moment Chase thought Goetz might laugh again. He didn't. He put his glass to one side, as if he'd had enough.

"I got a call from him," Chase said. "Maybe him. They want it back."

"They mention the amount?"

"Why should they have to?"

Goetz retrieved his glass and drained it. "Tell me something, Frank, how much did you walk away with?"

"A hundred."

"A hundred grand. And Kale?"

"The same."

"You sure?"

"I'm not sure of anything now."

"Tell me how it went down."

"I grabbed the stuff, Kale the payoff."

"It should've been the other way around."

"No. Kale would've been tempted to stash the cocaine and resell it on his own. I wanted to make sure it went into the Charles."

"Smart, but did you look at what you were dumping?"

"It was a suitcase. I didn't open it."

Goetz rolled his empty glass around in both hands, raised it in one, and studied it. "What if I was to tell you the payoff was a half-million bucks, meaning the street value of what you threw in the river must've been fantastic."

Chase sat eerily silent.

"Frank, it's what I heard. I did some checking, and that's why I was late getting here."

Chase dropped his head, as if to doze and forget everything. Goetz reached for the bottle.

"Let me pour you one."

"No." Chase smiled grimly at the ceiling. "I told him I didn't want to go near anything big. All I wanted was a cushion. In my mind it was severance pay. No silk sheets, Rupert. Percale was OK."

"I know, Frank." Goetz poured what was left in the bottle into his own glass and finished off most of it with a single swallow. His eyes looked tired. They were specks. "But to be fair, I don't think Johnny Kale had the faintest idea it would be that big. He must've done a double-take when he saw what he had. And it couldn't have taken him long to find out you never checked the suitcase. Put yourself in his shoes."

Chase brought his head forward, with a pain in his back from the way he'd been sitting. Goetz's voice was a mere noise thinning away. "What took them so long?" Chase said.

"Kale must've been clever. Up to a point. A reasonable amount they'd have written off. Not a half-million bucks."

"Who are they?"

"I'm still checking."

"Rupert, don't blow on my neck. If you know, tell me."

Goetz appeared honestly injured. "Frank, you're forgetting something. I'm on your side. Yours and Ida's and David's. Nothing's going to mess up their lives if I can help it. Let me handle it, huh? You know I've got ways."

Chase, stroking his unshaved jaw, no longer seemed interested in what Goetz was saying. His eye sought a fresh pack of cigarettes where he knew there was none.

"Say something, Frank. Maybe say thanks."

Chase said nothing.

Dearborn and Dix met near a tree and then cut across lawns through pinpoint explosions of fireflies. They didn't speak until they reached Wildwood, and then Dearborn said, "What was that noise you made before you got to me?"

"Cat. Scared the shit out of me."

"Could've been a skunk."

"It was a cat."

"What about the Gundermans?"

Dix's teeth flashed in the dark. "I can tell you what I think they were doing."

"You kidding?"

"Sure looked like it. Her on him."

"Nice people," Dearborn said. "What a way to act."

"Takes all kinds," said Dix.

They reached their car, which was parked under a canopy of pines and facing the road. Dix started for the driver's side, but Dearborn stopped him with a gesture. Slipping behind the wheel, Dearborn squinted hard at his watch. "Jesus," he said with a partial yawn.

They didn't go anywhere. They waited, listening to the high-frequency hiss of insects, but not for long. Lights washed the road, and then a large silent car glided by. Dearborn said, "That's him, Goetz."

"He can probably sleep late," Dix said.

Dearborn started the motor and switched on the headlights, the long beams immediately flooded with moths. After a moment of thought, he nudged the shift into drive and cocked his head. In the next instant the car squealed onto the road, with Dix grabbing the dash for support.

"What're you doing?"

Dearborn sped to the end of Wildwood, swerved onto South Main, and soon had the hot taillights of Goetz's car in sight. Goetz was traveling at a moderate speed. Dearborn accelerated, caught up to it, and then dropped back a bit.

"He's looking in the rearview," said Dix. "He knows we're

following him."

Dearborn grinned. "Good. I want him to. Let's shake him up."

"What for?" Dix was nervous. He watched Goetz take the cutoff toward Route 93. "You can tell where he's headed. We aren't going to tail him all the way to Boston, are we?"

Dearborn laughed and speeded up some. "Did you see his shoulder move? I bet he's got his gun on the seat. Hot shit!"

"Don't get too close," Dix said, his anxiety rising.

"Why not?" Dearborn sounded high, exhilarated as if from a subtle rage.

"He's not running," Dix said.

" 'Course not. Didn't think he would."

"Don't get too close," Dix said, his anxiety growing.

"Why not, you afraid?"

"He doesn't know we're cops. You don't know what the hell he might do."

Dearborn laughed again, the sound profane, and flashed on the high beams. "Now he doesn't know what the fuck is happening."

"Lionel, for Christ's sake!"

A car's length behind, headlights blazing, he kept speed with Goetz. The stretch was deserted, no houses but much moonlight and many trees, and then a sign up ahead: Route 93 South. Goetz used his directional, slowed. Dearborn did too, while Dix got ready to duck, certain that if anything was to happen it would happen here.

Goetz made the turn.

Dearborn coasted by it.

"Mind explaining?" Dix said with sudden anger.

"I know who he is," Dearborn said quietly. "Pretty soon that sonofabitch is going to know who I am."

Neither man spoke on the way back to town. Dix, tired and disturbed, sat in a slump; Dearborn was rigid, both hands tight on the wheel, as if ready to race again. The square, bathed blue in the moonlight, was deserted except for a dog trotting across the street. Failing to see it, Dearborn nearly hit it and muttered something about the leash law.

They left the unmarked car in the police station lot and tramped toward their own cars. Dearborn was now tired too and ran a slow hand over his face. Their cars were parked side by side, one facing in, the other out. They cut between them, and Dearborn said, "You don't have to come in till noon."

"Yuh."

"What's the matter?"

"I just don't think you had to do what you did," said Dix petulantly.

Dearborn regarded him calmly and said, "I don't do anything unless there's a purpose."

They climbed into their cars. Dix's faced in, and he stared for a moment at darkened Friendly's and then at the street. He saw what Dearborn didn't. Dearborn was rubbing his face, knuckling his eyes.

The car that glided by the station and away from Friendly's belonged to Goetz.

11.

HOUSES

A few weeks after their divorce, Goetz phoned Ida and said, "Can I talk to you without us getting into an argument?"

"Yes, talk." He talked, and she grew angry. "Where I move, if I move, is none of your business."

He said, "I mentioned Andover only because I know you liked the town those times we drove through it, and my cousin's there. He'd make sure you got a good buy. Ida, I want more than anything for you and Frank to start off right. And, hell, I admit it, I've got a selfish reason. I don't want you moving so far away I can't see the kid."

"That's a laugh. When have you found time to see him lately?"

"I've got him something. A baseball glove."

"That's great. There's eight inches of snow on the ground. This spring maybe you could get him skis."

"Ida, let's stick to the subject."

"Absolutely nothing is definite."

"Now you sound like Frank."

"And I'm busy. Could we talk about this later?"

"Ida, please. I'm sorry, but I'm not exactly an outsider, am I?"

"Yes, you are," she said harshly, "but you won't accept the situation. You don't want to give up control of anything, do you?"

He tilted back. He was at his desk, which was clear of work, everything put away for another day. "Maybe you're right," he said, altering his tone. "I guess I'm too used to doing things for you. Hard habit to break."

She was silent, and he shifted his position in his chair, sitting sideways and slinging a leg over an armrest. He cleared his throat.

"Ida, let me ask you one more thing. If Frank quits the department as I think he will, what's he got lined up. Anything?"

"Why are you asking me? Ask him."

"I can talk to you better. If I can do anything for him in the way of work, will you let me?"

"You're impossible. You just won't let go."

"Will you let me?"

"Rupert, I've got marketing to do."

"Ah, Frank must be coming over."

"Right!"

He let her hang up.

A half hour later he was back on the phone talking to a cousin he had never been close to and seldom saw outside of weddings and wakes. He remembered little about the man's wife other than that she was thin, intense, provocative, and probably approachable, and he knew they had a son about David's age. He explained the situation, but Gunderman had trouble grasping it.

"You mean, you and, ah, Ida, are separated?"

"Separated and divorced, yes."

"And she's marrying someone else?"

"That's what I said, and that's why I called you. They'll be scouting around for a house. I figured you could help them."

"Sure I can," Gunderman said exuberantly after a moment's pause.

"I figured too you might be able to take Frank on as a

salesman. Not right now. Give them time to settle in first."

"Wait a minute. What are we talking about here? You're going too fast."

"They'll be buying a pretty decent house, the kind with a pool, I suppose. By the way, Karl, how much do you get for a commission—six percent?"

"I charge seven, but they don't pay that. That comes from the other end."

"That so?" said Goetz, sitting back and dropping his feet on the top of his desk. "What if you were to get something from both ends?"

"What? I don't follow you."

"Call it a gratitude fee, strictly between you and me. I feel responsible for them, and I want to make sure they fit into that town of yours—for my son's sake. He'll be with them. You following me now?"

Gunderman started to say something and stopped. His desk was cluttered, and he fiddled with things on it, including a leather-framed picture of Lee and one of Brian and his brother. At the same time he computed hypothetical figures.

"You think about it," Goetz said, "And I'll get back to you."

He clicked off.

In May of '78 in a back booth in Finn's, Gunderman said, "If you've got the drive to make money in this business, you'll make it, no two ways about it, and how much you make depends on how hard you push yourself. Get me?"

Chase nodded.

"But you can't get by with just drive," said Gunderman, sitting forward and exuding too much aftershave. "One of the women works for me is getting an ulcer, and I'll tell you right now I don't trust anybody with an ulcer. Means they're all knotted up because the job's too much for them. Peter principle. Right?"

"Most likely," said Chase.

"If I hire you, it's that woman's place you'll take."

"I don't want to put anybody out of a job."

"Don't worry about it. She's on her way out whether I take you on or not." Gunderman's arm shot up, and he fluttered a hand at the waitress. "Sweetheart, two more coffees, huh?"

Chase lighted a cigarette, and Gunderman flexed large soft shoulders, as if he'd once had muscles in them.

"Another thing," he said. "You have to know how to handle people. I can count on one hand the times I had to lower my commission to turn a sale. No need of it, not if you're a good talker, and I am."

The coffee came, and Chase stared at the waitress, whose expression was aloof and sulky, as though she were working past her time. "Thank you," he said as her eyes swept past his.

"Of course," said Gunderman, reaching for the sugar, "I've been in this business so long everything comes natural. For instance, I can't look at a house, for sale or not, without assessing its value. And I hate seeing an uninhabited house. Means somebody isn't doing his job."

Chase half-nodded.

"You don't seem enthusiastic," Gunderman said, stirring his coffee.

"You're wrong. I am."

"Good, because that's vital. And the final thing is you have to know this town inside-out, all thirty-two square miles of it. It's got no slums, but it's got distinctions, believe me. Ballard-vale is your bad area, still shacky in spots, especially along the river, and no one worth his credit card wants to buy there. It's a good place, though, to sell to young marrieds and people you have your doubts about. Shawsheen's OK, but it's still got a mill reputation from years back when it was a model village in the textile industry. West Andover is hokey and too near Lawrence and Lowell, but that doesn't mean you can't get top dollar for the houses. You sure as hell can, and I do! Prime is any-where near the academy and east of it right into Harold Parker

Forest. Sky's the limit, which is the reason you paid a little more for your house than you probably planned, but you still got a whale of a deal."

"We have water in the basement," Chase said.

"What? Oh, well, that's happened to houses that've never had the problem before. It's from the bad winter, all that snow. Then we had the freak storm last week. Wasn't that something! Anyway, I wouldn't worry."

Chase lifted his coffee cup. Gunderman looked at his watch.

"I don't want to rush you," he said and rocked the booth getting out. He left a tiny tip, and Chase added to it. The waitress, unmindful of them, was wiping down ketchup bottles, as if in her sleep. Gunderman stopped to talk with somebody, and Chase waited for him on the sidewalk. The sunshine was thin, more March than May. Chase watched the Boston bus pull in across the street and take on two passengers.

"What's the matter?" Gunderman said, appearing abruptly at his side. "You look like you're a thousand miles away."

Chase shrugged.

"Cheer up," Gunderman said, giving him a hearty slap on the back. "I guess we can safely say the job is yours."

12.

THREATS

"I wish you wouldn't smoke that thing in front of me," Goetz said and drew a soft laugh from Sherry.

"Why? Would you arrest me?"

He sat much too stiffly on a hassock and drank from a tall glass of Dewar's and water overloaded with ice cubes. A discarded copy of the *Herald American* lay unraveled on a rug near Sherry's sandals. She was stretched out on the sofa, half dressed, her toes drying. She had painted the nails.

"Loosen up, have a drag," she said, lifting the ill-made joint.

"Never," he said as she spilled an ash. "Don't burn the furniture!"

"No, sir!"

"Do you want to talk serious or not?"

"Yes, sir."

"Then put it out. I can't stand the stink."

She sat up with theatrical obedience and pinched out the joint, saving it in an ashtray. Her hair, washed a few hours earlier, cascaded past her shoulders, except for a single strand caught in her mouth. She wiped it free. "So tell me. What went wrong."

"What else? Johnny Kale was traced and made to say things."

"Poor Johnny," She said, more alert than she looked. She scratched a bare knee and, timing each word, said slowly, "But he didn't make much of a splash. Buried on page twenty-six."

"Means nothing."

"But why overreact?"

His eyes narrowed. "I never overreact. I just do what has to be done."

"Fine," she said, scratching both knees. "But you're suspecting the absolute worst."

"That's the only way to operate," he said, rattling the cubes in his glass. He drank hard and put the glass aside. She sat back with her legs stuck out.

"Tell me what you're thinking."

"Frank Chase thinks Johnny Kale was a message only to him."

"You know different?"

"Yeah, I think so."

"That's bad," she said. "But it's not the absolute worst."

He rose from the hassock and stood still, a taut figure, as if aimed at something. His suit, another new one, had an almost invisible red pinstripe.

"You going back to the office?" she asked.

"No."

"Somewhere else?"

"Yes."

She was on her feet, all of a sudden, as if someone had jabbed her. She had on only a T-shirt and underpants. "I'm going with you."

"The hell you are."

"The hell I'm not." She tossed her hair back. "I want to be in on it."

"In on what? That's dumb."

"I want to see how you operate," she said, standing with her thighs crossed, as if she had to use the bathroom. Her underpants were lacy, wedding-cake white, one of a surprise batch he'd bought her for their honeymoon.

"That wasn't in the agreement," he said.

"You didn't read the fine print."

He rocked in place. "You're looking for a fucking adventure, aren't you?"

"Oh, I'm always looking for that," she said, moving to him and slipping her arms around him. "That's how I found you, isn't it? Be a good guy and give me a minute to pee and another to dress."

He retrieved his drink, finished it off, and waited. She reappeared shortly, wearing smoky glasses, a different T-shirt, and a denim jacket and pants, with a leather bag hanging from her left shoulder. Something flashed in her hand. She unlatched the bag and dropped a .22-caliber automatic pistol inside. He had given it to her for her birthday.

"Jesus Christ," he said with a rueful smile. "What the hell have I done?"

"What do you mean?" she said, stepping into her sandals, her toes sparkling.

"We're fucking Bonnie and Clyde."

"Not bad," she said and kissed him.

An investigator from the Essex County district attorney's office questioned Frank and Ida Chase and then talked alone with Chase outside the house. Chase knew him. They had met some years ago during special training at the FBI school in Virginia and had run into each other occasionally during the course of police work. His name was Moynihan, and his hair, which had grayed prematurely, was turning white. His eyes seemed sad; Chase didn't trust him. He and Chase wandered under a large oak, where sunlight lay in odd places, like paint. He said, "How come I age and you don't?"

"Clean living," Chase said with no trace of irony.

Moynihan looked to his left. "What's that you've got back there? Pool?"

Chase nodded.

"Nice. We have one too, but ours is above ground. Our kids

don't like it now they're older. How long have you had this house, Frank?"

"We're into our second year."

"That long? I guess you could say you're a real suburbanite now."

"Getting there."

"I didn't realize you had a son."

"Stepson."

"Ah, yes. Matter of fact, Frank, I didn't even know you were married."

Chase suspected that was a lie. High in the oak an unseen bird made noises like somebody clipping shrubbery. Moynihan planted his hands in his pockets and toed the ground, as if capable of digging holes, deep ones. When he looked up, his eyes seemed sadder, which put Chase on guard.

"Anything you want to tell me, Frank? I mean, off the record."

"I can't think of anything," Chase said.

"You understand I accept your story, but I don't buy it."

"I suppose you have to keep an open mind."

There wasn't really anything more to say, but Moynihan lingered. He raised his eyes high searching for the sound in the tree. "You were a bird, Frank, you could fly away."

"But I'm not a bird."

"Neither was this fellow Kale."

Chase accompanied Moynihan to his car and stood by as he climbed into it. Moynihan fastened his seat belt, which made an enormous click, like a real lockup. He started up the car and glanced out at Chase.

"I hope I don't ever have to hurt you, Frank."

"I hope you don't either," Chase said.

He watched Moynihan drive away.

She had been home for a half-hour and was still in her waitress's uniform when she turned sharply to the sound behind her. "Don't you ever knock?" she said.

"I'm family," he said.

"How can I forget." Standing with her back to the sink, her arms crossed, she watched him take a seat at the table. "You want a beer?"

"No," he said, glancing about. "How come the house is so quiet? Where're the kids?"

"Go out in the back yard. You'll see two of them there. The older boys are working. They got jobs, you know."

"They all OK? No problems?"

She shook her head, her face expressionless. The skirt of her uniform was stained and soiled, as if she'd been in battle.

He said, "How's Chuckie?"

"You see him, don't you? He's fine."

"Not up to his old tricks, is he?"

"What are you talking about?"

"Telephone."

"How do I know?"

They stared at each other, her face now slightly sour, like his. He said, "You been taking care of him?"

"I'm his wife, ain't I? I take care of him."

"You give him what he wants?"

"This is horseshit talk."

"I asked you a question."

"Sure, I give him what he wants, but maybe it ain't enough. Wasn't enough for you, was it?"

His face darkened. "We're discussing Chuckie, not me. He's got strong needs."

"You should talk," she said with a strange laugh.

"Come on," he said. "You and I squared everything away a long time ago."

"Did we?"

"Yes!"

She turned her head and stared cold-eyed at the refrigerator door, her arms still snugly crossed. He got up and went to her, but her head stayed turned. He smiled and then placed hands low on her body.

"You got the hardest thighs, any woman I know."

"You don't want to take, don't touch."

"You're funny."

She looked at him. "No, I'm not."

His hands rose to her waist. "Mind me saying something? You're getting a little roll here. Ought to take care of it."

She pulled violently to one side, her arms coming apart. "How about minding your own God-damned business!" she said as he stood tall.

"You are my business—because of Chuckie. Remember that. And I don't want him bothering nobody but you."

"You know something, Lionel? That's a good way to put it. Perfect, in fact." She watched him wheel and head for the door. When his hand reached the knob, she said, "Am I supposed to tell Chuckie you were here?"

He glared over his shoulder, while his hand tightened on the knob, as if he were forcing himself to stay calm. "You don't tell him anything, but you damn well better take care of him."

Lionel Dearborn saw his brother crossing the street and hastened his step. They were each headed in the same direction, for Police and Fire shared the building next to Friendly's, blue cars on one side, red ones on the other. He caught up to him near a pumper and startled him with an arm-grab. "Chuckie, how are you?"

"Good. Why?"

Lionel Dearborn's stare was merciless. "I don't have to start worrying about you again, do I?"

"No. Let go of the arm."

Lionel Dearborn tightened his grip, though his brother could have broken it, being the stronger physically, though not in will and not in anything else. "You're not going to embarrass me, are you, Chuckie?"

"How many times you want me to tell you?"

"I'm talking serious to you. If you're using the phone again, I'll jam it down your throat."

Anybody says I am is a liar."

"That's what I want to hear." Lionel Dearborn gave up the grip. "I'm working on a big case, meaning I've got no time to be bothered by you."

Chuckie Dearborn rubbed his arm. "Don't treat me like a kid."

"Do I have a choice, Chuckie? You tell me."

Chuckie Dearborn pulled at the bill of his cap.

"Why're you wearing that thing? You look like an idiot."

Chuckie Dearborn glanced over his shoulder. Other firemen were looking at them. "You got anything else to say to me?"

"Remember when we *were* kids, Chuckie, we used to wonder when you're put in the cemetery is there any moving around. Or do you have to stay where you're put. Remember, Chuckie?"

"You threatening me?"

"Yes, Chuckie. I'm threatening you."

13.

THE ITALIANS

"What you're seeing is harps, nothing but harps," said Rupert Goetz, wheeling slowly past moon-faced men, plug-uglies among them, planted near a tavern that appeared defunct from the outside. "They know my car. Look at 'em look." He waved to one who had a newspaper and the hunched shoulders of a horseplayer waiting for a result. Farther up the sidewalk was a humorless collection of women, high-haired and heavy-armed, alternately eyeing a snarl in traffic and a glut of children confined behind the chain-link of a playground. Goetz hung an elbow out the window. "They used to be good-looking. Can you believe that?"

"No," said Sherry.

"I bet I grew up with some of 'em."

"A hun among harps."

"Right," he said, pleased. "Except there were those thought I was a hebe. That's when the fun started."

"Fun?"

"Fights."

He showed a fist and then took a sharp left, beating a light. They were in the heart of South Boston, in the converging vicinities of West and East Broadway, *NEVER* painted in huge letters on the side of a ravaged building: a message to blacks. Goetz pulled his elbow in. He had a queer look, as if an electric current were running through him.

"What is this?" said Sherry. "A sentimental journey or your love-hate week for the Irish?"

He laughed and made another turn, a shortcut down a changing street: neat tenement houses mingling with rotting ones, three-deckers with children playing on porches that did not look all that safe. Sherry adjusted her smoke-colored glasses.

"Where are we going?"

"You'll see."

He made two more turns and presently pulled up beside a place that was nondescript except for a long dark window with a neon artery forming part of a word and then quitting. There was a tingle of tags from a dog trotting by.

"Years ago I used to drink here," Goetz said, and Sherry, mildly bored, looked at him.

"That's not why we're here, I hope."

"No," he said, opening the car door.

It was dimly lit inside, like a dating bar, though it was hardly that, though there were plenty of tables and dark booths and a long bar and a sudden zany laugh that could have come either from a man or a woman. Then a hush. Sherry hesitated, and Goetz gave her a tap on the rump. "Move." They took a table, and Goetz, with no perceptible movement, counted the people he could see, the scattering at the bar, the glimmer of a face or two in a booth, the solitary shape of a man at a distant table. The barkeep was bald and big and busy with a towel that probably wasn't any too clean.

"Jesus," whispered Sherry. "Doesn't anybody talk?"

Goetz smiled and raised a hand. "Two Dewars and water," he said in a loud voice.

"Thanks for making up my mind," Sherry said.

"You wouldn't want anything else here, believe me."

Sherry placed an elbow on the table and propped her chin. "No women," she said. "I could've sworn I heard one, but I don't see any."

"Too early. You might see one or two in the evening."

The barkeep appeared with their drinks. He had the towel with him, and it wasn't clean, as if he had wanted them to see that. He set the drinks down, and Sherry said, "Thanks." He left without looking at either of them. Sherry whispered, "Doesn't he know you?"

"Sure."

"You could've fooled me."

"His way."

Sherry sat back, taking her drink with her. "The place gives me the willies, but I like it. I feel like I'm on stage."

"You are," said Goetz, fingering his glass but not picking it up. "And you're going to see me perform. That's what you want, isn't it?"

"Sure. How long do I have to wait?"

Goetz picked up his drink and took a modest swallow. "Don't look, but sitting where you can't see him too well is an old snitch of mine. The problem is he's not going to make a move while you're sitting here."

"So what am I supposed to do? Hide under the table?"

"Take a trip to the ladies' room. I know there's one way in back. You'll see a light."

"Oh, I get it. I should go in there and pretend to pass water."

"You can do that, or you can read what's written on the walls. I'd be interested."

"I can't think of anything more boring. I'll piss."

He watched her wend her way around vacantly and disappear into the dark. He waited a moment and then gestured. The man at the distant table rose disjointedly and ambled forward, swaying to one side, as if it hurt to walk. His graying hair was combed high, giving him the crested head of a young bird, but his face was loose and sloppy. He sat in Sherry's chair and said, "You wanted to talk to me, you should've called. We could've met someplace not going to make me look bad."

"I haven't got time to meet in alleys."

"Let's get something straight. I don't owe you nothing."

Goetz smiled thinly. "That's right, you don't. I'm going to have to owe you."

"It don't work that way."

"Yes, it does. Because I'm still your friend." Goetz smiled again, finished off most of his drink, and glanced about. "Place hasn't changed much."

"Changed some," said the man. "You don't see Johnny Kale here."

Goetz sighed, as if in respect. The man shook his head, his face like rubble.

"But you ain't changed, Rupert. Sitting there half-crocked but looking at me like I'm the only rummy. You do it good, maybe even better than you used to. I like to remember when we were kids, Johnny Kale too. You were the one always had snot on your face. Didn't know how to blow your nose right. Remember?"

Goetz let that all pass, though the strain showed. His face resembled dough, the blue eyes baked in. He said, "They hurt Johnny Kale pretty bad."

The man whistled. "I'll say. They killed him."

"Identification isn't official. *Herald American* shouldn't have printed it till it was."

"Fucking Hearst paper. What d'you expect?"

Goetz scratched his chin while glancing at the fixed figures at the bar. They seemed unalive, their backs turned. They could see what they wanted to in the mirror, which included Sherry reemerging out of the dark and quietly taking a table where Goetz could see her but the man couldn't without stretching his neck. Goetz said softly, "Wasn't right, the way Johnny Kale was wasted. Nobody should go out that way."

"You should be on the street looking for the guy," the man said with irony. "You must have an idea who did it."

"The guy I got in mind," said Goetz, "he only works for harps when he's in town. That's what I really want to know. Which harps?"

The man snorted. "You out of your mind? How would I

know something like that?"

"I'm not out of my mind," Goetz said, laying his hands on the table. "So I figure you know. You'll save me a lot of time, and that way nobody gets hurt. Understand?"

"You didn't hear me," the man said. "I don't know nothing. Total zero."

Goetz's shoulders stiffened with impatience. From the corner of his eye he took in Sherry, who sat with her tightly denimed legs crossed, her painted toes sticking out. She had lit a cigarette. He could smell it, and he reddened. She was smoking a joint. The man turned in his chair and then looked back at Goetz.

"Who's the cunt?"

"What cunt?" said Goetz, whose eyes, face and tone of voice told the man to back off fast. Instead the man smiled.

"That ain't the new wife, is it?"

Goetz struck him with the flat of his hand. The man's head snapped back, and his hair fell in his face. No one at the bar moved. The barkeep's head was down and stayed that way. Somebody showed himself from a booth but quickly drew back. Goetz struck again, harder than the first time, and the man toppled off his chair.

"You dumb fuck!" The man came off the floor with a snarl and a smile. "It ain't harps. It's the big leagues. It's the fucking Italians!"

"That's bullshit," said Goetz, but he saw the truth in the man's triumph. He pushed back in his chair and rose with a swift gesture to Sherry, who was already on her feet, cat-quick, and cutting toward him. "Let's get out of here," he said and tossed a bill onto the table. "That's for you," he said to the man.

In the car she embraced him. "You were beautiful," she said. He shrugged her away and started up the car. The car made hardly any sound and rolled forward as if it had always been in motion. "What's the matter?" she asked, staying close to him.

"This isn't a game anymore," he said. "We're dealing with big people."

She did not seem impressed, and he sighed.

"Very big."

Chuckie Dearborn held an unscheduled practice for key members of the team. David Goetz was not there, but Brian Gunderman was. While the infield threw the ball around, Chuckie Dearborn took Brian to one side. Brian had a brand-new ball and was socking it into his glove. Chuckie Dearborn squeezed his big hand into a small catcher's mitt and said, "You know how to throw a curve?"

"Sure," said Brian with a squint. "But I thought we weren't supposed to throw those."

"That's right, you're not," Chuckie Dearborn said gruffly. "Just like you're not supposed to lose games either, but you do, don't you?"

"It's not all my fault."

"I didn't say it was, but a lot depends on you."

"I can wreck my arm throwing curves, right?"

"Who the hell told you that?"

"My mother."

Chuckie Dearborn wiggled his hand out of the undersized mitt and appeared ready to hurl the mitt away. "You want to believe that, kid, go ahead."

"You mean it's OK to do it?"

"I was throwing curves when I was eight, even younger. Nothing wrong with my arm."

"But you didn't become a major leaguer or anything."

"I could've. I had the stuff. Instead I got married. Took on responsibilities. Understand?"

The boy fingered the ball and crooked his wrist. "OK, why don't I throw you some. You can tell me how it breaks."

Chuckie Dearborn gave him a sour smile. "You better ask your mother first. Go call her."

"I don't have to."

"Yuh, I want you to."

"She's not home."

"No, where is she?"

"I don't know."

Chuckie Dearborn made his voice casual. "She go out someplace?"

The boy nodded, refingering the ball, anxious now to do what the coach wanted and to do it well.

"Where'd she go?"

The boy shook his head and backed away, cocking his arm, wanting to throw, but Chuckie Dearborn gazed off, profoundly preoccupied, as if he could see another ball field, different players, another kind of game. Finally he glanced back at the boy, whose arm was still poised.

"Forget the curve, kid. Your arm ain't like mine was."

"Let me try."

"Naw," said Chuckie Dearborn with a brutal smile. "Tell your mother she's right."

Karl Gunderman rose from his desk and greeted Detective-Sergeant Lionel Dearborn as if he were a client, giving him a two-handed shake, which was meant to convey that if he, Gunderman, were not friendly, honest and sincere, nobody was. Dearborn took a chair beside the desk, and Gunderman reseated himself, tipping back.

"Smoke if you want," he said. "I don't."

"I don't either," said Dearborn, speaking almost through set teeth. He was neither friendly nor unfriendly, which annoyed Gunderman who, as a businessman and a relatively substantial resident of the town, expected a degree of deference. Dearborn produced a pocket notebook and a gold pen. "A few questions about Frank Chase," he said.

"Terrible thing to happen," Gunderman said. "Right on my street. God-damn upsetting for everybody. I told Frank to take a couple of weeks off."

Dearborn lifted his eyes. "With pay?"

"What's that got to do with anything?"

"I'm curious."

"Yes, sure. With pay. I take care of my employees."

"Doesn't he work on commission?"

Gunderman cleared his throat. "Sure, but I'll give him something against future earnings."

Dearborn nodded. "So actually it's not with pay."

"Call it what you want," Gunderman said sharply. He felt he was purposely being rubbed the wrong way and sized up at the same time, and he didn't like it. He also didn't like Dearborn's face, too long and too pocked. He couldn't read it.

"What were his net wages from you last year?" Dearborn asked, ready to write in his notebook.

"Well, now," said Gunderman, tipping farther back in his chair, "that's confidential information. Sorry."

Dearborn closed his notebook and tucked it away. Then he rose stiffly and headed for the door. Gunderman watched him.

"Hey, where you going?"

Dearborn turned deliberately. "I'm getting a warrant for your arrest. Obstruction of justice in a murder case."

Gunderman gave out a loud nervous laugh and sat forward. "What the hell are you talking about?"

"I came here for answers," Dearborn said in a deadly tone, "and I've no time to fuck around."

Gunderman shot up from his chair as Dearborn reached for the door. "For God's sake, sergeant, come on back and sit down, will you!"

Dearborn stayed for more than an hour. He had many questions, and Gunderman answered them all as well as he could.

14.

FAMILY TALK

"You ever whack anybody out?" the boy asked, sitting at the pool's edge, his plump legs dangling in the slightly over-chlorinated water. Frank Chase, deep in a deck chair, with a towel slung around his neck and his swim trunks drying, leaned forward sluggishly, as though he might not make it. The boy waited for an answer.

"I don't like your terminology," Chase said, an edge to his voice. "It's television talk."

"But did you?"

"No."

"My dad did."

Chase sank back. "Yes, I know. It was a long time ago, David."

"He didn't have any choice," the boy said, dropping back on spread arms. "He said it was either him or the other guy, and he wanted to make damn sure it wasn't him."

Chase nodded. "That's the way it happened. That's the only way it can happen and not be wrong."

"What if some guy was running away and you had to stop him? I mean, like again, you didn't have a choice."

Chase smiled at him. "What if I was to tell you I don't particularly like this conversation?"

"I'd say you were just like my mother."

"Is that bad?"

The boy dragged his legs from the water and got to his feet, slipping a little. His floral trunks were plastered to his skin. He had a fat behind and his father's wide shape, lacking only the muscles. He grinned at Chase with his mother's face and the sun in his eyes.

"The kids think I'm a big deal now. I mean, that's what they think you are."

"Because of what's happened?"

David nodded vigorously. "That was scary at first. It's not now."

"David, it's still scary, OK? Nobody should find what we did on the lawn."

"But you're not scared."

"Come here," Chase said, and the boy approached warily because of the solemnity of the voice. Chase held out his right hand and made it tremble. "I'm not scared like that, David. But I'm scared."

The boy had been holding his breath, and now he let out air as if he'd been punctured. "Me too!" he said.

"He's not here," Ida said, keeping her voice level.

"Where is he?" said the man on the line. "We don't like he should not be there when we call."

"He's outside."

"Get him."

"What kind of a creep are you?"

"Careful, sweetheart, we can hurt you. We can hurt you in a way you'll never have another kid."

Ida hung up hard and took a moment to compose herself. Then she went outdoors. Chase and David were playing catch with a new ball bright enough to see in the fading light. Chase threw the ball high and hard, and the boy made a good grab. Chase said something to him, and the boy beamed. Chase glanced Ida's way.

"Want something?"

"When you're finished."

She wandered toward the pool and sat in a chair, closing her eyes. When she opened them she saw Chase's bare legs. He had a shirt on over his trunks, and the shirt was coming apart at the right shoulder seam. His feet were bare and grass-stained.

"You look elegant," she said, her face failing the quip, and he squatted beside the chair.

"What's the matter?"

"I'm tired."

"You look more than tired. What's the matter?"

"Where's David?"

"In the house."

She gazed beyond the pool to great trees rearranging themselves into the dusk. The scent of mown grass was pervasive, a whole neighborhood of it. She took a slow deep sniff, her head dropping back and her hand reaching out. The top buttons of Chase's shirt were undone, and her fingers rubbed into his chest hair. "We've got a nice little world here, Frank. What's going to happen to it?"

"Ida, please. What's the matter?"

She told him.

For a long time his face gave away nothing, which reminded her too much of Rupert Goetz, and she pressed higher into his shirt toward the exposed shoulder.

"Say something, Frank."

"He calls again I want you to hang up right away. I don't want you to listen to him."

"I think you should tell me absolutely everything, so there'll be no surprises."

He reached to his shoulder for her fingers.

She said, "I want to know exactly what to expect."

"Why not?"

"That's what I say, Frank. Why the hell not?"

With her knees pressed to his chest, Sherry had no trouble coming, but Goetz did. He dug in, toiled, went slow, and then speeded up until he was pounding, but still he failed. "Rest,"

she said, but he shook his head. "Yes," she said. He broke from
her and collapsed on his back, his chest heaving, a hand hurled
over the edge of the bed. She propped herself on an elbow and
beheld him.

"I'm all right," he said with a cough.

"Such macho."

"I'm waiting for a second wind," he murmured.

Her eyes pored over him. "You deserve a treat."

He reached for her.

"No, don't move." Her hair brushed him, and a fingernail
nicked him. She smiled. "There's not a man in the world doesn't like this."

His breath caught as her mouth clenched him, knotting and
reknotting, and he threw his head to one side, giving in to the
rhythmic squeeze. He came with a slow shudder, as if waking
from a bad dream, of the sort children have.

He stared for a long time at the ceiling.

"Hey," she said and prodded him. She was sitting crosslegged near his feet. "Don't I even get a thank-you?"

"You're an expert," he said, and the tight tone of his voice
brought him a sharp look. She waved a warning finger.

"That's the wrong route, Rupert." She swept the hair from
her face. "How can you be beautiful one moment and boring
the next?"

He closed his eyes, opening them when he felt her leaving the
bed. He watched her cross the room, her bare buttocks like two
eggs bubbling from the boil of water. She became busy at her
bureau and spoke to him with her back turned.

"I'm all loose, and you're up-tight. Why?"

He didn't answer. She returned to him with the scented smell
of smoke and sat on the bed's edge.

"Here," she said. "Take a few hits off this. You need it."

He glared at her. "God-damn it, no!"

"I'm not going to waste it." She took a deep satisfying drag.
He stared at her. She stared back. "You're like a kid who won't

take his medicine."

He sat up. "Give it to me!"

He drew on the joint as if he'd done so a hundred times before.

"Move over," she said. She swung her legs onto the bed and sat next to him, pulling the printed percale sheet to their waists. They passed the joint back and forth.

"Did you do other guys just like that?"

"Yes, Rupert, just like that. I wasn't Snow White. I thought you'd gotten that through your head."

"It was only a question," he said as a dry ash tumbled to his chest. He blew it away.

They smoked the joint down, and she said, "Well?"

"Well what?"

"Anything?"

"Something, not enough to talk about."

"But you're a hell of a lot calmer, have you noticed?"

He slid his head down to the pillow. She followed, snuggling against him.

"Tell me about this Dance," she said.

"He's not the one I'm worried about."

"Tell me anyway. Is he an animal?"

"He's a fruitcake used to be a hit man, worked with a silencer, but he doesn't anymore. Never carries a gun now."

"Why not?"

"That's a story in itself," Goetz said, running a scratching hand over his flat hair. "Seven, eight years ago he rented a little house all for himself out near Chicopee, which is where he's from, one of those places. Maybe he had a woman with him because he wasn't hiding out, just taking it easy. Anyway, he takes a liking to the birds he sees and rigs up a fancy feeder for them on this big branch."

"Birdman of Alcatraz," Sherry said with a laugh, and Goetz's hand shifted from his hair to hers.

"Except he's got a problem with squirrels, and he goes bullshit over them stealing the seed. But he's got a worse problem with this old guy for a neighbor looking out his window, nothing else to do. The old guy sees squirrels dropping to the ground and bleeding for no apparent reason, and he sees Dance come out and kick the squirrels around. Then one time Dance comes out and he's still got the gun in his hand, silencer and all. The old guy calls the cops, and they catch Dance cold, possession of a piece that will take your heart out but won't pierce your ear drums."

Sherry laughed again. "Fruitcake is right."

"You asked me if he's an animal. Yeah, he's an animal. Johnny Kale was alive he could verify it."

"What does he look like?"

"He's a big guy, the kind you see working in a carnival or on the side of a road. Don't worry, you're not going to run into him."

"Are you?"

"There's more important people I have to deal with first. Everything depends on them."

"Is that what worries you?"

"Honey, I'm tired."

He kept his hand in her hair, and she watched him fall asleep like a baby.

Ida lay on her back with the covers pulled to her chin, windows wide open. The night was moonless and unnaturally quiet, so that sudden sounds carried, and from the distant dark she heard a bird thumping its wings. The stinging sound of insects was muted, not there if she didn't tune her ear to it. She sensed that Chase was not asleep and said, "I did the same thing with you, Frank. I repeated the mistake."

"What was the mistake?" The voice was fully awake.

"I always knew Rupert and I lived better than we had a right to, but I didn't say anything. Maybe once I did, but I wasn't forceful. I felt he deserved whatever he took because of the

danger and dirtiness of the job, especially when people started
calling police pigs."

The bed creaked, and she was unsure whether he was moving
toward her or away from her. Neither. She turned her head and
made out the shape of his face and then his eyes, which were
like bright stamps on an otherwise foreboding envelope. He
said, "I don't want you to think what I did was for you. It was
for me. I wanted the cushion."

"Frank, you wanted me. I wanted you. We didn't need the
cushion."

"You were coming to me with all he'd given you, including
support for David. I wanted something of my own there."

A silence fell between them, and she tuned her ear back to
the insects, their concerted sound somewhat sad.

"Then, too," he said, "I was past where I expected to make
anything of myself. I never had Rupert's ambition."

"Frank, I know what you're saying."

The silence fell again and spread, and for a time she was
caught somewhere between wakefulness and sleep. The cry of
a cat brought her back.

"There's something you should know, Frank. I don't think
you can depend on Rupert. I don't even think you can trust
him." When he did not respond, she said, "I'm not telling you
anything you don't already know, am I?"

His voice came without inflection. "No, but I'm glad you told
me."

"Did you think I wouldn't."

"I didn't think about it."

She put a hand near him, and his cock seemed to pour into
it.

"Frank," she said, and they made love.

15.

THE LAWYER

"Why can't I go?" Sherry asked.

"Because I said," Goetz murmured with a scowl. "That's it."

He finished off his Dewar's. He felt more confident after a drink and more alert after two. He had ended up having three, for the extra bounce.

"That's the wrong medicine," she said.

He didn't deign to answer. He slipped on his suitcoat and armed himself.

"That doesn't look very big," she said.

"Big enough," he muttered, shoulders squared.

"You remind me of a Hollywood version of a German officer —S.S. or Gestapo." Her eyes were partly sardonic, partly admiring. His were sour, cynical. She said, "What if somebody from your office calls?"

"I've taken care of it. No one will." He stepped toward the door.

"Rupert."

He turned. She was smiling.

"I like a man who makes hard decisions."

"You don't know what I've decided."

"Yes, I do."

His expression was ugly. "No, you don't."

She slipped forward and reached the door the same time he did, her hands creeping up his back, as though she expected to grab a ride. Her face became that of a kewpie doll. "You haven't kissed me."

He did, then opened the door.

"What am I supposed to do all this time?"

"Nothing that'll make me mad."

"Maybe I'll have lunch with Betty."

He gave her a penetrating glance. "Yeah, I'd like to meet this Betty sometime. See what he looks like."

Then he was gone.

Parked cars narrowed the little streets, and he left his where he could, half on a sidewalk with the back bumper pressing a hydrant that had paint from another car on it. The sidewalk was scarred and chewed up, his step careful. Up ahead two boys were hurling rocks at each other. "Cut the shit," he said to the nearest one, and the boy, button eyes snapping out, knew better than to give him the finger. He crossed the street under a zinc sky, corroded clouds, and no sun, the air muggy, almost unbreathable. When he sought to enter a dry-cleaning shop, a heavy woman in black stood in his way, her face fierce, as if nothing fitted her mood. "Excuse me," he said and forced his way around her. He strode past the counter, through curtains of clothes, and in and out of a back room.

"Who you looking for?" asked the proprietor, who received no answer.

Back on the sidewalk, he paused to consider his direction, sweeping a hand to his face, protection against a tentacle of poison from an idling van bearing no lettering. He went left on Hanover Street and gazed through the window of the Cafe Felix, which was shallow enough for him to see everybody, and for everybody to see him. Turning right at the next corner, he saw the person he wanted near a pizza parlor and immediately approached the man. The man lifted his chin.

"Jesus, you walk just like the United States Marines. Welcome to little fucking It'ly."

"Let's talk."

"Not on your life," said the man, who was bantam-sized and looked as if he suffered from a chronic sour stomach. "I never talk to a cop unless he's stark fucking naked."

"I'm not wired."

"How do I know that?"

"Since when does the chief of Homicide go around wired, and who the hell are you that I should?"

The man laughed. "You ain't changed, Rupert. But I been hearing bad things about you, something about you roughing up an old friend over in Southie. I said, no, I don't believe it."

"Believe it," Goetz said, edging closer to the man.

"You hit me you'll be dead in a week."

"I hit you you'll be dead in the fucking instant."

Both men smiled.

"What do you want, Rupert?"

"Direction."

The man gave Goetz an appraising look, long and cool. "Yeah," he said, "I been hearing a lot of bad things about you. Kinda surprised me. Me and some other guys, you know?"

"Don't dangle me."

"Don't rush me."

"Who do I see?"

The man regarded a passing woman with legs thickset but shapely. Then he rubbed his chin with the back of his fist. "Something like that, I'd say you oughta talk to the lawyer. Maybe he can tell you. Me, I don't know."

Goetz nodded slowly. "I thought it would be him."

"What's the matter? You don't look so good."

"Make me an appointment."

"Make your own. Me, I wouldn't be surprised he takes you right off." The man glanced over his shoulder. "We done? I don't like us putting on a show."

Goetz was already walking away.

"Why the hell shouldn't I fire him?" Karl Gunderman said.

Lee ignored him. She was at the breakfast table with the two boys. "Don't wolf your food," she said to Brian, whose face was practically in his bowl.

"I asked you a question," Gunderman said, standing by the cabinets and clenching a coffee cup. "What's the matter, you got something going with him?"

She threw him a contemptuous look. "Leave it to you to think of that."

"Do you?"

"Karl, dear. I don't think the boys want to hear this."

Brian glanced up from his bowl. "David's my friend, sort of."

"Of course he is, and I don't want you to say a word. Karl, let's talk about this later."

Later was as soon as Brian and his brother left the table. Gunderman poured himself more coffee and glared at a wall. Lee lit a cigarette.

"What I want to know," he said, "is why it's important to you what I do with Frank Chase."

"Because I like the Chases, and I like him even more than I like Ida. He's an odd quiet guy and basically nice."

Gunderman rolled his eyes. "It's me that's supposed to like him, and you his wife. That's how it's supposed to work, not the other way around."

"Oh, God, Karl." She seemed on the edge of either screaming or laughing, and he backed off, made a face, as if to show he'd been only half-serious.

He said, "Houses aren't for him. He should find something else to do."

"You hired him, dear."

"Then I should have the right to fire him."

"Do what pleases you," she said much too sweetly.

"That's what *you* do, isn't it?"

She puffed on her cigarette. "I put on a good act, Karl. That's all."

He was not a lawyer. He only acted like one after a single
semester years ago at Suffolk Law. He was tall and gaunt,
gray-skinned and noticeably false-toothed, in his fifties, though
he looked much older, seventy at least. He said to Goetz, "You
did a few nice things for us in the past. That was good. Good
for you too."

Goetz agreed with a flickering of blue eyes. He sat before a
desk in a high-ceilinged room that looked like a law office. It
had the books, also the odor of the ocean wafting in from the
harbor. The color photograph on the desk showed a family. The
rest of the desk was bare except for a pencil, more or less the
way Goetz kept his. If there was a telephone, it was in a drawer.
Goetz suspected there was none.

"That's why we didn't want to bother you personally with
this matter," the lawyer said with macabre humor solemnly
delivered, speaking through set teeth, which were square.

Goetz said, "I swear to God, I didn't know you people were
involved."

"All this time gone by, you must've stopped thinking. That's
the worst thing can happen to a man."

Goetz stared silently at shadows from the scalloped leaves of
a rubber plant.

"To tell you the truth," the lawyer said, "we never figured
Johnny Kale. Somebody not smart enough to tie his own shoe.
Him you should've sent out of the country for ten years, at least.
You should've known he'd finally let something slip to the right
people." The lawyer's laugh was quiet, hardly there. "I natu-
rally don't mean the right people for him."

Goetz brushed his knee, a place for him to put his eyes.

"You feel bad about him?"

Goetz gave a nod. "Sure I feel bad."

"I'll tell you something," the lawyer said. "Somebody gets
himself wasted means he's accident-prone. It's a situation like
a Negro hollering about things. I say a guy's dumb enough to
be born black, that's his fault."

Goetz, suspecting he was being put on, smiled. The lawyer didn't. Goetz said, "I want to make it right."

The lawyer gazed toward the open window, his face lifted to the sea breeze, as if the office doubled as a health club. "That was high-grade and uncut stuff, what a congressman would be glad to blow."

Goetz shifted uneasily in his chair. "Everything was lost on that end. It was thrown away. Chase."

The lawyer gave Goetz an amused look. "That's another thing we didn't figure. We always took Chase for Mr. Clean. It was you, Rupert, was Mr. Stink."

"He threw it in the Charles, my right hand to God."

"Did you see him?"

"No, but I know he did it."

The lawyer abruptly exhibited all his teeth in a broad smile. "Let's eat, Rupert. We can do it right here and talk some more."

Goetz did not see him move a muscle, but within seconds the door opened. The man who entered had Goetz's gun in his jacket pocket for safekeeping and a menu in his hand for the lawyer, who waved it way.

"My usual," he said.

"Whatever he's having," Goetz said when offered the menu.

"You'll be surprised," the lawyer said. "Good food, what you call organic. My wife laughs at me."

When the man left, Goetz said, "My right hand to God, what I've told you is true."

"Later, Rupert. What we've got to talk about could hurt my stomach. We'll wait."

Goetz sighed imperceptively and brushed his knee.

"I heard you gave up the old wife for a young one," the lawyer said in a tone that did not indicate approval, and Goetz nodded. "Not good, Rupert."

Goetz said nothing.

"Then they tell me the old wife marries Chase." The lawyer

seemed to shudder. "That goes right over my head."

Goetz felt the back of his neck redden, and he started to speak.

"No," the lawyer said. "I don't want to understand." Then he swiveled closer to the window and tipped his head back for the full smell of the ocean, his eyes closing. A protracted silence followed.

Goetz, sitting erect, waited for the food and the talk that would follow, with no appetite for either.

Two hours later, his weapon returned, Goetz left the wharf building and crossed congested Commercial Street with a terrible detachment, two drivers banging horns at him. He walked idly in the wrong direction, toward Atlantic Avenue, stopping in his tracks when a young woman stepped out of the Rusty Scupper. For a second he mistook her for Sherry and nearly grabbed her arm. He wanted a drink. He needed one, and he stepped into the Scupper, which was noisy, smoky, full of young people, a hundred conversations going on at once. He backed out.

He made his way back toward Hanover Street, an uphill climb under clouds that threatened rain. Three times he was startled, first when somebody smirked at him from a doorway, a boy flashing signs of imbecility, and a second time when he glimpsed the bloody apron of a butcher and didn't know what the man had in his arms—the carcass of a lamb. The third time was when he reached Hanover Street.

He saw Frank Chase.

16.

PLAYERS

"He's not here," Ida Chase said. "He's working."

"You mean selling houses?"

"That's right, sergeant."

Lionel Dearborn viewed her sharply, and she crossed her arms, feeling exposed and vulnerable in her bathing suit. They stood on opposite sides of the gate to the swimming pool, with great chunks of light falling around them as the sun shattered the cloud cover. He placed a hand on the gate.

"No, I don't think he is, Mrs. Chase."

"Then I don't know where he is. Sorry."

"Sure you know," Dearborn said, attempting to stare her down and, to a degree, succeeding.

"I said I didn't."

"You don't have to tell me where he is, Mrs. Chase, but you don't have to lie to me either."

"Look!" she said, coloring, but immediately she regained her composure and spoke in a hard polished voice. "I'm not sure where he is, so I'd rather not hazard a guess."

He stepped back a little, his arm dropping, the sun slanting into his face. He gave her an empty smile while shielding his eyes with a stiff hand, like a salute. "The point is, he's not out selling houses."

"He might be."

"Don't be hostile."

"You make it impossible not to be."

A heavy silence followed. He was still shielding his eyes, his stance crooked, the smile still there. Then she realized he was looking at her body, and she felt naked and foolish.

"Anything else?"

"No," he said, his voice playful. "Just tell your husband I was here."

Ida cursed softly, watching him disappear.

"This guy we're using. What's his name?"

"Dance."

"Pay him off, but tell him to stick around."

"How long?"

"Till I say so." The lawyer turned toward the window. Instead of the expected rain, a burst of sunshine flooded the office. He basked in it, eyes half-closed, and murmured, "Like a gift." Then he gripped the arms of his chair.

The man in the jacket stepped forward.

"I don't need help!" With agonizing effort the lawyer rose into a stance that made him look arthritic from head to foot.

The man in the jacket stood by, just in case. He had large apathetic eyes, like those of a stunned fish.

After a while the lawyer straightened up, a taut figure, as if every bone had been tightened. He looked cruelly at the man in the jacket and said, "I gave you something to do."

Alone, in a blast of sunlight, the lawyer practiced walking around the office, until his step was nearly normal.

"Frank, I'm not denying anything."

"You played me like a violin."

"Frank." Rupert Goetz observed him sympathetically. "Frank, you carried the tune."

"I did. I'm not disputing it."

They were parked on a short street in the South End, unoccupied buildings on each side, some burnt and skeletal. They had driven there from Hanover Street in Chase's wagon at Goetz's urging, Goetz's car left behind, anything to get Chase out of the North End. Both men froze because of a sudden shadow, but it had nothing to do with them. It was from a silent runner, a spindly man in shorts passing them in a wink. Goetz's eyes smarted from the sweat in them. He felt the strain and the heat.

Chase said, "You also took advantage of the way I felt for Ida, but I'm not mad about that either because I have her and you don't. I see myself as way ahead."

"Frank, you are. I never knew what I had in Ida."

"Let me do the talking, Rupert. You got Sherry, and you got the real money. But I still got the best of the swap."

"Frank, it wasn't a swap."

"You're right. You were parceling out. This for you, that for me. And something for Johnny Kale because you needed him. Poor Johnny, right?"

"You think it doesn't tear my heart out, what happened to him? Frank, I grew up with him."

Chase was silent. Then he pulled the keys away from the ignition switch and opened his door. "Let's walk. It's better than sitting."

Their steps were lifeless, as though both men were being manipulated by the lazy pull of strings. Goetz had trouble breathing. His chest was hot. He said. "How'd you happen on to Hanover Street?"

"I saw the same guy you did, except I didn't have to beat him up for answers."

"Frank, don't go two-face on me. You socked guys around in your time."

"Never a friend."

Goetz shielded his eyes. "Fucking sun. I could've sworn it was going to rain."

They reached the end of the street and stopped, keeping the wagon in sight, as if it were a spaceship, Chase's only means of returning to his home planet. They heard rapid Spanish voices from an abandoned building, something being sold or traded, an argument brewing.

"The old days we'd go in there and bust 'em," Goetz said.

"What old days?" said Chase.

They fell silent, retracing their steps in the same slow pace, the sun at their backs. Chase's manner was remote. A short elderly woman with bobbed hair gave them a hostile glance in passing, as if they were landlords. Goetz ran a quick hand across his mouth.

"Go back to Andover. Please."

Chase shook his head. "That was a bad call Ida took."

They approached the wagon, the sun exploding off its glass and polish. Chase leaned against the front fender and folded his arms. Goetz stood solidly on the asphalt, as if about to square off at him.

"I'm working things out, you understand? Moynihan from the DA's office. He talked to you, remember? Later I talked to him. You've got nothing to worry on that end."

Chase's silence revealed no appreciation.

"Listen to me," Goetz said, speaking fast. "The Italians bankrolled what you ripped off. You understand what I'm telling you? You and me, Frank, we went against impossible odds and didn't know it. Harps I can deal with, I'm like one of 'em. Wops are something else. The lawyer, you've heard of him."

Chase nodded. "Of course I've heard of him."

"I was yelled at like a little kid. I had to eat shit."

Chase glanced away. "I'm sorry you had to, Rupert, but I have to talk to this Dancewicz character. I want to impress upon him he should never call my house again, never come near it."

"You don't have to. The lawyer's given me his word the guy's going."

"I still want to talk to him myself. I'll feel better."

"Let me get permission," Goetz said quickly and colored as

Chase gave him a curious look. "You still don't understand, do you? I've signed my life away. I owe favors!"

"From what I've heard," Chase said mildly, "you've owed them before."

"Not like this!" For a moment Goetz looked helpless, even old. "Can't I make you understand? The lawyer even wanted to make me accountable for the coke. He didn't think anybody in his right mind would've thrown it in the river."

"That's his problem."

"No, Frank. It's mine."

Chase gazed up the street and saw lithe men running from the building where he had heard the voices. He looked back at Goetz, who was absently toeing the sidewalk, as if marking out a space between them. "Come on," Chase said. "I'll drive you back to your car."

Traffic was heavy. Anchored in it near the Public Garden, Chase lighted a cigarette and listened to distant sirens wailing from two different points in the city. Goetz, eyeing a young woman with an ice-cream, said, "Sherry's going to think I skipped the country."

"She figured into it, didn't she?"

Goetz gave Chase a slow look. "Not in the way you think. Frank, she's a kid."

"Your wife."

"I know. Ida was good for me. No unknowns. With Sherry, it's different."

"There are always unknowns. Always."

"You telling me something, Frank?"

"No. Nothing."

"I wouldn't want to hear anything like that."

"OK, Rupert. You never will."

Goetz's car had been vandalized, a fender gouged, a side window cracked. Both men climbed out of the wagon to look at the damage. "It's OK," Goetz said after a silence. "As long as I can drive it." Then he smiled. "Ever feel that somebody's got your number? That's how I feel around here."

Chase returned to the wagon but didn't climb in. He looked over the roof at Goetz, whose face had turned jowly, unequal bulks upsetting the balance.

"Frank, will you go home?"

"I can't," Chase said quietly.

17.

LOVERS

In the fall of '75 Rupert Goetz wore leather heels that made important sounds when he entered the classroom. An evening a week he lectured at Northeastern University to a small group of homogeneous males and one female who sat with a slack posture and a strand of her luxuriant hair caught in the corner of her mouth while now and then taking notes. The male students, Viet Nam veterans among them, were youngish policemen. A few were from Boston and the others from nearby communities, all of them working for credits that would raise their salaries. The young woman, a distraction, the skin of a hip showing through a hole in her jeans, was there for no discernible reason, except maybe to amuse herself. Goetz, reckoning her age at eighteen or nineteen, seldom looked her way, but when he did his gaze was cold and level, slightly insulting, and obviously meant to intimidate her, which it didn't. She returned the infrequent challenge with a tidy smile and, her hip hung out, sank into a deeper commitment to the student chair she occupied. Goetz's lectures were supposed to deal with the role of the policeman in a period of changing social values, but often he digressed to other considerations, such as the efficiency of a high-velocity rifle and the effect of a fusillade on the human body.

"It's like a dance," Goetz said, speaking from experience. "The suspect rises and falls at the same time. Graceful, because for a second everything stops. You guys in the war probably know what I'm talking about."

A couple of them nodded as Goetz momentarily shifted his attention to the young woman, whose smile was tidier than ever.

That was when he suspected she was high.

Headlights leaping at her, she stood on Huntington Avenue with a thumb out for a ride, her other hand dug into the pocket of her parka, her jeans rolled to the height of her boots. Goetz, leaving the university, saw her and lunged at her as a car skittered toward a stop. "What the Christ are you doing?" he demanded, pulling her to the sidewalk and furiously waving the car on. "A great God-damn way to get yourself raped and murdered! Don't you read the papers? That's what's been happening." His eyes burned into hers, and she gave him the classroom smile.

"The Blue Knight. You don't even need a uniform."

"You want a ride, I'll give you one."

"I had one, but he didn't show."

"Come on!"

He drove slowly under hazy tracks of light, letting other cars honk and whip by. The general direction was Cambridge. She lit up a Tareyton Light, and he said, "What else do you smoke?"

"Read me my rights first," she said, casting him a half-glance.

"How old are you?"

"Old enough to have had an abortion. It hurt."

He threw her a bored look. "That supposed to shock me?"

"That's what you try to do to me in class, isn't it?"

He laughed. There were two ashtrays, but she leaned over to use the one near him, giving him the herbal scent of her hair, which brushed his hand. His fingers felt it. "What do you do, wash it every day?"

"Sometimes twice. Clean head, clean mind."

"That the way it works?" he said and electrically lowered her window a little to let out some of her smoke. They cruised over Harvard Bridge into Cambridge, and she pitched the cigarette out the window and pointed to the right.

"It would be shorter if you went that way."

"I'm in no hurry," he said and continued straight. "What are you doing in the class, anyway?"

"Slumming." Her voice was sweet.

"I don't like your mouth."

"How would you know?"

She lived off Kirkland Street, almost into Somerville, old houses in a high-rent district, people walking dogs in the dark, here and there a bark. He double-parked next to a Volkswagen that looked as if it belonged in a repair shop, and she pointed to a lighted third-story window.

"That's it." Her voice was still sweet. "I'd ask you up, but I live with somebody."

"The guy who didn't pick you up?"

She nodded past him. "That's his car. He probably couldn't get it started."

"He should've found a way." Goetz's smile was nasty, and his hand went past her parka to the bare spot on her hip. "A girl old enough to live with somebody ought to start wearing underpants."

"What kind do you suggest?"

"Lacy ones, a few frills."

"I'm not the type, but thanks for the ride." Before she could turn, the lock on her door clicked, and the car moved ahead. As he wound his way back to Kirkland Street, she looked at him with amazement. "Are you kidnaping me?"

"Right," he said.

He drove into Harvard Square, parked the car illegally, guided her out of it, and ungraciously prodded her arm to get her moving in the right direction, which was toward the fiercely bright lights of a Brigham's. She began to laugh.

"This isn't a kidnaping. It's a date."

"You a junkie?"

"Do I look it?"

"No, junkies don't wash their hair. You're a beautiful creature."

"I know. I've been told."

"Tell me about yourself."

"Oh, Jesus," she said, pushing away the remains of a banana split. Then, as he sipped black coffee, she recited a quick story about a childhood in Chillicothe, Ohio, and a father who seldom approved of anything she did. "He was a Mason. My mother was in Eastern Star, and I was in Rainbow." She spoke of an academically disastrous year at Radcliffe, or rather at Harvard with its integrated classes, and a bearded and bookish man who desperately tried to press marriage on her and in a show of strength impregnated her. She got rid of them both.

Goetz studied her. "How much of that is true?"

She drank water and smiled. "Some of it."

"I'm not just a cop. I'm a big cop. I can check on everything."

"Why should you want to?"

His eyes never leaving her, he took a cigarette from her Tareyton pack, lit it, and blew smoke over her head. "What d'you do for work?"

"I'm between jobs."

"Meaning you don't do a God-damn thing. What about this guy you're hooked up with now?"

"What about him?"

"What's he do?"

"Not much."

"I can check on that too."

"Wow."

He ignored the sarcasm. "Comfortable with him?"

"I wouldn't be with him if I weren't."

His eyes wouldn't let go. He sat with a shoe in the aisle, a nice one, Scotch-grain, and people had to edge around it, though nobody said anything to him. She retrieved her banana-split dish, picked up the spoon, and scraped syrup.

"We have basic agreements," she said, "one being we don't breathe all over each other."

He placed his cigarette in the ashtray and dropped his hands on the table, his manner vaguely menacing. He wore a large wedding ring on one hand and black onyx on the other.

"Now I have a question for you," she said, tasting her spoon. "Why this third-degree?"

"I have a hard-on for you."

"Let's not tell the world." A woman at the next table was staring.

"What's your answer," he said.

Her laughter was sudden, full, open-mouthed, and sustained. The woman at the next table got up and left, and two foreign students, Pakistani or Indian, took the table. Goetz rose and helped her on with her parka, awkwardly, all thumbs, as if he had played out his hand.

They drove back to her street, and she said, "I don't think he's up there." Goetz left the car behind the Volkswagen and followed her into the house and up two flights of stairs, conscious of every step, as if each were clumsy. She tried the door, then used a key. Taped to the refrigerator was a note, which she tore off and crumpled without reading. He uncrumpled it and tried to read it, though he could scarcely see it. "Jesus, you're suspicious," she said with a laugh. In the shadows of the bedroom he gripped her legs and widened them. About twenty minutes later a young man with a quart-bottle of beer appeared in the doorway.

"What the hell's going on?" he said.

Goetz did not stir, perhaps did not even hear the voice, but Sherry raised her head slightly, showing a luminous patch of face. "Billy, you'd better get out of here."

"No!"

Goetz was moving on her again, pumping slowly, making a small sound.

"Billy, he's bigger than you."

The young man left reluctantly.

"I understand he's moving you into a big apartment. Charles River Park."

Sherry Abbott exhibited pleasant surprise. "Did he tell you that?"

"He didn't tell me anything," Ida Goetz said coldly.

The two women stared at each other from across a small table in a Newbury Street coffee shop, where they had agreed to meet, Ida's request. The request had been another surprise, flattering to Sherry, who had agreed at once, quite cordially.

"I found the deposit slip," Ida said. "Your name on it."

"Ah," said Sherry, her heavy hair alive with waves of light. "That's how you found out about me. He's told you nothing?"

"Nothing."

"Poor guy." Sherry toyed with her coffee cup. Two men at another table could not take their eyes off her. "It hasn't been easy for him."

Ida forced herself to remain calm. At the same time she wondered why she had arranged the meeting. What purpose? What profit? She wished she were home. Then she noticed that Sherry was studying her.

"You have a very interesting face," Sherry said. "I bet you're one of those women who get more attractive as they grow older." Her hand shot forward, almost touching Ida. "Please, I meant that as a compliment."

"I'm not here for compliments."

"But I'd like us to be friends."

"Don't you know how ludicrous that sounds?" Ida said with a grimace. "Are you taking any of this seriously?"

"God, yes. Otherwise, why am I here?"

"I'm wondering why I'm here."

Sherry tasted her coffee. "Because you wanted face-to-face contact, which is only natural. And I was dying to meet you. Rupert has told me so much about you."

Ida stiffened. "This is ugly, do you know that?"

Sherry shrugged. "Why can't we be civilized?"

Ida could not bring herself to respond. She lighted a cigarette and blew the smoke out fast. Sherry was studying her again.

"You have beautiful black hair. Coarse but stunning. I like it better than mine. Really."

Ida's eyes were sardonic. "Would you like us to take a shower together? Then we can compare everything."

"Now you're being nasty. You don't understand me, do you? I'm an original. I think you might very well be too."

Ida snuffed out her cigarette. "This is ridiculous."

"Your husband wants me. *Really* wants me. Does that scare you?"

"Yes, of course it does."

"Are you going to fight for him? I think you should."

"What the hell kind of talk is that? What's *your* feeling for him? I guess that's what I want to know."

Sherry smiled lightly. "I love him, of course."

"Oh, shit," said Ida, glancing impatiently away and suddenly feeling very weary. She took money out of her shoulder bag and placed it on the table for the check. Sherry took another taste of coffee.

"Does Rupert know you're here?"

"No, honey, he doesn't," said Ida, preparing to make a quick departure, and Sherry gave her a smile that seemed entirely impure.

"Then I won't say a word. We'll let nature take its course."

Frank Chase took Ida Goetz to a performance of the Pops, and she watched and listened with a fixed smile, as if coldly committed to enjoying the evening. She sat stiff-shouldered and deeply decolletaged, and when she spoke her voice was low. Half the time Chase did not hear her. At intermission she let out her breath and touched his arm. "Do you mind."

They walked. They thought it would be warm enough, but it wasn't because of the wind, which was strong and carried her a step backwards. Old newspapers charged out of the gutter. Chase craned his neck for a taxi, but she tugged his sleeve. "It's all right," she said, punching a hand into the pocket of his overcoat while tightening her own coat, a fur. They walked faster, into a stampede of paper, and hurried across Massachusetts Avenue against headlights beating up in the distance and then surging forward, spreading. Youths hooted on the sidewalk, their shadows leaping by like galloping horsemen.

"You don't really need this, do you?" Ida said in a breathy voice. "An old married woman hanging off your arm."

"It's comfortable," he said, giving the hand in his pocket a squeeze.

They made their way past Boylston and Newbury Streets and turned down Commonwealth Avenue, which took them out of the wind. Ida slowed her step, a relief to Chase, who had been on his feet all day, a case that had kept him moving through alleys and up and down stairs. His hams hurt. She clung to him like a comrade in arms.

"I despise November," she said under a spill of street light. Her eyes were ink stains in a face startling white, as if carefully chalked.

"Same here," he said. "The days start sinking away as soon as they start."

"That's dismally good, Frank."

"I remember as a kid I believed willows truly wept."

She smiled, which was what he wanted. They approached the vicinity of her apartment building, which was on the opposite side of the mall dividing the avenue.

"You cold?" she asked.

"No," he said, though he was, and they continued walking, silently, eyes down, the wind shooting at them when they passed crossways, Hereford Street, then Gloucester. She sniffed and dabbed at her nose with a pale-green tissue dug from her purse.

"I only have the one," she said. "Want to share?"

He took it, used it, and let it fly away.

"That was intimate, Frank." Her smile was droll as they stayed in perfect step, passing another couple, much younger, walking as they were. "For some reason Rupert has always considered you and me totally safe together. Why is that?"

"I've never thought to ask him."

"He has somebody on the side again. Did you know that?"

Chase shook his head, a bit too hesitantly.

"Oh, yes. I've met her. She's truly gorgeous and quite young. Rather strange, though. Rupert might find it hard to keep up with her."

Chase refused to meet her eyes, which he knew were on him.

She said, "He's going to trade me in, Frank. I'm pretty sure of it. But it's possible I don't care."

Chase gave her a slow sidelong glance. "You could be wrong about everything."

"Shall I pretend he's in Chicago at a seminar I know for a fact isn't scheduled till next month."

"Ida, don't put me in the middle."

"You *are* in the middle. You're his stand-in, his good buddy. My good buddy too. Isn't that so?"

Chase chose to ignore the deep bitterness of her tone. As their step slowed to nothing, her hand emerged from his overcoat. They stood still. Warm fingers touched his cold cheek.

"I'm sorry. I'm in a lousy mood."

They embraced briefly and broke clean. A taxi roared by, discharging smoke. Chase was ready to walk on, but Ida stood rooted and, with a cynical smile, gazed through him.

"He won't like scenes of separation," she said. "He'll want

everything to go smoothly. And he'll be generous to a fault. That's his way."

"Ida, cut it out."

"Don't worry. I'm not going to cry. That's not my way. But I could use a kiss. It might make me feel better."

He kissed her lightly.

"No. I want a real one."

He kissed her hard, took her tongue. Cars passed, one with its horn blowing. A man walking his dog crossed the street rather than approach them.

"I wish we weren't such good friends, Frank. I wish we could just go somewhere and—" She looked up at him. "Am I embarrassing you, or am I hard to take?"

"Ida, don't."

"I'm not all that bad. Rupert says I have such a hot ass you could fry an egg on it."

"Ida."

"I'll never be what you call thin, but I'll never let myself get fat either. I have a tiny bit of a pot, just enough to let you know it's there. But I'm working on it."

"Ida, for Christ's sake." He embraced her again.

"You *are* embarassed."

"No, just uncomfortable. Probably because I've had a crush on you for years."

"You've said that many times, always as a joke."

"How else could I say it to you?"

She was quiet for a moment. "I have a confession, Frank. I've always considered you my ace in the hole. If anything happened, you'd be there."

They began walking, no longer touching, no longer feeling the cold either, though their silence was intimidating.

"Say something, Frank."

"I might be a king who beats queens."

"And I might be a joker."

"Ida, we might both be fooling ourselves about a lot of

things," he said, and then he told her where he wanted to go.
He lived one street over, Marlborough. She squinted at her
watch, her thoughts on her son and the sitter.

"All right," she said. "Let's go to your place and see what
happens.

"Nothing might."

"You don't believe that, do you?"

They linked arms and walked faster.

18.

MARLBOROUGH STREET

Frank Chase held Ida Goetz's bare feet in his hands, lightly squeezing them. He wanted to kiss them. She was seated in the soft chair where he usually sat to watch television, read the papers, sip coffee, doze off. She was still in her coat. The only things he had removed were her shoes and stockings so that he could warm her toes.

"I don't have pretty feet," she said.

"God, you do!" he said from his knees and kissed both of her feet, very quickly.

"Frank." There was a break in her voice, and he was blushing, as if he had humbled himself into a foolish figure. There was an uncomfortable silence. She shifted her eyes to different corners of the apartment. She could see into the tiny kitchen and the bedroom. "It's so neat. I though it'd be a mess."

"It usually is."

"You cleaned it up?"

"Yes."

"You anticipated our ending up here?"

"Way in the back of my mind, where I didn't have to think about it." He still had her feet in his hands. He was simply holding them, as if he would soon have to give them back, which he didn't want to do. Her eyes had left him again. They were on the Picasso print on the wall. "It's called *Three Bathers*," he said.

"Why three? I see only two."

"I don't know," he said, "but the two there each remind me of you."

Her smile was wry. "Am I that buxom?"

"I don't know," he said with the shy impulsiveness of a schoolboy. "I've never seen you with your clothes off."

She stared at him. Then she closed her eyes to think. Her lids fluttered. "Suddenly I'm scared. Isn't that funny?"

"I'm not exactly calm."

Her eyes opened. "But you're not afraid."

"Yes, I am. This is the first time I've been so close to a best friend's wife, perhaps because I never had a best friend before, not even as a kid."

"Is Rupert your best friend, Frank? Really? I know he's not mine."

"You have to understand about us."

"I understand perfectly," she said impatiently. "You're brother officers. What I don't understand is why you became a cop in the first place. Rupert was born to be one. Not just an ordinary cop, but a detective, so he could throw his weight around, strut. That was his goal since he was a boy, and I thought it was cute. Remember, I knew him back then. I didn't know you, Frank, but I can't imagine you with the same burning ambition."

"Why not?"

"For one thing, you don't strut."

"I could learn."

"You'd look silly. You have to be born to it."

Chase freed one of her feet but held firmly on to the other, as if only half-surrendering. She smiled at him from her fur. "You must be warm in that," he said.

"I'm roasting, but I'm afraid to take it off."

"Do you know why I became a cop?"

"Do you want me to guess?"

"You never would."

"Then tell me."

"I didn't want to lose track of you."

"Frank, you're kidding. Come on."

"It was a good fifty percent of the reason."

"What was the other fifty?"

"It seemed like a good idea at the time, and I've had no regrets."

"Neither has Rupert," she said, closing her eyes. She lay her head back, and the lamplight provided a varnish for her pale face and gave a reddish tone to her black hair. Chase's free hand moved up her leg. "Frank, don't."

His hand stopped but did not retreat. Her eyes were still closed.

"I'm not trying to tease you," she said.

"But you are," he said, and his hand moved well under her dress. He felt her quicken. Her eyes were open.

"This is what he wants us to do, Frank. You understand that, don't you? He's dumping me, and he wants you to take me. This is his game, and it's bizarre. Terribly bizarre. Do you want us to play it?"

Chase's face was morose, his hand stilled. He said, "The question is, How do you feel about it?"

She was quiet.

He said, "It's an easy decision for me. I happen to love you."

"The coat, Frank. Get me out of it."

She spilled cigarette ash on her belly, and he blew it off. Strands of her hair were smeared across her cheek. He peeled them away. She held her cigarette to one side and slipped her other hand under her head. "The pillow slip, Frank, and the sheets, they're all new. I can still smell the store."

"I can only smell us."

"When did you buy them?"

"This afternoon."

"I think I was taken," she said with only faint irony. She looked at him in the half-light. "You're something."

"I hope so." He took the cigarette from her fingers and snuffed it out in a saucer serving as an ashtray. Then he put his arms around her.

"Again?" she said.

"Again."

"I have to call the sitter. She probably thinks I've been murdered."

"Ask her to stay the night."

"Frank, take it slow. Can you?"

"I doubt it," he said and slipped down on her, a bee into the flower, the intimate odor filling his nostrils and the taste taking him. She held her breath, her top teeth tooled into her lower lip. He said something.

"I can't hear you."

"I want to be a husband to you. Phone's beside you."

"Not while you're doing that."

He stopped.

He moved up as she groped for the phone, and he settled into her as she made the call, jiggling her voice when she spoke, a quick conversation, the sitter agreeable. When she tried to cradle the receiver she missed, and it fell to the floor, a thump on the worn carpet, which concerned neither of them.

Later, still stuck to her, he dropped an arm over the edge of the bed and retrieved the phone, his mouth brushing a question into her ear. She lay still. It was not a question she felt he should ask or she should ever answer, so she merely pressed fingers against him.

"Is that an answer?"

"Frank."

"I need an answer. Don't ask me why."

She gave in. "It was good."

"I want it to be better."

"Do you always get what you want?"

"This might be the first time."

They smiled, they measured.

He said, "I'm trying to make it sexually impossible for you to go near him again. I'm trying to rub myself all over you. Does that make you uneasy?"

"I don't know if it works that way, Frank. I really don't."

Toward dawn he opened his eyes to find her sitting up, crosslegged, and staring toward the window, her skin like marble in the ash-gray of the room, no covers. The apartment was overheated. He studied her profiled face, trying to determine her thoughts. She felt his eyes.

"It's snowing."

"Let it," he said. "Why are you smiling?"

"Do you mind?"

"I can't answer that until I know what you're smiling about."

She turned to him, the smile still there. "I was thinking that I had a good reputation, virtuously earned, but I did indeed want to get laid tonight."

"Just laid."

"By you, Frank. Who else?"

She reached for his hand, looking at him with dark direct eyes that in small measure reproached him. Moments later the phone rang, an ugly burst that tore them apart. Seconds of silence brought them back together. The phone rang again.

"Who would call you at this hour?" She spoke into the moist hair of his chest. He didn't answer, and he didn't move. The ringing persisted, with something hysterical about it at that vague hour, neither night nor day. "Frank, answer it!"

"You answer it."

Her eyes widened. "You know who it is?"

"I'm only guessing, like you."

"Frank."

"I want a commitment. I want you to answer it."

The ring became a blast, and her arm jerked, as if from the prick of a pin. Her hand reached for the phone, and his traveled down to the warmest part of her. She tilted the receiver to her head but for the longest while didn't speak. Her face glistened in the dim, the heat of the room clinging to her skin. Then, finally, her voice surprisingly husky, she said, "Hello."

Chase's fingers pressed into her.

The person on the other end disconnected.

Sherry Abbott, still half-asleep, came out of the bedroom and for a moment looked older than she was despite the frilly little nightdress. She reached for cigarettes. She lit one with a wooden match from a tiny box, *Davio's* inscribed on the top. Rupert Goetz stood at a window with his bare back to her. Aiming her eyes at his broad neck, she said, "I don't like waking up alone."

He shrugged.

She said, "What's the matter? Couldn't you sleep?"

"I don't need much sleep."

"As you get older, you don't."

"You trying to tell me something?"

"Don't be touchy."

"I've never needed much sleep."

"I'm just the opposite."

"Then go back to bed."

She took a seat on the sofa, drawing up one leg. Her hand holding the cigarette dropped over the knee. "What's it doing out there?"

"Snowing."

"Nice. Do you ski?"

"No."

"You can learn."

"Too late."

"It's never too late." Her tone was teasing. "I'm young enough to tell you that."

He turned around. "And I'm old enough to tell you it is."

"Why are you in such a pissy mood?" She patted the next cushion. "Come here."

He approached her with a slow step, his stomach pulled in, his boxer shorts worn low and loose, and sat beside her. He was not a smoker, but he shared her cigarette to get rid of it.

She said, "You afraid you're going to miss your kid?"

"What d'you mean, miss him? I'll see as much of him as I ever did. Maybe more. You mind?"

"Of course not. I think he's kind of cute. Looks an awful lot like your wife."

"You mind *that?*"

"Honey, I like your wife. I wish she'd let me know her better."

He looked away. She placed a hand on the spread of his thigh.

"We can always call this off, you know."

"You think that's what I want?"

"Luv, look at me. I want you to tell me."

"I love you, OK?"

"That's not an answer."

"Yes, it is. Nothing's off."

She grinned. "Good. Because we can make it work. You and I, Rupert, we're different from other people."

"That so? How?"

"We take chances."

"Wrong. I set things up so I don't have to take chances.

She pushed her hair back on one side. "Honey, you're taking one on me."

He was studiously casual in the way he regarded her. "How big a chance?"

"As big as you want to make it," she said.

Back in bed, they watched snow accumulate on the outside window ledge, a sealing effect. They lay quite still, as if tethered, the covers pulled up to their chins, Sherry with two pillows under her head, Goetz with one.

"By the way, luv, who were you phoning?"

Moments passed. It did not appear that he would answer. His mouth was not set to open, and his eyes were now closed. "Marlborough Street," he murmured, scarcely moving his lips.

"Ahhh. And?"

"And nothing," he said, his tone telling her what his words did not. "Go to sleep."

She did. He stayed awake.

The snow turned to rain, which didn't last, and the day abruptly became mild, sunny and windy. Frank Chase knew where Goetz was. Goetz had mentioned the address, even the apartment number, in case he was seriously needed. Chase, his trench coat open, hailed a taxi.

Charles River Park: *If you lived here, you'd be home now.*

He got into the building without using the buzzer. Someone coming out held the door for him, a trusting soul. He used the elevator, rehearsing in his mind what he would say to Goetz, something simple, declaratory: *I want Ida.*

There was a button he could have jabbed, but instead he rapped. He had to rap several times, hard, knuckles hurting, before he received a response. The door opened a bit, and he saw a wildly glorious head of hair and a sweet face peering at him, though he was not sure the eyes were truly taking him in. The pupils appeared punched out. The rest of her was hidden behind the door.

"I'm looking for Rupert," he said.

"You are?" Her smile was slightly silly.

"Do you know who I am?"

"I think so."

He saw her fingers. They were suddenly gripping the edge of the door, the nails a bright red. He seemed to feel her presence through all his pores, and he wondered why. He said, "I'm Frank Chase."

"Yes, that's what I thought. You're his man Friday."

"Is that how he described me?"

The smile was back. "That's how I described you. Do you want to come in?"

She drew back and opened the door wide enough for him to pass through. His eye went to a painting on the wall, an abstract with a vague likeness to a fetus floating in amniotic fluid, and his nose drew the sure scent of smoked marijuana. The door closed behind him.

"I'm afraid I'm naked," she said. "Do you mind?"

He stood with a foot forward and honestly tried not to look

at her, but she drifted into his line of vision, long legs tapering
down to fine feet, lacquered toes, the same red as on her fingers.
And he understood all at once Goetz's madness for her. He
tried to force his eye back to the painting.

"Do you like the picture? Rupert doesn't. Hates it."

He didn't answer.

"Don't be embarrassed. I'm not."

"Get Rupert."

"Rupert said you were standing in for him. We both thank
you."

He tried to convince himself that he need feel no belittlement
because she had no brains, only a body, but he did not believe
himself, not even a little. He felt instead that she was one up
on him and that her brains were her trump. "And put something on," he said.

"You didn't give me a chance. The aggressive way you
knocked." She turned. "I'll only be a second."

She retreated to the bedroon, nonchalantly, and he watched
her every step of the way, couldn't stop himself. He heard from
Storrow Drive a blare of horns from snarled traffic. He heard
her in the bedroom say, "Gimme that."

Then a nervous male voice, not Goetz's: "What?"

Her voice: "That!"

A coldness ran through Chase. For a second he thought he
had gotten into the wrong apartment and the young woman had
taken it into her head to play upon his mistake. He leaned far
to one side. He saw her sitting on the edge of the bed and fussing
with her feet. A pair of male hands held what looked like a coat.
The coat dropped beside her. Chase straightened and stepped
back.

She emerged from the bedroom in a fur-collared storm coat
and shiny knee-high boots, with her friend reluctantly behind
her, his head bobbing, as if he were trying to hide it. He wore
sunglasses like a mask. She drew him gently beside her.

"This is Billy."

Chase scrutinized a gangling half-handsome youth in an untucked shirt and with a jacket over his arm, his legs tightly denimed. One of his shoes was not tied.

"I was just going," the youth said, but Sherry held his arm.

"Don't be scared. This isn't who you think it is." She kissed his cheek and then looked at Chase. "Billy lives in Cambridge. We've been saying goodby. It's the last time we'll be seeing each other. Right, Billy?"

The youth nodded fast and broke from her. "Nice to meet you," he said to Chase in passing. He fumbled with the door and exited in a stumble. Chase did not watch. Sherry's voice crept toward him.

"Billy and I used to live together."

Chase raised his chin. "That's nice."

She stuck her hands in the pockets of the coat. "It wasn't too exciting."

"Sorry to hear that."

"Do you like my coat? Rupert gave it to me. The boots too."

"Where is he?"

"He's here."

Chase was startled. "He's here?"

"I mean he *was* here. Hours ago. Is it important?"

Chase decided he no longer had a reason to stay. He made himself turn to the door.

"Frank."

He looked back.

"May I call you that?"

"Sure."

"You won't mention Billy to him, will you?"

Chase found himself smiling easily. He said, "I could tell him and do him a favor. Or I could *not* tell him and do myself a favor."

Her smile came just as easily. "Want my advice, Frank? Think of yourself for a change."

19.

VIOLENT ACTS

Dance lived in Dorchester, the top tenement of a tilting three-decker in a neighborhood rapidly going black. Dance said to his visitor, "Guy had this place before me weighed four-hundred pounds, that's what I'm told. He died in bed and the body bloated up, and they couldn't get him through the door. Fire Department had to use ladders and rope to bring him out the window. Halfway down they dropped him."

Dance's laugh was loud. The man in the jacket said, "White guy?"

"What do you think."

"I think the place should be fumigated. It still stinks."

"That's garbage," said Dance.

"You eat here?"

"Sometimes."

"This the guy's furniture?"

"Yeah."

"That means you sleep in his bed."

"It ain't the same mattress," Dance said defensively.

They were sitting at a scratched formica-topped table. A mammoth set of keys on a tug of metal lay between them. The man in the jacket nodded at the keys. "I'm interested. You ever kill with them before?"

Dance laughed but didn't answer.

"You've got a lot of imagination, but you should throw them

away." The man's eyes were dull and flat, and his voice had a sleepy quality. "They become a trademark. You don't want that."

"I paid good money for 'em. Second-hand store in Springfield."

"You don't like to take advice?"

Dance hesitated. "You want me to throw 'em away, I'll throw 'em away."

"That's what I want you to do," the man said. "You been staying away from the sauce?"

"A jolt now and then, nothing you got to worry about."

The man let that register slowly. Then he said, "I recommended you. Don't make me regret it."

"No sweat."

The man rose, and so did Dance. The man was six inches shorter than Dance, sixty pounds lighter, and perhaps ten years older. His hair was black, the gray colored out. He said, "You don't need to do any more telephoning."

Dance smiled broadly. "I must've done OK."

"You did too much, but we're not blaming you. What you want to do now is just sit tight."

"How long?"

"I knew how long I'd tell you," the man said and turned to leave.

"You got something for me?" Dance asked.

The man glanced back with an odd smile, as though he'd been waiting for those words. His hand slid into his jacket pocket. "Yeah, I got something for you."

Dance froze.

The man tossed a roll of bills at him.

The killings took place shortly before dusk on Prince Street, off Hanover, starting with a sudden and savage encounter between two youths who, from their polished manes of hair to their high-heeled shoes, looked enough alike to be brothers.

They used not fists but fingers, going for the eyes and grabbing for the throat, until the taller of the two, taking the worst of it, produced a .45-caliber pistol and fired off two shots, his arm climbing. The first shot lifted the other youth off the sidewalk and threw him into the street, blood spinning through a shirt that looked like tissue paper. The second shot shattered plate glass across the street and dropped an unseen woman in her tracks.

Within seconds whatever people had been around were gone, shops that had been open were closed and shaded, and the street lay eerily deserted, trashy from the day's leavings of tourists, dogs, and residents. The only sound came from a child until some ten minutes later when the wail of sirens was heard.

The man in the jacket was parking his car on Hanover Street as the sirens grew louder. He slipped out of the car and stood in shadows, shifting his weight from foot to foot as police cruisers tore by, more on the way, as if the whole city were on the alert. Soon two men joined him and told him what had happened. They gave him names. He blanched and then cursed.

Shortly later he rode the elevator to the fourteenth floor in Harbour Towers, where the lawyer lived with his wife. The wife viewed him through a peephole that worked on the principle of a periscope and gave her wide-angle views extending to the elevators. On the outside the device looked like a decorative design of the door, though the man was aware of its function. The wife let him in. His eyes, as always, strayed to large oil paintings he didn't particularly appreciate but knew cost a lot. The lawyer was settled in for the night in a soft tip-back chair in front of a color television tuned to the public channel, an opera by Verdi. The expression on the man's face revealed the gravity of his business, and the lawyer kept the television on so that his wife would not hear.

"Your nephew," the man said, kneeling next to the chair so that he would not have to shout and quickly relating what he had been told.

The lawyer was quiet, as if more interested in the opera and the immense man who was singing at the top of his voice, bellyaching in rich Italian about a son who did not know where his duty lay. Finally the lawyer said, "I don't remember one time that kid ever showed good sense. Where is he now?"

"I don't know anything more than I told you," the man said. "I came here first thing."

"Find him."

The man nodded.

"Three things," the lawyer said, ticking off arthritic fingers. "I want the kid under wraps. I want flowers and money sent to the families. And I want Rupert Goetz to see me soon as possible. Sooner!"

The man rose.

The lawyer said, "I don't think you're going to get much sleep tonight."

The man smiled. "I ought to belong to a union."

"Yes," the lawyer said. "Teamsters."

The man let himself out.

Dome lights from parked police cruisers flashed from one end of Prince Street to the other, as uniformed officers and homicide detectives invaded buildings and ascended to rooftops. Two detectives took time to relieve themselves in the dark against a chimney, and the younger one said, "I hear the chief's showing up for this one."

The other detective grunted, pulling in and zipping up. After a moment or so they both moved away from the chimney, ducking clotheslines and stepping around small gardens contained in big boxes. They made their way to the roof's edge, and the younger one pointed down.

"That's him, isn't it? Standing there next to Donovan."

The older detective squinted. "Yeah, I'd recognize that cannonball head anywhere."

"What's the story on him anyway?"

The older detective snorted. "Biggest manipulator in the world, bar none. You knew Frank Chase, didn't you?"

"I didn't know him, but I've heard of him. I mean, Christ, he married the chief's wife. The chief married someone else."

"That ain't all, kiddo."

They moved away from the edge and, stepping on a blanket somebody had used for sunbathing, made their way to the ragged door that was coming off its hinges.

"So what else?" the younger one asked.

The older detective laughed. "You wouldn't believe me if I told you."

"What's the matter, don't you trust me?"

"Sure I trust you. Took a leak with you, didn't I?"

They made their way down the stairs, back into the building, revolvers drawn, just in case.

Rupert Goetz arrived late and was briefed by his second-in-command, a man named Donovan who looked like a tough marine out of uniform. Goetz viewed the body on the street and then the one in the store. The body of the youth didn't bother him. The woman's did.

"She must've got it by accident," Donovan said.

"I figured that out myself," said Goetz, guessing that the woman, whose hair was in curlers, all of them tightly in place, never knew what hit her. "Who was that little kid I saw?"

"Hers. Someone's looking after him."

They stepped carefully out of the store, over broken glass. The flashing lights silvered Goetz's face and purpled his hair. He said, "There's not going to be one fucking witness, you realize that."

"The woman might make a difference."

"No difference," said Goetz.

"We might get a break."

"We'll get nothing except maybe by leaning."

Donovan nodded. "I'll do more than lean. I'll break some fucking heads."

"I didn't hear you," Goetz said and walked away.

Something woke Dance. He lay quite still in the dark, naked except for baggy boxer shorts, and listened to the whispers of a breeze and the sound of a passing car. Then he heard a noise out at the door, the lock slipping, clicking loose, and knew that someone was entering the tenement, penetrating the blackness of the kitchen. His mind clothed the figure with the shine of a jacket, a loaded hand easing out of it. Everything hit him at once: fear and outrage, pity for himself, giddiness. He lay catatonic, a weakness in every muscle. Then it all passed, and he leaped off the bed.

For a split second, while deciding what to do, he stood pale and poised, noble in one way, for he seemed ready to fight with his bare hands, and ridiculous in another, for his penis hung out of his shorts. He slapped it back in. He had no gun, nothing, not even keys. They were out on the table. He was nimbler than he looked, and no fool. He leaped to the open window and with scarcely a sound lifted the screen and flung it far into the night. A leg flew out first, then the rest of him, a long ghost. Gripping the sill with one hand and the rotted edge of a porch with the other, he dangled three flights up, too far to fall. But he did.

He struck rubber—loose junk tires left in the alley—and skidded headfirst on a twisting ankle, his right shoulder scraping asphalt, losing skin, and crunching bottle glass. Then he hit a plastic sack of something that became a cushion for his head. He lay on his back, shivering and hurting, with a dazed eye on the window he'd fallen from. Each second he waited for something to happen. Nothing did.

He held his breath when a dog appeared from nowhere. It didn't bark. It merely sniffed his throbbing shoulder and then backed off as he rose haltingly on one foot. The other foot was on fire. The dog disappeared as he hobbled toward a fence and tried to push himself through it. He failed.

Groping toward the sidewalk and losing strength, he heard footsteps, somebody leaving the building, a hurried pace, and the figure that crossed the street was too tall, not the man he thought it was, which relieved him and confused him. He saw the car the man slipped into, a ranch wagon, which confused him more. Not till the wagon vanished down the street could he place it.

"You scumbag," he whispered and vowed vengeance.

20.

FRIENDS

Sergeant Lionel Dearborn's sister-in-law stood with pencil and pad in front of the booth, and Dearborn without looking up said, "We'll both have coffee. Unless you want something else."

Frank Chase shook his head and lit a cigarette.

"You should quit."

"I've been thinking about it."

"Maybe it's a bad time to try. You must have a lot on your mind."

"No," said Chase. "But you obviously do."

The coffees came, and they took turns with the sugar shaker, Dearborn last. He said, "I thought it better us talking here. I kind of upset your wife yesterday. She tell you?"

"She didn't mention being upset."

"Maybe I read her wrong."

Chase returned Dearborn's thin smile with a thinner one. Dearborn picked up his cup and sipped.

"Best coffee in town, don't you think?"

"Friendly's and Ford's isn't bad," Chase said, reluctantly playing the game.

"No, I've been to them all. Finn's is the best, including service. You saw how quick the waitress took care of us."

Chase lost patience. "Let's get to the point."

"I like to set the scene."

"It's set."

Dearborn sipped more coffee, taking his time. "I'll tell you what bothers me, Chase. I'm not getting any cooperation, not even where I should. Moynihan, the guy from the DA's office, acts like he couldn't care less."

"That's odd," said Chase.

"That's what I thought. Then, too, I was bothered how you said you didn't know the victim."

"There was no face, remember?"

"Right. That wasn't pretty."

Chase put out his cigarette. "Few murder victims are."

"You've probably seen more than I have."

"I was in Homicide."

"Right. Miss it?"

"I'm happy."

"Frank," said Dearborn, as if Chase's words were too flagrant to let pass. "I know how much you make. I don't think you've got your heart in it. Selling houses, I mean."

"I do my best."

"Frank, I even know how much you put down on your own house. Twenty percent. That surprised me. I thought you might've paid cash for it. Then again, that wouldn't have been smart."

"Maybe you should explain that," Chase said in a hard tone, as if to bring matters to a head or to call a bluff. Dearborn leaned forward, confidentially.

"Frank, some things aren't for me to know. I'm starting to realize that. I guess you could say I'm maturing as a cop."

Chase's face was expressionless, and Dearborn smiled.

"I bet we could be friends, what d'you think?"

"What's your name—Lionel? Lionel, I'll be truthful with you. I hadn't given it any thought."

Dearborn nodded toward the waitress who had served them. She was counting slips. "That's my sister-in-law. What d'you think of her?"

Chase gave her a slow glance, and their eyes met. Hers told him absolutely nothing, and he imagined his did the same. "A good-looking woman."

"And she works hard. She's got a bunch of kids. I have too, as a matter of fact. Five. People like her and me, we have a tough time surviving in a town like this, even though we were born here. I'm talking financially. What's my sister-in-law? You can see what she is. A servant. That's what I am. And you used to be, Frank."

"I think it's time you made your point."

"The point is, Frank, I think you're going to have a tough time surviving here. Not financially—I think you're real OK there—but in other ways. People who live in this town, in houses like yours and bigger, are wondering who the hell you are, somebody dumps a dead man on your lawn."

"I don't blame them. I'd wonder too."

"Then there's your boss, Gunderman. I don't think he likes you anymore. Of course there're other realtors in town. There's Darling and Dodd, Victor. Hell, a whole lot of them, but I'm wondering if any of them would want you."

"What are you telling me? To leave?"

Dearborn sighed. "I'm trying to make a point, and you're missing it. What I'm saying, Frank, is you and me should stick together. I don't think we're that different, do you?" He took time to finish the last of his coffee and wave back his sister-in-law when she started to come forward. "We should help each other out, Frank, because I think you've got enemies enough. What you need now is a friend, especially if somebody wants to put anything more on your lawn. Maybe put you there."

Chase rose, leaving a dollar on the table. "My treat."

Dearborn stared up at him. "Will you think it over, Frank? So I can help you, not hurt you."

Chase started to leave. Dearborn called him back.

"You'd better not be carrying anything, Frank, because I know you don't have a permit, not with us. If I catch you with a piece, I'll arrest you."

Chase left, and Dearborn's sister-in-law came to the booth. "Here's a dollar," Dearborn said. "Keep the change."

"What were you two doing?" she asked. "Fighting?"

"Did it look it?"

"No, but I could tell."

"Don't you know who that was?"

"Never saw him before."

"That's a guy who's sitting on anywhere from a hundred grand to a million bucks, I'd stake my life on it."

"You should've introduced me."

"You've got enough to worry about. How are you treating Chuckie?"

"Why don't you ask how he's treating me?"

"All right, tell me."

"Like a piece of shit," she said and strode away.

The phone rang. Lee Gunderman answered it and received no response, but she had a good idea who and what it was. "Look," she said, "this used to be cute, but I'm getting tired of it."

She waited.

"You might as well know," she said. "I've taped your other calls and played them at parties."

She half-laughed.

"You could be put away, fella."

She heard not a peep and was no longer sure anyone was on the other end.

"I've decided not to let my son play on the team anymore. You're not a fit person."

The impression that she was speaking to nobody grew stronger. She was near a mirror and smiled pleasantly at herself.

"I've heard about you Dearborns. You breed like rabbits. You're probably all inbred. You wouldn't know what to do with a real woman if you had one. You'd have to be taught."

Her voice rose. "Do you hear me, peckerhead?"

A click sounded in her ear and in time a dial tone. She replaced the receiver slowly, her hand faintly trembling.

Later, while she was polishing silver, it occurred to her that the caller might have been Karl. She polished harder, as if to smudge out the thought.

Ida Chase returned from a two-hour bicycle ride in Harold Parker State Forest and joined her husband near the pool. He was sitting in a deck chair with an unread copy of the Andover *Townsman* in his lap.

"Everything all right?" she asked.

"Everything's fine. You look ready for a dip."

"Do I dare?"

"David's not here."

She gave him a fast kiss, quickly slipped out of her clothes, and plunged into the pool, a substantial woman who turned wraithlike in water. Chase tossed the paper aside and watched her smooth unhurried stroke and odd sort of kick. She swam the length three times and floated near him.

"Join me."

He smiled but shook his head and watched her draw herself out of the pool, water sparkling off her like shards of glass. She wrapped up in a bright blanket of a towel, used a large corner to give her soaked hair a swift scrub, and kissed him again, her lips still wet, a smarting taste of chlorine.

"You should've biked with me."

"The hills hurt."

"Feel."

His hand sank through folds of terrycloth and felt a cool belly, almost a solid muscle.

"See," she said. "That's from making the hills."

A sudden gusting breeze left a nice smell dangling in the air. Somebody in the neighborhood, way ahead of anybody else, was charcoaling steaks. Ida stared at him.

"Hungry?"

He shook his head.

"I am, and you should be. How about a cold plate of bar-becued chicken wings?"

"Not for me."

"All right, something simpler. Wait here."

She snatched up her clothes, rearranged the towel around her, and barefooted toward the house. She was back in twenty minutes wearing a striped jersey and white jeans and carrying a tray. Chase brought himself forward in his chair, as if slowly surfacing from sleep, while she arranged the tray in front of him, two small plates of garden salad, Russian dressing on his, low-cal stuff on hers. She drew a chair for herself.

"Eat," she said. He picked. "Frank, what's the matter, and don't try to kid me."

Quietly, while scraping his fork against a wedge of tomato, as if to extract the seeds, he told her about Lionel Dearborn, and she too began to pick at her food. Chase said wryly, "He thinks I scored big, like a million dollars. I almost wish I had, for his sake."

"Oh, Frank."

"He's trying to do one of two things. Con me or shake me down. Or who knows, maybe both."

"Frank, don't do anything foolish."

He lifted his eyes. "What do you think I'd do?"

"I don't know."

"I'm not Rupert."

"Haven't we agreed to that, maybe a hundred years ago?" She reached over the tray to caress the back of his hand, the one with the fork. "But I still don't know all you did in Boston yesterday. And there are other things you still haven't filled me in on."

"You know about the money, you know how I got it, Johnny Kale and I. I have his blood on my hands. But so has Rupert."

"Frank, I suspected that a long time ago. Rupert was behind

everything, wasn't he?"

"Every detail. I think I knew it all the time, but it was easier pretending otherwise. That way I could just let things happen."

Ida shifted her feet around but kept her eyes on her husband. She said, "Tell me about yesterday."

He told her everything, slowly, in detail, still holding the fork, at times using it to eat. When he finished he expected to see fear in her eyes. Her face was blank.

She said, "Is that really a name—Dance?"

"Dancewicz."

"And this lawyer person?"

"He's not really a lawyer."

"Jesus, I hope not."

"He's Mafia."

"Oh, my Christ." Now he saw the fear. She said, "Frank, are we going to be all right?"

"If not, we'll have only me to blame." He put the fork down. "I'm handling it now. Really. No more Rupert."

Ida reached for his hand again, this time gripping it, her nails digging in. "Let me rephrase the question. Are *you* going to be all right?"

"I think so," he said.

21.

FAVORS

"Yes or no, do I still have a job?" Frank Chase said, sitting in front of Karl Gunderman's desk and wondering why the man seemed so tired and listless, as if it were too much of an effort for him to speak. He had shaved badly and appeared not to have combed his hair. "I'm not going to fight about it," Chase said. "I'd just like to know."

"Frank, you're a good man."

"Is that an answer?"

Gunderman tried to look wise, first with a smile that was too weak to last and then with a tilt of the head that did not look comfortable. "Do you know why I gave you a job in the first place? I mean, the real reason, what clinched it."

"I don't want to know. I just want to know if I have a job now."

Gunderman straightened his head. His hands were hidden. He said, "It's not a good business, Frank. Ten years from now —hell, not ten, probably only five—people like me won't be selling houses anymore. Corporations are gobbling us up— Century 21, Gallery of Homes, Realty World. That's a few. There's more, Frank. Too many. You can't stop them, and no way can you compete with them."

"You're not starving."

"You want to buy my business? I'll sell it to you in a minute."

"I think you've answered my question," Chase said and rose. Gunderman did too, but with trouble. He weaved a little and had to steady himself with a hand on the edge of the desk.

"You've still got a job, Frank, but I want you to take a little more time off. People are still talking. You understand, don't you?"

Chase lowered his gaze. "What happened to your hand?"

"Nothing," Gunderman said and shoved it into his pocket. "The job's still yours, all right?"

"Yes, that's what you said."

"I mean it. I'm glad you came in. I feel better."

Chase hesitated. He felt that Gunderman had more to say. Gunderman pulled the hand out of his pocket.

"See this, Frank? I took a poke at Lee. From a distance. Missed her by a mile."

Chase said nothing.

"Are you fooling around with her, Frank?"

Chase still said nothing, but his face gave an answer. Gunderman looked exhausted, the exhaustion permanent.

"I'm sorry," he said. "I know it's not you, but maybe it's Ted Dowell. Can you tell me?"

"Karl, don't ask me that crap."

Blushing, Gunderman closed his eyes and nodded. "That's what it is. Crap."

Chase got as far as the door.

"Frank." Gunderman's voice was broken. "Come back to work anytime. Today if you want. I don't care what people are saying."

Rupert and Sherry Goetz lunched at Davio's on Newbury Street, graciously served by a waiter who knew Goetz. Sherry was hungry and ate big, veal smothered with eggplant and mozzarella, and Goetz ate little, soup followed by salad. He ordered a second drink but ignored it when it arrived. Sherry buttered bread and smiled. Goetz said, "I love you."

"Ditto," she said.

"Do you remember what you said right after we started going together?"

"Luv," she said, chewing the bread. "You had me on my back all the time. How can I remember?"

"You said the scary thing about us is we might be two of a kind."

"And you said nobody's two of a kind."

"I was wrong." He went for her hand and held it hard. "That's why we've always got to stick together."

"Something heavy is on your mind, Rupert. What is it?"

"I have to give the money back," he said and watched the changing color of her eyes.

"Bullshit," she said.

He spoke quietly. "I don't have a choice."

"The money's as much mine as yours."

He stared at her. She was wearing an elegantly plain blouse with blown sleeves and a deep unbuttoned front. The blouse was new. He had been with her when she bought it. He said, "All right. *We* don't have a choice. *We* have to give it back."

She dabbed her mouth with a linen napkin. "What about our plans, Rupert? The place at the Cape. Right on the beach, you said. What about the year in Europe? How are you going to retire now, Rupert?"

"Something else will come up."

She snapped her fingers. "Just like that?"

"Maybe."

"Bullshit."

Goetz tasted his drink, conscious now of the others around him, the ringing silverware, the waiter slipping by to serve the next table. Sherry's lips twisted oddly.

"What about what we've already spent?"

Goetz put a hand to his jaw. "That too. I'll have to borrow."

"Terriffic. And what about them in Andover? What do *they* have to give back?"

He didn't answer.

"I see."

"No, that's the problem," he said. "You don't see."

"What I see, Rupert, is a man running scared."

Goetz sighed with patience that seemed utmost. "It's not a question of running scared, Sherry. Only of not being stupid."

"Finish your drink."

He did, as if he deserved it, while she smiled, seeming to look through him. Her smile widened.

"All right. What's funny?"

She refocused her eyes. "I'm sorry, Rupert. What?"

"I asked what's so funny?"

"Just that shit about you and me being two of a kind. That's all."

Frank Chase showed a New Jersey couple houses on Oriole Drive, Cheever Circle, and High Plain Road, pretending that none of the houses had water problems, though fairly certain that two of them did. He tried to pressure the couple into a decision, but the woman, who wore tinted oversize glasses and appeared sharper than her husband, said, "Don't rush us." Chase found himself blushing.

He dropped them off and drove home.

David was cutting the grass with the power mower, a job he liked, and Ida was working in her flower garden. Chase waved to them and entered the house through the garage, hurrying because the phone was ringing. He grabbed it, and a voice said, "I don't like what you did."

"That so," Chase said, recognizing the voice. "Couple of things you did I don't like."

"If I'd known it was you, I'd have stayed instead of going out the fucking window. I hurt myself."

"That's too bad."

"Let's meet."

"Be glad to," Chase said.

"How about next to the Charles, so I can dump you in?"

"How about in the Common?"

"Name the fucking bench."

"I have a feeling the only place we're going to meet is in the dark."

"You've got it, buddy."

The line went dead, and Chase put the receiver down as Ida entered the house, her face flushed and her forehead smudged. "Who was that?" she asked.

"A client," Chase said. "I'm selling houses again."

"You don't look pleased."

"Half-pleased," he said.

Slowly she stiffened. "That's not fair, Frank."

"What isn't?"

"You're lying. You're not telling me everything."

He gave her a curious look.

"That wasn't a client," she said. "Who was it?"

"Our friend," he said.

Rupert Goetz squeezed into the noise of Haymarket, squashed fruit and vegetables underfoot, the push and pile of people at times impenetrable. Italian youths wearing open shirts and shorts tossed empty crates and cartons to one side, building a barricade, but Goetz found a way around it and crossed the street to Faneuil Hall Marketplace, into the thick of a tourist crowd. He found a bench to sit on near the glass arcade of a cafe. The man in the jacket joined him within minutes, and for a while neither spoke. People edged by them, a constant procession, with a surprisingly large number of scantily dressed women, all ages. "The place is a gold mine," the man in the jacket murmured, as if he had a stake in it, an interest in one or more of the shops. "And not bad for looking at tits and asses."

"This why we're here?" said Goetz.

"Thought you might be a connoisseur."

"I'm here to hear what you've got to say. And I'm in a hurry."

"Everybody is." The man stuffed his hands into the thin pockets of his jacket and pulled his feet in fast as somebody nearly stepped on them. "You were supposed to see the lawyer again, soon as possible. Didn't you get the word?"

"Yeah, I got the word. I've been busy."

"Where's his money?"

"It's spread around. I already told him that. I'm getting it together, which takes time."

"What have you got it in—a hundred banks?"

"Something like that."

The man scratched his head. "You're taking too much time to suit him. That bothers him."

"Don't threaten me."

"Take it easy, chief. I'm only telling you what he said.

"He'll get the money. He knows that."

The man nodded. "Another thing. He wants to know who the hell this Donovan thinks he is, pushing people around, slapping them. Did you hear about it?"

"We talking about the Prince Street thing?"

"That's what we're talking about."

"Does it touch your people?"

"That's not the point. The lawyer's concerned about individual rights."

Goetz looked at him sideways. "I think you'd better talk plainer. I told you I'm in a hurry."

"The lawyer thinks you should write the Prince Street thing off. He says you can count it as one of the favors you owe him."

"I see."

"He said you would."

Goetz was quiet for a few seconds. "Tell him this favor's big enough to cover any others. Tell him he gets the money and this favor, and we're square."

"Sure," the man said, rising slowly. "I'll tell him."

Goetz watched him pass into the crowd.

The hardware store was deep in Dorchester. Dance entered it and nodded to the heavy man who owned it. The store was small and dark, and the man had an extravagant mustache, like that of an old-time Turk. He said to Dance, "Long time no see. You walk funny. What the hell happened to you?"

"I fell." Dance glanced around to make certain they were alone. "I need a favor."

"That kind, huh?" The man toyed with his mustache, which had dried bits of shoe polish on it.

"Yeah, that kind. Can you help me or not?"

The man emerged from behind the counter and led Dance into a back room. They stood near a tool bench. Dance made a face.

"Something smells."

"I got a cat."

"You oughta change the box."

The man folded his arms high against his chest. "Tell me what you want."

"A piece like I had before."

The man grinned, showing unnaturally bright teeth. "I remember you saying you weren't ever going to carry again."

"I also want the attachment."

"That's going to cost you a hell of a lot more than what you used to pay. Prices have gone up. Inflation."

"You don't hear me arguing. I guess you haven't heard who I'm working for now."

The man nodded. "Yeah, I heard. Congratulations."

"How soon?"

"The piece you can have right now, you want it. The accessory will take a week. I've got work I've got to get out first."

"I want it faster."

"You sound like you got a hard-on for somebody. OK, maybe three, four days, but don't count on it."

"I'll pick up the whole item then. Where's the cat? I don't see him."

"He hides."

"He should."

They left the room, and the man accompanied Dance to the door. The man grinned again. "I heard you got a set of keys belonged to a castle. Someone told me that."

"Someone did, huh? Funny thing there. Some guy came in

off the street one night and stole them right off the table. But maybe I'll get them back. Never can tell."

The man slapped Dance on the back and opened the door for him.

As soon as Rupert Goetz settled at his desk, Donovan came in and said quietly, "The commissioner himself called. Sounded pissed off. Says he can never get you when he wants you. He asked if you ever come in at all."

Goetz tipped back, as if unconcerned. "He knows how I operate. I'm a field soldier, right?"

Donovan smiled, an effort for him. Goetz yawned, loosened his striped tie, and undid a few buttons on his vest.

"He say what he wanted?"

"He just wanted to know how it's going on Prince Street. He's upset because the *Globe* ran the picture of the dead woman again. I told him you were working on it personally."

"That calm him down?"

"I don't know. He hung up."

"How *is* it going?"

"I'm still banging heads."

"You can get yourself in trouble doing that."

"Never bothered you."

"Times have changed."

The two men studied each other, and after a while Donovan caught on.

Goetz said, "Don't worry about the commissioner. He's my problem."

Donovan said, "I'll work by the book."

"It's the only way to stay out of trouble," said Goetz.

Donovan nodded and left, closing the door behind him.

After several minutes Goetz got up awkwardly from his chair and walked to the window, where he stared down at the brutal Boston traffic.

For the first time in a long time he allowed himself to think about Johnny Kale.

22.

JOHNNY KALE

They met near the Ritz and shook hands, squeezing to the point of pain, conspiratorially, as if still involved in the violent teamwork of football that they had played together at South Boston High, both of them in the line, tackle and guard. Rupert Goetz appeared trimmer than he was in a dark overcoat, neatly fur-collared and fitted, and could have passed for a banker had he worn a hat. Johnny Kale was a chunky figure in a three-quarter-length leather coat over a polka-dot shirt and double-knit pants, and he was what he seemed to be: a kiter of checks and a filer of false claims, a placer of bets and a loser of too many long shots, a handler of questionable goods and a mishandler of himself. He was aging too fast, with a couple of internal organs already wasting away.

"You look good, Rupert."

"You look lousy."

"Thanks a fucking lot."

They went into the Ritz and into the bar, Goetz leading the way. Removing their coats, they sank into big chairs at a tiny table, and Goetz ordered for the both of them. They were boyhood buddies, and Kale, a quiet spectator at sordid gatherings and events, was Goetz's most reliable snitch. Now he was a co-conspirator.

"Not bad," he said, tasting what Goetz had ordered, a dark Wurzburger that was nice and nutty, ice-cold.

"Glad you like it," said Goetz, his attention a couple of tables

away on a young woman whose adventurous smile reminded
him of Sherry's. A handsomely dressed man with white hair
and a faint resemblance to Cary Grant had both her hands in
what appeared a deep discussion.

"You picked a classy place to meet," Kale said.

Goetz leaned forward because of poor acoustics. "What did
you say?"

"I said I just farted. I hope nobody heard."

Goetz tasted his beer. "You don't change, Johnny-boy."

"That's right. Happy-go-lucky during the day, but I cry at
night. What you're looking at over there, I bet when they finish
their drinks he takes her to his room. Wanna bet? We'll follow."

"No bet. They're obviously traveling together."

"Yeah, obviously." Kale dug his fingers into a bowl of salted
nuts, spilling some. A few made it to his mouth.

"You nervous?"

"Yeah. I ain't got laid in over a month. That's why I cry at
night. Add the fact, I'm a fucking failure. Not like you. A big
shot."

"You want to talk business?"

"Sure." Kale raised the glass mug and drained it. "Do I just
yell out for another, or will somebody see it and come?"

"Finish mine. I don't want it."

Kale lit a cigarette. "The young guys we been talking about.
They're still only amateurs, but suddenly what's going on between them is big. The one making trips to Colombia is supposed to be coming back with a shitload in a special suitcase,
and the other guy's got the cash to buy it. Somebody's bankroll-
ing the whole operation, no doubt about it."

"Who?"

"That's a fucking mystery. Might be somebody down in
Florida. They both got contacts there around Miami. Might be
a Cuban."

Goetz studied his fingernails. "Could be somebody here just
as easily."

"I don't know."

"Is it still going down in the same way, the same place?"

"Absolutely. These college kids live charmed lives. They trust each other and the world. They ain't even armed."

"That's good because I don't want you holding either."

"You kidding? I wouldn't carry a gun even if you put a knife to my neck. What I'd do is faint."

Goetz reached into the bowl of nuts and took one, examining it before putting it into his mouth. "So what you're saying is it looks better than ever."

Kale drank Goetz's beer. "Yuh."

Goetz studied him. "Does it scare you?"

"Lot of things scare me, Rupert. Doing something like this is one of them."

"We can forget it if you want."

"No, you've got me out of jams, and I owe you too much. I know that."

"You don't owe me anything."

Kale smiled over Goetz's beer. "You say it, Rupert, but you don't mean it. I'll do this thing, don't worry."

Goetz motioned to the waiter and again ordered for the both of them, Dewar's. His attention strayed briefly to the bar, where a man was overcome with quiet laughter, others joining in, even the bartender. Kale was quiet. Goetz said, "Lay it out to Frank like I said. Don't push him. You push him, he'll look at you sideways."

"I like Frank."

"I like him too. He trust you?"

"He trusts *you*, Rupert. He knows you and I go back."

"He's not to know I'm involved. You understand that?"

The drinks came. Kale lifted his and rattled the ice near his ear, as if the sound were a stimulant. "I understand only what you want me to, OK?"

"When you lay it out, act like you want him to grab the money and you the stuff. He won't like that. That's where he won't trust you."

"Seems a shame, letting that stuff get dumped."

"He wouldn't have it any other way. I know him."

"How much am I getting out of this, Rupert?"

"Same as Frank."

"Meaning we're both getting screwed, except he don't know it."

"Like you said yourself, you owe me."

Kale downed his drink, sucking in some of the ice. The white-haired man and the young woman were on their feet, the woman standing in a way that gave prominence to her breasts. The man eased around the chairs to help her on with her coat. Kale said, "How come I never get anything like that? Not once, not ever in my whole life."

Goetz said, "Calm down. You bitch about one thing when you're worried about another."

"Nothing's fair." Kale spoke with the ice still in his mouth. "Look what you're doing. Throwing away the kind of woman that would never come my way. Why don't you give her to me? Why should Frank have her?"

"Johnny, shut up."

"I'm out of line, huh?"

"I want you to relax. When this thing happens, I'll be there where nobody sees me. Just so nothing unexpected hits you."

Kale lowered himself deep into his chair and watched the white-haired man and the woman leave. "Rupert, I don't want to get hurt."

Goetz, though he didn't hear all of the words, said, "Trust me."

Frank Chase crouched at the back of a building, behind cars, beyond a squirt of light from a doorway. His head was bullet-shaped from a tight watch cap pulled down to his eyebrows, and the rest of his face was shielded by the hiked collar of his lumber jacket. His crouch brought cramps, and the cold cut through the legs of his pants. Not far away, in the shadows between two long cars, two men approached each other.

Chase did not budge, as if weighted into place, lead in his shoes, second thoughts in his head. The two men were talking. He could not hear their words, but he clearly saw the bursts of mist from their mouths. Somewhere else in the dark, similarly crouched and cramped, was Johnny Kale, whose record Chase had read. According to it, Kale had once lumbered into Liberty Mutual as though he were a repairman and tried to waltz out with a typewriter. Chase half-laughed, as if the humor were just now reaching him. He pictured Kale sweating in the cold because he, Chase, had not yet made the move.

They were not college kids, not any more. He saw that right away as he slipped between the cars. They were in their middle twenties, and one was tall and lanky, like a basketball player, his left elbow cocked near his shoulder, support for the loaded garment bag he draped behind him. His right hand clutched the suitcase. The other young man wore heavy glasses that magnified his eyes and lifted them out of his face. The eyes were plastic, like a cat's. He held the briefcase.

"The odd couple," Chase said, baring a five-shot Smith & Wesson Chief.

Both men froze.

"The briefcase," Chase said lightly. "Put it on the hood of the car. Do it slow."

The one with the briefcase did not move except to adjust his substantial glasses, a gesture to buy time. His grip on the briefcase remained firm.

"Please," Chase said tonelessly.

The tall one let his garment bag slip down his back to the ground, and his free arm fell casually to his side. His carelessly groomed head lolled high and loose in a thin sweep of light. He had the long dried-out features of a flint-eyed Yankee coming of age, a new generation, and he appeared tightly wound, ready to spring in the defense of property, which threw Chase off stride. He had figured the one with the glasses for potential trouble, not this one.

"It's not worth it," he said, angling the revolver, which was a bluff. He didn't intend to use it except as a club to protect himself, though he had visions of it going off, their young blood on his hands, in which case the ripoff would turn into a legitimate bust, his badge flashing. He had other visions of his head on the asphalt, their fists and feet hammering him. He said, "I'm even dumber than you two. So you can understand the danger we're in."

"Don't argue with him," the one with the glasses said and suddenly tossed the briefcase onto the hood, the noise more than Chase had wanted.

"Take it," Chase said, giving it a quick shove as a hand flew out of the dark. The briefcase vanished, as if it had never been there, and the sound of fleeing footsteps faded fast.

"Who are you?" the tall one said.

"The suitcase," said Chase, ignoring the question.

"Do you know what you're getting yourself into?" The tall one had a brisk accent, boarding school.

"Let alone the trouble it gets us into," said the one with the glasses.

Chase sighed, as if time had run out, including his own.

"Don't!"

"Don't make me."

"Do what he wants, Horace."

"Yes, Horace. Drop the suitcase."

The tall one did, reluctantly, letting it plop to one side. Then they ran. Chase told them to, pointing the way and then watching their flight for only a moment. He kicked the garment bag under a car and for a second considered doing the same with the suitcase. Then he picked it up. He entered the building through the lighted doorway, bumped his way down a dim corridor, and emerged on a narrow street, where his car was parked.

He drove toward the Charles River.

What amazed him in one way and frightened him in another was the relative ease with which he had performed the criminal deed.

Rupert Goetz slipped into his darkened car, wedging the briefcase between himself and the steering wheel, his eyes turning murderously to Johnny Kale, who sat shamefaced against the passenger door. "I'm sorry," Kale said. "I fucking froze."

"You sure as shit did," Goetz said, unsnapping the briefcase. He swiftly inspected the contents with a pocket flashlight and whistled softly to himself. Then he snapped the briefcase shut and tossed it into the back.

Kale from his corner said, "Don't I get a look?"

Goetz started up the car.

Sherry from the back seat said, "Ah, hell, what difference does it make? Everything came out OK."

Kale turned around and looked at her lovingly.

The car shot forward, jolting him against the door.

23.

THE PARTY

The Chases stayed little more than an hour at the Gundermans' party, a large gathering, more people than usual, many of whom they didn't know. As Ida was introducing herself to one woman, another turned sharply and said, "You're who? Who did you say you are?"

At the drinks table a man from a rival realty office shook Frank Chase's hand and said, "You're a celebrity, you know that?"

"A celebrity?"

"You know what I mean." The man had a loud voice he would not or could not modulate. "A lot of people ask if I know you."

"What do you say?"

"Sure I know you. That's what I say."

They were joined by a banker, Andover Savings, where Karl Gunderman had helped negotiate Chase's house mortgage at a favorable rate. The banker was as big as a bull. He thrust an empty glass at the youth tending the table and turned his eyes on Chase.

Chase slipped away without a drink for himself, none for Ida either. Ida was escaping a past president of the garden club and fetching a drink for herself, another table, another room, where Lee Gunderman was embracing people, moving from mouth to mouth, her face a shiny blade. She kissed Ida.

"I'm so glad you came. Are you meeting people?"

"Yes."

"Where's Frank?"

"He's here." Ida stepped back to admire Lee's long smooth dress. "You look great."

"I feel great. I love parties, sometimes too much. Is that bad?"

Ida's smile was warm. "I wouldn't think so."

"I won't flirt with Frank. Promise."

"It's all right. You can."

"That's because you know he won't flirt back."

Ida smiled again. Then she edged sideways to the table and picked up a glass of white wine. Holding it high, she inched deeper into the room. Under a hanging coleus, she chatted with an economist from some state agency, who stood as if practicing posture. Then she realized it was his way of looking at her cleavage, which gradually got on her nerves.

"Excuse me," she said.

In the kitchen she helped Karl Gunderman reload a couple of ice buckets and slice lemons. Gunderman looked at her out of the corner of his eye and said, "Is Frank circulating?"

"I'm sure he is."

"Good. I want people to meet him. That way they'll know he's not a bad guy."

"Then I should circulate too."

He stopped what he was doing and gazed at her full in the face, his eyes a little sad. "I didn't mean anything by that."

She touched his arm, more like a brush. "I know you didn't. I was just being funny."

"Frank's only got eyes for you," he said suddenly, apropos of nothing. "That's the very first thing I noticed about you two."

Ida didn't quite know what to say and said nothing. He was sweating, his shirt collar sticking to his neck. The silence grew heavy between them. Ida lowered her eyes.

"Should I cut more lemons?"

"If you don't mind," he said and handed her a sharper knife.

Frank Chase, squeezing through the throng, saw a wild curve of leg from a slit dress as a woman rose from a huge reclining chair. She reached for him as if taking it for granted that he would know her, know who she was, the banker's wife, a Faye Dunaway face. Fingernails polished to look like pearls touched his sleeve. Her other hand was jiggling. She had cocktail peanuts in it, as if she might feed him one. Instead she fed herself and mumbled, "You're the Chase fellow."

"Yes," he said after a pause, scenting an enemy. She was chewing and smiling, looking at him closely, watching him breathe, as if he were some odd sort of creature, like a boxer. She wore a choker of pearls that matched her nails.

"You don't have a drink."

"No," he said, as if he were in training.

"You're in real estate?"

"Yes."

"My husband says you have an interesting background."

"Not really."

She licked salt from her lips, deliberately. He knew exactly what she was doing, which in no way flattered him.

"Can you talk about the murder?"

"I don't know that much about it."

"Come now. That's for the newspapers." She reached behind her for her drink, which looked like a screwdriver. "I'm dying to know the details. Was it your wife who found the body?"

"She saw it."

"Head blown off, something like that?"

"Something like that."

"You're being very mysterious," she said with a bare hint of impatience.

"I don't mean to be."

She sipped her drink. "You must come to our house for

dinner. You may bring your wife."

Chase simply stared at her, so strangely that she laughed. "We won't bite you."

"What guarantees do I have?"

"My husband bites only those who cross him."

"And you?"

"You mean, do I bite? I leave that to him."

Chase glanced away. "My wife and I are the stay-at-home types."

"You're not very clever, Mr. Chase."

"I'm aware of that."

"A shame."

"You'll excuse me?"

"I already have."

Picking his way through the crowd, one room and then another, he caught sight of Lee Gunderman and avoided her. He avoided others too. He loosened his tie because the noise and smoke was getting to him. The smoke seemed to hang in threads.

Rubbing an eye, he stepped into the kitchen and saw Ida. He saw the shape of her more than anything else, and he saw a man putting a knife to her throat. Or at least it looked that way. He reacted fast.

"Frank, it's all right!"

He was gripping the man's wrist, squeezing as if to break it. The knife fell to floor, and Gunderman's face seemed to expand, the eyes wide with pain and astonishment.

"I'm sorry," Chase said, letting go. "I'm really sorry."

A window was raised, and Rupert Goetz listened to light traffic from Storrow Drive, the sounds as soothing as those of the sea, the random screech of a horn reminding him of a gull, except the sounds did not lull him to sleep. After a while they got on his nerves. He moved a sudden and almost hostile hand over Sherry, hard, as if to reshape her and more than enough to wake. She was on her stomach, and she rolled over with a

bit of alarm. He said, "That crap about you coming from Chillicothe—you come from New Hampshire where the cows are."

"You woke me for that?" She blinked at him, almost making
out his face in the dark. She stretched, starting at the small of
her back and raising her elbows. "I'm a long way from the cows
now, luv."

"Your father works in a fertilizer factory."

"I'm a long way from that too." Her voice was starchy, not
fully awake. She yawned. "It's not really a fertilizer factory, if
that's what you're worried about. It's a chemical plant."

"I know exactly what it is. I knew before we were married.
I even talked to your father, made a trip up there once. Didn't
know that, did you?"

More awake now, she ran a hand through her hair and
rubbed a side of her mouth. Then yawned again, while shaking
a leg free and raising the knee.

"Your name's not Sherry. It's Shirley."

"Don't you like Sherry better? I do."

"That's not the fucking point."

"You married me knowing this. What is the point, luv?"

He said nothing, his face burning softly. She could see it
better now. She tried smiling at it, which made it burn more.

"What did you tell my father?"

"That worry you?"

"Not in the least."

"I didn't tell him anything. Figured you were ashamed of
him."

"Not so, luv. I simply cut my ties up there a long time ago."

"You cut them pretty easy, don't you? That kid, Billy. That
didn't seem to bother you either."

She drew up against him, the knee falling over him. He was
indifferent, as if much in him were frozen. "What's wrong, luv?
Tell me."

His voice was deliberate. "I just want to know if I can trust
you."

Her voice was playful. "What makes you think you can't."

"Don't do that! Don't answer me with a question. How many times I got to tell you this isn't a game? A man was snuffed because of us."

"Oh, Rupert." Her head jerked. "Don't lay that on me. You said yourself he was a loser."

"But I don't want to be one, you understand?"

"You're big leagues, luv."

Quite gently, he began stroking her hair.

24.

SURPRISES

Rupert Goetz spent twenty minutes talking on the phone to Frank Chase, first about his son and then about other things. Lowering his voice, he said, "What have you done on Dancewicz? Nothing, I hope."

"I visited his place. He wasn't home. I think he left by a window."

"That doesn't sound like him. He'd fight first. He's a crazy fucking bohunk, in case you don't know."

"I know."

"The guy isn't tilted right between the ears."

"You already said that."

"I'm trying to pound the point home. I don't want my wife a widow."

"Whose wife?" Chase's voice was dry as a bone.

"I got that mixed up. I meant Ida. Your wife."

"Is that what you meant?"

"Come on, Frank. It was a slip of the tongue or whatever you call it."

"I don't know what you call it."

"Let's get back to Dancewicz."

"I have something of his might interest you. Keys. The ones you told me about. They look like they're out of another century. Do you want them?"

For a while Goetz did not speak. Then he said, "So what do

you want me to do, bust him? Then watch him get a good
lawyer and walk while you go down the tubes? Use your head,
Frank."

"I didn't have that in mind."

"What the hell have you got in mind? You going to sprinkle
those keys in his face? If you try that you'd better make sure
both his hands are tied, his feet too. He's the type of guy, if you
miss, he'll come after you. He doesn't need those keys. He'll get
a gun."

"Let me worry about it."

"You're not doing Ida and the kid any favors by messing
with him."

"I'm thinking more of Johnny Kale."

"You didn't know him that well."

"Well enough."

"Maybe we better talk about this later, not on the phone. I've
got a lot on my mind, Frank, and you're not helping. Let me
talk to the kid."

Chase called David, who took the phone shyly, gripping it in
both hands and clearing his throat before speaking. Chase made
his way to the sun porch, where the shades emitted only a few
hot slivers of light, enough to read by. He picked up the *Globe*
and scanned headlines. David appeared presently with a small
pleased smile.

"He wants to watch me play. Tonight's game."

"He's coming tonight?"

"That's what he said."

Chase put the newspaper aside. "That's great, David."

"I told him where. I gave him directions."

"I'm sure he'll find it."

A look of uncertainty passed over the boy's face. "You don't
mind, do you?"

"He's your father, David. I never in the world would mind."

The boy brightened. "I just wanted to make sure."

They shared a wink.

"You surprise me," Dance said, handling the hardware. Didn't think you were so fast."

"A job fell through, so I did yours," said the man with the moustache. "Go ahead, put them together. They were made for each other."

Dance turned the two parts into one, and the weapon looked like a blowtorch. Dance raised it, aiming it at a multicolored cat sleeping atop a box on the tool bench.

"How's it feel?"

"Like a fishing pole with something big on the line."

"You'll get used to it."

"How much?"

"What we said."

"What'd we say?"

The man's expression didn't change, though some tiny light in his eyes did. He said, "You going to make me argue over something we already agreed on?"

Dance paid him from a roll of fifties, peeling slowly with a wet thumb.

The man counted with a dry one. "Like I explained. Inflation."

"That's why I asked again about the price. I read how the government's got guidelines. I didn't want for you to get in trouble."

The man smiled.

Dance disassembled the weapon. He put the two pieces into a paper bag advertising "True Value," and the man stuck in a free box of bullets, a customary courtesy. The two of them moved to the front of the store, the owner taking his place behind the counter and Dance stepping toward the door with the bag firmly under his arm.

"I see you're still limping."

"A couple of days I'll be fit. I'm in no rush."

"That's wise. It's never good to play hurt. Only bushers do that."

"I'm no busher," said Dance.

"If I thought you were," said the man, "you'd never walk out of here with that."

Frank Chase sneaked a glance at David while taking a sharp turn onto the private road between Doherty School and East Junior High. He drove slowly past parked cars to the chain-link fence bordering the front of the ball field. David sat silently with his glove in his lap, his Red Sox uniform freshly laundered, his cap clamped squarely on his head. Chase gave him another look.

"What's the matter?"

"He's going to know I don't play all that good. He'll see."

"You do all right."

"No, I don't."

"Your father's coming to see you. How you play doesn't make any difference."

The boy lowered his eyes and slipped on the glove, pounding a fist into it. "I hope I don't strike out all the time."

"Take each pitch as it comes. Forget the misses."

"The coach says I can't hit anything unless it's lobbed."

"Surprise him."

"The coach is mad because Brian Gunderman can't pitch. His mother won't let him."

"Why not?"

"He doesn't know."

The motor was idling. Chase readjusted the boy's cap, though it needed no readjustment. "Don't be nervous. Have you got your chewing gum?"

"Four sticks. You going to drive me home?"

"Your father will want to do that. He'll probably even want to take you somewhere first. Tell him about Friendly's."

Reluctantly the boy climbed out of the car and made his way past the fence, moving as if to an ominous drumbeat. Chase backed the station wagon down the road and parked in a space where he could watch for Goetz. Sucking a Lifesaver instead of smoking a cigarette, he watched assortments of parents and grandparents straggle by. None glanced his way except a woman with white hair that looked like cake frosting. Her eyes filled with suspicion: a lone man in a parked car.

Then Goetz arrived.

Chase saw two shapes in the long dark car as it drifted by in search of a space, and he waited until it angled into one before climbing out of the wagon. Sherry emerged first, looking even younger than he remembered, the hair more luxuriant, the legs longer. She was in white walking shorts, thong sandals, and she immediately drew the eyes of a passing man. Then Goetz appeared, his face somewhat drawn, his hair more gray than blond, and he seemed out of character, no three-piece suit. He had on a yellow jersey and loose chino pants. He saw Chase first, but it was Sherry who greeted him.

"Great," she said.

She pressed close, as if Chase were a blood cousin or even a brother who had been separated from her by events. She smiled, with her teeth pointing at him, almost as if she expected a kiss. Goetz was less exuberant. He nodded. The three of them stood close together, like a family.

"You do look great," Sherry said. "Is it the air here?"

"It must be," said Chase.

"I think Frank wants to talk with me," Goetz said curtly.

She shrugged off the words and continued to smile at Chase, her eyelids painted to look bruised. Suddenly a cigarette was in her hand, a Tareyton Light. "Will you light it for me, please?" Chase did, unsure how much of her manner was mockery. He watched the end of the cigarette flicker into an ash. She said, "If you were a little darker, you'd remind me of Peter Gunn. Remember him?"

"I'm surprised you do."

"Reruns. Rupert and I watch them sometimes."

Goetz said, "You going to let us talk, Sherry?"

"Surely." She kind of peeled away from Chase and glanced toward the field. "The game hasn't started, has it?"

"It will be," said Goetz. "Find a place for us in the stands."

Chase smiled a goodbye and watched her walk away, the bare-legged stride as free as she could make it. Goetz also watched her.

"She was flirting with you, Frank. She does that to get my ass."

"That's your problem, Rupert."

"It's no problem. I was just telling you. Sometimes she can be a little bitch. It's what makes her interesting." Goetz's smile was for one second superior. "You wouldn't know about that, Frank."

Chase ignored the comment. He said, "David's really excited, your being here."

Goetz nodded, pleased. "He likes that glove I got him, huh?"

"It's a little big for his hand, but he does OK with it. I mean, no worse than anybody else."

"What are you saying, he's not a good ballplayer?"

"I'm saying he'll be trying awfully hard to impress you, maybe too hard."

"So?"

"So just be gentle."

"One thing, Frank. Don't ever tell me how to handle my kid. OK?"

Chase glanced away. "OK, Rupert, let's talk."

They moved from the fence and began walking along the road, past Goetz's car, toward Chase's ranch wagon. Small boys at play cut abruptly in front of them and raced out of the way. Goetz said, "Are you going to be smart about Dancewicz?"

"Forget about Dancewicz. It's my worry. What I want to know is whether you're making restitution to the lawyer."

Goetz sighed. They were standing now behind the wagon, out of sight, East Junior High behind them. Goetz accepted a

Lifesaver and sucked on it. He said, "I'm getting it together."

"What about Johnny Kale's share."

"The way I figure, the lawyer already got that back, what was left of it."

"Then there's my share, Rupert."

"You forget that. I'll handle it."

"How will you handle it?"

"I'll find a way. I always do."

Chase shook his head. "It's not that easy. You know better than I do you can't play games with the lawyer." He opened the rear of the wagon, lifted the storage lid, and removed a green shoe box from the sunken storage compartment. "Two-fifths of it is gone, Rupert. We used it for a down-payment on the house, but I'll make it up as soon as I can. I'll sell the house if I have to."

"No, you won't." Goetz would not accept the box or even look at it. "That money's yours and Ida's. Call it a wedding gift if you want."

"Ida doesn't want it. And it's no wedding gift. Take it."

"No. Do something with it for David. Put it in a trust or something."

"Take it and give it to the lawyer. I'm making my own decisions now, Rupert."

Goetz stepped back. "Shove it up your ass, Frank."

Chase watched him go in the direction of a few fierce cheers, a team taking the field. Then Chase returned the box to its hiding place. He drove away from the school, but he did not drive home.

"Are you all right?" Sherry asked.

"Of course I am." He sat with a hand covering one side of his face, the victim of a sudden nervous tic. They were sitting in the second row of the stands, near the smell of grass, clean sweat, food from a vendor, with a good view of home plate, where David took a final swing, more of a brutal chop, and threw his bat away in disgust.

"He's not doing so well."

"He's doing great."

"Rupert, that's the third time he's struck out. He's a little pudgy. Maybe that's his problem."

Goetz shot to his feet, making a megaphone out of his hands. "Next time, kid! Out of the park!" The voice was a boom. "Hey, you hear?"

David hurried to the bench.

Sherry tugged at Goetz and drew him back down to his seat. "You're embarrassing him."

"What d'you mean?"

"For one thing, no more next time. The game's almost over."

The paunchy man in front of them, licking the drip of a raspberry ice-cream, slowly turned around.

Goetz said, "What the fuck are you looking at?"

Sherry nudged him, not hard, nearly a tickle, the sort she gave him in bed. "Shhhh. You'll get us kicked out."

"In a pig's ass."

"Calm down."

Goetz went into a hostile silence, a bit of brooding in it. David shifted from one part of the bench to another as if to escape the eyes of his father and the coach. The coach's face was concealed by the bill of his cap. So was David's. Goetz moved his feet.

"It's not the kid's fault."

Sherry looked at him with amusement. "Whose fault, then?"

"Frank's. Frank doesn't know how to teach him anything."

Sherry was no longer amused. But she smiled.

Dance, who owned one necktie, wore it and dined with a high-priced hooker who ate like a horse. So did he. Anthony's Pier 4. She drank wine, and he had beer, then a shot. She had the biggest lobster in the house, cracking it to pieces and ferreting and sucking out every morsel of flesh. He had a cut of sirloin

big enough for two men, maybe more, plus a platter of French
fries. Extra bread. He chewed hard. She said, "You sure you
can afford this?"

"I look like I can't?"

She grinned. "You look like you got the world by the balls."

"I do all right."

"What did you say your name was?"

"You call me anything you want."

She went light on dessert, a small fruit dish. He had shortcake, the fat strawberries bleeding into the cream. He liked it
so well he had another. She said, "You celebrating or something?"

"No. This is the way I live."

"A big shot."

"Big enough." He wiped his mouth, using the napkin as if it
were a towel. "Actually this is the way I prime myself for
something I gotta do."

"What's that?"

He gave her a mysterious shrug and scraped his second dessert plate clean. "You're not going to believe this."

"I'll believe anything you tell me. I'm that way."

"I'm going to have another one of these things."

"You're right. I don't believe you."

The third shortcake came, and she took a bite from it, then
watched him eat the rest. She had Irish coffee. He said, "You
Irish?"

"No, I just like the stuff. You like Jap food?"

"I eat anything," he said, giving the words double meaning,
which she ignored.

She said, "We could go to Benihana sometime. Stuart Street.
Been there?"

"Naw. C'mere."

"What?"

"I said c'mere." She leaned toward him, and he whispered
into her hair, which was several tones of red, all natural. "I hear

you go right out of your tree for wise guys."

"Who?"

"You know."

"No, I honest to God don't."

"Italians who're connected."

She understood. Then she dropped back with a mocking smile. "You trying to tell me you're a wise guy?"

"Could be."

She laughed, which he didn't like. She said, "You don't look like one."

"That's because of my coloring. Ever hear of Joey Gallo? He was from Brooklyn. They called him Joey the Blond."

She remained unconvinced but much amused, which annoyed him more.

He said, "All wops ain't black."

"All the ones I know are."

"C'mere." She bent her head toward him, her scented hair brushing his face. He said, "Ever hear of the lawyer?"

For a moment her expression turned serious. "Yes, sure. Who hasn't?"

"I'm his shooter."

"Honey," she said, touching his pants, "I think you've been shooting this too much."

Her smile, more mocking than before, froze in the flash of his hands, one gripping her hair to hold her head in place and the other cracking against her face. A brutal backhand. No one saw him do it, and he did it again, expertly, with lightning speed, the ring he wore doing damage.

"You want to say you're sorry?"

She couldn't speak. Blood leaked down her chin. She grappled for a napkin and buried her mouth in it. He rose and, casually buttoning his sports coat, bent over her as though to press a cheek to her head.

"I've got a surprise for you."

Her head stayed lowered.

"The meal's on you," he said and left.

His car, a Dodge Dart, was delivered, and he gave the attendant a dollar and sped off with an elbow out the window, a dark breeze cooling him. It was a nice evening, with a pungent smell from the harbor. He drove through South Boston into Dorchester with the radio playing, kid music. He stopped at a neighborhood package store to buy a bottle and then drove straight to the tenement. The bottle was in a bag beside him on the seat. The other bag, True Value, was wedged deep beneath the seat. He dug it out, which gave him two bags to carry.

He hummed his way up the stairs, no hurry, and juggled the bags to unlock the door. Shouldering the door open, he stepped into the dark kitchen and reached for the light switch. Somebody beat him to it.

"Surprise," said Frank Chase.

25.

MACHO

Frank Chase kicked the door shut. He held a .38-caliber revolver in one hand and a great bunch of keys in the other. The keys were rusty rods with shiny teeth at the end. The teeth were sharp, having been honed. Chase stood still, but the keys jangled. The hand holding them appeared steady, but it wasn't.

Dance said, "This is kind of funny. I won't tell you why." He moved. "You mind?" He put the bags on the table. The one with the bottle clanked against the other bag. He said, "You want a drink? Plenty here."

"Sit down."

"Sure." Dance sat down and reached toward a bag. "You want a drink or not?"

"Let it alone."

"Sure. Don't get excited." Dance relaxed in the rickety chair, one leg flung out, an arm on the table, while Chase stood a reasonable distance away. "That's a lot of gun you got there," Dance said.

"This was my off-duty piece, meaning it's untraceable."

"You ain't a cop anymore. I'm reminding you."

"That's funny. I feel like one. Feels good."

Dance drummed his fingers on the table, as though Chase needed humoring and time to settle himself. The light in the kitchen was not good, its glow weak and off-color. Dance, wiggling his foot, said, "You're over your head. I'm working for the Wops."

"I know."

"I know you know, but I figured you forgot."

There was a moment of silence. Each man seemed faceless and in a way sightless. Chase was pale, paler than Dance thought normal. Dance also paled.

He said, "Why don't you relax? I could tell you a hundred fucking sad stories going back to when I was a kid. Make you feel sorry for me."

Chase stood like sculpture. The gun in one hand and the keys in the other resembled offerings.

"My mother was cracked," Dance said with a little laugh. "She kept hens in the house, can you imagine that? Think first of the stink. She wasn't from the old country, but you'd of thought she was. Never knew my father. Did you know yours?"

Chase jangled the keys.

"Yeah, I see 'em," Dance said, dragging in his foot. "Listen, when you come right down to it, you and I got no fight. The Wops have paid me off. Understand?"

Chase jangled the keys again. "If you were going to punish somebody with these, how would you do it? Little by little?"

"What am I supposed to say? You want to fight a fucking cripple? That's what I am. You already hurt me."

Chase let the keys hang silent. "I suppose you did Johnny Kale a favor by finishing him off. He couldn't have used what you left him for a face."

"I don't know what you're talking about." Dance forced a smile. "You understand I got to say that. You're taking things too personal and acting like you're fucking pure in all this."

"You threatened my wife."

"I must've been drinking. The Wops warned me about that."

"You didn't listen."

"I should've."

There was another silence, much more intense, as if both men, all their senses concentrated on each other, were coming to decisions. Dance did not like the way Chase was gripping the revolver.

Chase said, "I've never killed a man."

"You want me to beg? Hey, I don't know how." Dance tensed himself. Then he sprang.

The gun didn't go off. The keys did. They splattered against Dance's face, brightening it, and drove him instantly to his knees, a praying position. The barrel of Chase's revolver pressed into his forehead, though he scarcely felt it.

"Don't ever bother me again."

"OK, I promise," Dance said, bubbling blood. The top of his nose was gone.

Chase left.

Dance groped for the table and clawed at the bags. He had trouble getting the right one and more trouble tearing the weapon loose. The weapon was loaded, the silencer attached. Chase had left the door partly open, and Dance banged past it, staggering, dripping, pain blinding him. He forgot about his bad ankle and went crashing down the stairs.

An old woman peered up from the ill-lit first landing and screamed.

Chase, who was born and bred in Boston and knew it better than most, took wrong turns, at times his hands shaking so much he feared the wagon would veer out of control. How in God's name he had ended up in Mattapan he would never know. He wanted a cigarette but had only Lifesavers. He sucked several at once and reversed his direction, taking it slow and staying on Blue Hill Avenue, which led him back into areas of Dorchester designated "Badlands" by the city's two dailies, stricken streets where he had no business and was fair game. At a set of signals a band of black youths hovered in the shadows waiting for him to stop. Instead he raised his window and went through a red light.

He made it to Columbia Road and then to Washington Street, lowering the window in order to breathe. The boiling blue turret light of a parked cruiser startled him in a way he would not have thought possible, and he passed it with his eyes straight ahead, while a taxi recklessly roared by him for taking too much time. As he drew closer to downtown the evening sidewalk crowd seemed to squawk at him, though in a way the noise was soothing. In the tightened remains of the Combat Zone, traffic clogged, two figures, one slender and the other ample, approached the wagon from his side and smiled in on him. They were prostitutes, still young, one white and one black, offering him a good time, two for the price of one, a mixed bag. The black one was willowy, wore her hair in a great wire ball with chunks of gold in it, and in another culture could have passed for a princess. The white one, swelling out of her unbuttoned brocaded shirt and showing freckles on her breasts, winked at him. Her eyes were blue and seemingly too pure for the business she was in. She reached through the window and prodded him.

"Come on, honey. We're *bi*-racial and *bi*-sexual, and *by*-gawd we're good."

He stared at them from the secrecy of his silence, and the black one stared back from the secrecy of hers. Then she said, "I think he's a cop."

The white one pulled away as if burnt. "Jesus Christ—in a station wagon!"

They hurried off, and he watched them, warmed by their words, in a way thrilled by their mistake, horns blowing behind him.

Several minutes later he crossed Longfellow Bridge to the Cambridge side of the Charles and followed the river to the same accessible area where he had once thrown a suitcase into the dark water.

This time it was a ring of keys.

Lieutenant Donovan, second in command, homicide, deposited a large Styrofoam cup of coffee on the desk, a midmorning gift to his chief, who sat hunched over a list of names, men whom he might recommend for promotion, most of them Irish. Donovan remained standing near the desk, and Goetz, finally glancing sideways at the coffee, said, "Thanks."

Donovan said, "About the Prince Street thing. I've been playing it like you said."

Goetz did not look up. "By the book?"

"Right. By the book. I heard something from a guy ninety percent reliable. He gave me a name. Spitaleri. Ring a bell?"

"No," Goetz said, checking off three names.

"The lawyer's nephew."

Goetz looked up without a readable expression.

Donovan said, "I'd like to get him."

"By the book?"

"I wasn't thinking along those lines. He's the type would go to pieces. I know him."

Goetz rubbed his eyes and left them red. "I'll think about it." His tone was a dismissal. Donovan stayed.

"Chief, there was something in the *Globe*. Mike Barnicle there, he wrote something bad."

"You were dumb enough to talk with him?"

"He cornered me. Chief, did you read what he wrote? He said we're dragging our asses. He used those exact words in print, a family newspaper."

"I read the thing. You don't have to tell me about it."

"Chief, there's worse. Jeremiah Murphy there, I understand he's coming out with a real sob story on the woman who went down. I guess he went to her funeral."

Goetz flipped his pencil to one side and creaked back in his chair, his expression readable now and quite sour. "OK. What's coming from Higgins at the Herald? Banks. Sullivan. Who else is there? Let me think."

Donovan ignored the sarcasm. "Higgins already wrote something bad a couple of days ago. I'll check on the others if you want."

"Check on the fucking *Phoenix* first. Tell them to get my

name right. Also tell them what I eat for breakfast."

Donovan showed patience, his major strength. "What about the commissioner? Did you handle him OK?"

Goetz shifted forward slowly in his chair, his eyes a brutal blue. "Get off my ass."

"I try to look out for you, Rupert."

Goetz's face softened, and he lowered his eyes. "I know you do."

"Then you also know you have to return the commissioner's calls," Donovan said and waited vainly for a response. Goetz's head was bowed. "Rupert, you can't ignore him."

When Donovan left, Goetz picked up the unopened cup of coffee and threw it into the wastebasket. When he made the call to the commissioner, he had a bottle of Dewar's on the desk, a double shot poured. The commissioner said, "The mayor wants to know if it's personal. Something about him we don't like."

Goetz said, "I'm doing my best."

"That's not enough."

Goetz's lips were pursed, as if to whistle loudly for Donovan and have him handle the call.

The commissioner said, "Is something the matter? Do you have personal problems?"

"No, sir."

"Then carry on a conversation with me, so I'll know you're there."

"The case is tough."

"That's an excuse?"

Goetz stared at his drink, wishing he had a glass of chilled water to go with it. Then he raised it to his mouth and merely wet his lips.

"A woman was killed, Rupert. She was a mother and an innocent bystander, which makes the case popular with the media, and that makes it political. That means we give it priority. But I'm not telling you anything you don't know, am I?"

"No, sir."

"You're a professional. A professional covers his ass."

Goetz downed the drink, which made his whole body shrug. Then he put the bottle away to keep himself from pouring another.

"I *am* talking to a professional, aren't I?"

Goetz put a hand to his forehead and tipped back. He needed a neck massage, the kind Ida used to give him, her fingers rearranging muscles and removing every knot, her body pampering his, making him a boy again, the biggest on the block. He said, "Yes, sir, I am a professional."

The commissioner didn't hear him. He said, "Tell me something. Haven't I been good to you?"

"Yes, sir, you have."

"I asked you before if you have problems. And don't blow smoke up my ass. I'm too old for that."

"No problems, sir. And I'll put more men on the case."

"You already should've done that. What I want to know is whether I can depend on you. Whether the mayor can."

"Yes, sir."

The commissioner rang off.

Ida Chase read her husband's face and said, "Is it time for a talk?" He nodded, and they carried their morning coffee out to the pool and sat at a miniature metal table still moist from the night. Chase was dressed for selling houses, Ida for gardening. Chase lit a cigarette and immediately gave out a small smoker's cough.

"I've been trying to quit," he said.

"I've noticed," she said.

"One of these days."

"Me, too." she said and lit up. The early sun was painting the pool and already throwing off great streaks of heat. "Maybe when things settle down."

"What things?"

"Everything." She smiled at him over the edge of her coffee cup. "Sometimes you look very young, Frank. As if you were back in Northeastern and wearing your navy shoes."

"You remember them?"

"They looked like police shoes."

"Like Rupert's."

"I guess so."

He glanced away. "I don't feel very young. I feel incompetent, impotent, and venal, all at once."

"Frank, you've never been any of those things with me." She put the cup down. "We're talking around something. Please come out with it."

He put his own cup down. "I want to know if you're happy here."

"You mean in this house? This town? Yes, but I would have been happy moving into your place on Marlborough Street. Maybe even more happy."

"There wouldn't have been room for David."

"We'd have made room. You wanted to give me too much."

Chase shook his head. "I've been trying to convince you it wasn't that grand. I went into the thing with Johnny Kale because I thought the score was small, something that would never make any noise and would give me an edge while I got used to the outside. A down payment on a house, and maybe I wanted the house more than you, and I wanted a little in reserve. Right or wrong, I saw it as severance pay."

"I'm not judging you, Frank."

"I'm judging myself. When I saw Johnny Kale lying on our lawn I almost heaved my guts out, and I wanted to go into Boston with a gun, although I didn't know who I wanted to shoot, maybe Rupert. That was when I first suspected he had dealt from the bottom and taken from the top."

"Frank," Ida said in a small voice, "I never asked, but how much did he walk away with?"

Chase made a fist. "Too much. But now everything goes back

to the lawyer. It has to. He has no choice, and I don't either."

"Frank, it's what I wanted you to do."

"I know." He lit a fresh cigarette. "We may have to sell the house."

"I can't worry about that."

"But Rupert has other ideas." Chase's voice was dry. "He thinks he's still calling the shots. He wants us to keep the money and let him make good on it. His gift to us."

Ida after a silence said, "I'm not surprised."

"You know him better than I do."

Ida shifted her feet. "Frank, he's macho. It's his image. He should've been born Italian. He thinks he's our godfather. He still thinks our marriage was all his idea."

"I'd like to set him straight."

"Is it that important to you? Maybe you're being macho."

"Maybe."

"Frank, the same way you wanted to provide me with a house, he wanted to provide me with a husband. It solved problems for him, one being guilt. We all finagle. I reached the point where I let him believe what he wanted. It made the divorce easier."

Chase pitched his cigarette away and tried to smile. "I'm not macho," he said. "What I am is scared. I'm scared that I have you only on loan, and pretty soon he'll want you back."

Her eyes grew fierce and in a way frightening. She said, "Don't you know what commitment means?"

His eyes filled without his knowing it. "Tell me."

She kissed him. "I shouldn't have to."

Chuckie Dearborn assaulted Lee Gunderman. He didn't hurt her, but he laid hands on her and pushed her against the wall and acted indecently. It happened in the garage. She had entered it from the house and saw him standing near her car, the overhead door pulled down. The bill of his cap was yanked low, and his hands dangled at his sides, the fingers curled. She stared at him with utter disbelief and then with contempt that verged on laughter. That was when he pushed her. Her shoulder struck the rough wall, though not hard enough to bruise her or make her fall.

"You're going to be in a lot of trouble," she said in a tight voice, fear spreading through her.

"This ain't a rape," he said, and now it was he conveying the contempt. "I just want you to take a look. You can decide for yourself."

She controlled her face and said, "My husband's home."

"You're a liar." He shifted his feet. "You're not looking."

She put a fist to her mouth, as if to scream.

"You got kids in the yard," he said. "You don't want them in on this."

Seconds passed. "What do you want me to say?"

"It's up to you."

She tried to keep the fear out of her voice and even brought forth a weak smile, as if they were in a locker room, she by mistake. "It's a big fellow," she said and then held her breath while hearing him take one. He was waiting for her to say more. "Interesting, but I haven't seen that many. Honest."

"Who the hell are you kidding?"

His tone was hateful, and she closed her eyes because she thought he was about to strike her. He spoke again, a single explosive word, what he thought of her, perhaps what he thought of all women, but a hum in her head prevented her from hearing it. She kept her eyes closed even when she sensed the hard upward rumble of the garage door and knew he was fleeing.

She stumbled into the house and racked her brain for a name and finally remembered it. Dix. She phoned the police station, but he was not there. The officer who answered promised Dix would call her.

Then she phoned Chase. There was no answer, but she did not hang up, not even when her two sons crowded against her and the younger one began to cry.

Rupert Goetz stepped out of a barber shop on Boylston Street and was approached by the man in the jacket, who said, "He wants to see you."

Goetz patted his flat fragrant hair and scratched the back of his naked neck, scarcely looking at the man. "Haven't got time."

"He'd like you to make time."

Now Goetz gave the man his full attention. "Do you know what burns me? Someone like you thinking he can tell me what to do."

"It's him telling you. Not me."

"That's right. You're just his lackey. That ever bother you?"

"I do what I'm told."

"That's the difference between me and you," Goetz said, rising on his toes, gathering strength. "Spitaleri," he said. "Think that name means anything to your boss?"

"I don't know," the man said impassively. "You can ask him yourself."

Goetz's right hand floated forward and for an instant seemed severed from the arm. Two fingers lightly thumped the man's chest. "No, you ask him. And tell him that favor he wants is getting bigger all the time."

The man, stuffing his hands into his pockets, watched Goetz swagger away.

26.

BARGAINS

"You want to see him, you hand it over," said the man in the jacket, his voice crusted, his tone indifferent, and reluctantly Chase surrendered his revolver. The green shoe box he kept under his arm. He entered the wharf building and climbed a single flight of stairs, the man behind him. At the top the man nimbly stepped ahead of him, rapped once on a door, and opened it. Chase stepped into a breezy office, a window wide open. The door closed behind him as he approached the desk, and a gnarled set of fingers offered him a chair.

"You'll excuse me if I don't get up."

Chase placed the shoe box on the desk and sat down, wondering how the lawyer made it up and down the stairs. He pictured him being carried. The lawyer, his head turned toward the window, ignored the box.

"Do you like the smell of that breeze?"

Chase nodded.

"Love it," said the lawyer. "Absolutely love it." Then he turned in his chair to face Chase directly. "I'm trying to place you."

"We've never met."

The lawyer smiled. "But we know of each other. And we have a mutual friend. How is Rupert?"

Chase nodded, an ocean of air washing over him. The smell was not that great.

"Strange man," said the lawyer, clasping his hands together

and laying them in his lap, out of sight. "Polite one time and arrogant the next. You don't know where you stand with a person like that."

Chase's eyes were empty.

"Actually," the lawyer said, "I do place you. I remember when you and Rupert worked Roxbury. That was a lot of years ago, and both of you, tough cops."

"I wasn't tough," Chase said. "Cautious. I stayed in one piece."

"No, you were tough, Frank, but well-liked. The way I heard it, those black fellows had respect for you. It was Rupert they wanted to cut up."

Chase made no comment. He watched the lawyer raise his hands to the edge of the desk and rest them there. The nails were manicured, but the fingers were impossibly bent, as if the damage to them had been malicious.

"I understand you're still tough," the lawyer said, his smile still quite friendly, almost jovial, as if Chase were a member of the family. "I'm referring to what happened over in Dorchester. I heard you practically peeled that fellow's nose off."

"He threatened my wife," Chase said coldly. "He didn't need to do that."

"Agreed," the lawyer said at once. "A person like that deserves what he gets."

Chase shifted forward, as if tired of the talk. "That box is for you."

"Yes, I see. How much is there, Frank?"

Chase told him, and he told him how much was missing and the time needed to make it up. The lawyer gave a sympathetic nod while not appearing pleased.

"I was expecting a much bigger box. Not from you, Frank. From Rupert."

"I can't answer for him."

The lawyer's expression of sympathy increased. "He's a problem to both of us, isn't he?"

Chase shook his head. "Not to me."

"Come now, Frank." The lawyer's tone was avuncular. "We both have our own knowledge of Rupert, and I'm aware of your special family situation. Rupert doesn't let go of things even when he seems to. Such a shadow over your shoulder, no?"

"No," Chase said and set himself to leave, though the lawyer clearly was not finished with him. The lawyer placed one twisted hand over the other and took a deep breath, almost a gulp, as if nourishing himself, a kind of private act Chase was being allowed to watch.

"I'm not well," the lawyer said. "I'm stiff in every joint. I probably need to get away for a while. What about yourself, Frank? How are you doing?"

"Fine."

"You're living out in Andover, I hear. Selling houses is it? That's a rough game, touch and go. Maybe I could find something for you."

"No need," Chase said and rose.

The lawyer realigned himself in his chair while gripping the desk, his eyes glazed, as if absorbing pain. Chase watched, waited.

"What I want to know," Chase said, "is whether things are right between me and you."

"No, Frank." The lawyer's eyes brightened and hardened, as if X-rayed into Chase. "Nothing is right until our friend makes it right. And if he doesn't I might have to depend on you."

"Is that a threat?"

"Somebody should've told you. I don't make threats. A waste of breath."

"Then what is it?"

"I guess you should know our friend isn't sensible like you. The fact is, he worries me, and maybe he should worry you too."

"I guess you don't understand why I'm here," Chase said, rising out of his chair. "I want you to leave me and my family alone."

The lawyer feigned alarm. "Nobody wants to hurt you and,

of course, not your family."

Chase stood tall. "Then I have your guarantee."

"I can't guarantee anything. You seem to think everything is in my hands. You forget our friend."

"Then I might have to come back and deal with you again."

"Deal with me?" The lawyer looked amused. "How will you deal with me, Frank?"

"With these," Chase said, showing his hands.

Goetz phoned home from a Boylston Street bar, and the voice of a young man came through. Goetz said, "What the hell! I must have the wrong number."

Then suddenly Sherry was on the line. "Hi."

"Who the hell was that?"

"Billy. You know Billy."

Goetz tightened his grip on the receiver, and his voice became guttural. "What's he doing there?"

Sherry laughed. "At the moment he's shivering. You scared him."

Goetz's free hand became a fist, and he delivered soft little hits to a glass panel, as if measuring its resistence. He said, "I asked you a question."

"Rupert, relax."

"Tell me what he's doing there."

"Grass. You told me not to buy on the street, so this is the safest way."

"Damn you," he whispered.

"What?"

"Get him out of there."

"Rupert, he's already gone. I was getting his money, that's why he answered the phone. Maybe I should have let it ring."

He was silent.

She said, "I hear music. Where are you?"

He didn't answer. His fist was still tapping the glass but only intermittently. His head turned as a waitress walked by, her step heavy and tired, subdued, a manifestation of his own mood.

Sherry said, "Tell me where you are. I'll join you."

"I'm nowhere," he said.

"What's that supposed to mean?"

"You don't know, do you?" His voice flattened out. With a dull kind of amusement, he said, "You've got a power over me."

"Is that bad?"

"You're the only woman in the world that can hurt me. Not even Ida had that power, or rather she did, but I knew she'd never use it."

"Luv, you don't know women."

"Maybe you don't either."

"If we compare notes, luv, I'll come out on top."

"You think so."

"Rupert, we're arguing about nothing."

"We're arguing about my life," he said and was suddenly gripping the phone harder than ever.

"That's a selfish statement," she said. "I'm standing here too. Now I have a question for you. What have you done about the money?"

Goetz laughed, to himself. "That's what it's coming down to," he said, also to himself.

She said, "I have a right to know. Have you given it back yet?"

"Sure."

"I don't believe you."

"All right. I still have it."

"Stop play-acting. Do you or don't you?"

Goetz gazed toward the bar. A young couple was sitting at the end. The man was biting the woman's ear, and she was laughing, her mouth wide open, brilliant teeth, her eyes dark and handsome.

"I'm coming home," he said.

Minutes after Frank Chase swerved off Route 93 to the road into Andover, he noticed a car behind him and knew that the shape behind the wheel was Lionel Dearborn. Dearborn flashed headlights, and Chase guided the wagon onto the soft bumpy shoulder of the road, stirring a small mustard cloud of dust. Dearborn pulled up behind him, each opening his door at the same time. They moved toward each other slowly, almost like old men. Chase studied the strain in Dearborn's pitted face. Dearborn said, "Let's talk."

They drifted away from the cars and stood at the damp start of a field flooded with purpling weeds. Dearborn said, "When I was a kid I shot rabbits here. Did it early in the morning, four, five o'clock. My brother and me. We got ourselves a family of pheasants that way. It was against the law."

"A lot of things are against the law," Chase murmured.

"That's why a guy should keep an open mind," Dearborn said, gazing absently at Japanese beetles glittering off the weeds. "Everything has to be in context. A kid shooting pheasants is different from a grown man doing it."

Chase, unsure what Dearborn was leading up to, said nothing.

"Then again, you've got grown men that mentally might still be kids, no fault of their own. I don't mean they're simple or slow. They're just not mature like you and me."

Chase said, "Are we talking about anybody in particular?"

"Don't rush me. OK? I've got this rehearsed."

Chase smiled. So did Dearborn.

Dearborn said, "You see I've a feeling I can talk to you. In ways, you know, I envy your background. Big-city cop. I don't mean I would've wanted to change places with you, but I wouldn't have minded the experience."

A breeze lifted Chase's hair. He patted it down.

"I guess I better get to the point," Dearborn said.

"Sounds serious," Chase said, smiling again.

"I need your help." Dearborn's voice was low. The two men gazed at each other, embarrassed.

"And I need yours," Chase said.

Chase left his car where it was and climbed into Dearborn's. Dearborn drove to Route 93 North and stayed in the inside lane at a leisurely speed, letting traffic swoosh by. Chase lit a cigarette. Dearborn said, "A buddy of mine, Dix, took a complaint from one of your neighbors. Lee Gunderman. She's a friend of yours, right?"

"I work for her husband."

"The complaint's against my brother," Dearborn said, driving with his hands at the bottom of the wheel, his fingers barely brushing it. "You know him. At least you know of him. Little League."

Chase gave a slow nod.

"You have to understand him," Dearborn said with effort. "He's the older brother but has always been regarded as the younger. Like I was explaining, he's not dumb, just different."

"You mentioned immature."

"I try to look after him."

"Is Lee all right?"

"She's OK. You know her better than I do, but I think she brought it on herself. Shoots her ass around at Little League. That's what my brother says."

"What happened?"

Dearborn spoke softly. "Indecent exposure, and he might've pushed her, not hard. All he really did was scare her and call her a name. Cocktease. He says that's what she is."

Construction was taking place up ahead. Barrels painted orange split the highway and narrowed traffic to two lanes. Maintaining the same light touch on the wheel, Dearborn eased the car to the left. The barrels seemed to go on forever. Dearborn drove near them, almost skinning them, absently playing a game. Chase looked at him.

"Witnesses?"

"Chuckie says no. Her kids were around, but they didn't see him. And I don't know this for a fact, but I don't think she's told her husband."

"What do you want me to do?"

"Talk to her."

"Tell her to forget it?"

Dearborn continued to skin barrels, increasing his speed, his eyes straight ahead. "Tell her it won't happen again. I give my word."

Chase snapped his cigarette out the window. Dearborn took the next exit, and moments later they were on the other side of 93, cruising south, free of barrels. The early evening sun remained hard and bright. Chase said, "I can't promise results, but I'll talk to her."

"That's all I'm asking."

Chase smiled at him. "Some people might think you're asking a hell of a lot."

Dearborn returned the smile. "That could depend on what you want from me."

Both men stayed silent until Dearborn pulled up behind Chase's ranch wagon. Dearborn killed the motor, and they listened to a chorus of birds emanating from the field. Chase said, "Did you eat those rabbits you and brother shot?"

"No."

"What about the pheasants?"

"I'm sorry we did it. Beautiful creatures."

Chase rested an elbow out the window and gazed at a hawk sailing high to the west, into the sun. "Someone might try to make a move on me."

"Ah," said Dearborn. "Same guy who laid something on your lawn?"

"That's the one."

"You want to tell me more?"

"I've already told you too much. I'd rather just be able to call you if I need you."

Dearborn didn't press the point. He said, "If he comes, it'll probably be at night."

"I wouldn't be surprised."

Dearborn pulled out a pocket notebook, jotted something in it with a gold pen he seemed proud of, and tore out the page.

He passed it casually to Chase. "Home phone," he said. "Unlisted number."

Chase left the car, watching the songbirds fly up. Dearborn backed up, swung swiftly onto the road, and was gone before Chase reached the wagon. When Chase arrived home, Ida was waiting for him at the door.

"Something's the matter with Lee Gunderman," she said. He kissed her. "I know."

The room was in shadows, and Sherry lay in a twisted sheet with sulky eyes and sullen face. She dropped a hand near Goetz and said, "You still haven't told me a damn thing."

"That's right," he mumbled from his far side of the bed, lying flat on his stomach, his head turned away from her.

"I can't hear you."

He was naked, no covers, one leg stretched straight and the other bent, as if he were fixed forever. "I didn't say anything."

"Yes, you did."

His head moved wearily. "Maybe I want to keep you guessing."

"What's that supposed to accomplish?"

He gave no answer, perhaps because he had none. When the phone rang neither made a move to answer it. It was on his side, and he acted as though he didn't hear it. The ringing became shrill. She reached past him and grabbed the phone, slicing the cord across his shoulders.

"Hello. What? Yes, of course." She smothered the mouthpiece. "It's Frank Chase."

"Tell him I'm out."

"He knows you're not."

"Tell him I'm asleep."

"You tell him."

Goetz snatched the phone from her and bashed it down.

27.

SICKNESSES

The lawyer shuffled stiffly out of his office and began descending the stairs with slow sclerotic steps, a tedious journey with his hand squeezing the rail as if for blood and with the man in the jacket ready to catch him at each step of the way. The day was brilliant, the sun a white flash. The lawyer donned dark glasses. His posture gradually straightened, and he became unnaturally erect, his face lifting to a salty breeze. Tourists crowded the wharf.

"I don't know why they come down here," the man in the jacket said. "They belong up at the Aquarium, that area."

The lawyer began moving forward in his unbending way. "They come to look at us," he said. "And they come to smell real fish."

The smell was from dead fish, actually just the heads, peering from a barrel: garbage. The lawyer scowled at litter underfoot: squashed cigarette packs, flattened Coca-Cola cans, scraps of newspaper. The man in the jacket adjusted his step to the lawyer's while keeping an alert eye on the crowd, which held a number of attractive women.

"How's your wife?" the lawyer asked pointedly.

The man nodded. "Good."

"She losing any weight?"

"She doesn't have will power. Nothing I can do."

"Tell her it's not good to be fat. This isn't the old country."

"She wasn't born in the old country."

"That's what I mean," said the lawyer.

"Maybe," the man said, "you could talk to her."

"You should be able to handle that yourself."

The crowd thinned. The man unlocked a gate to a chain-link fence protecting a secluded part of the wharf, private property, the lawyer's. The lawyer walked on through, head tilted back, and made his way to a rough wooden bench at the edge of the wharf as the man secured the gate. The lawyer studied the sun prickling off the water.

"Nice," he said as the man approached. Then, with the man's help, he removed his suitcoat, shirt and tie and sat naked to the waist, a collection of veins and knots, although something about him was steely, as if rods held him together. Gulls gathered. "Feed them," he said.

The man pulled a plastic bag of torn bread from his jacket pocket. He threw a crust into the water, and the gulls attacked it. The lawyer sat with his back arched, letting the sun's fire boil him.

"You keeping in touch with my nephew?" he asked, and the man nodded, pitching more bread into the water. The lawyer scratched an elbow. "No problems?"

"No."

"So the only problem is with Rupert, a man nobody can trust. He's not even true to his friends."

"You ask me, he's soft in the head." The man hurled the rest of the bread to the gulls and tucked the bag back into his pocket. Unthinkingly he reached inside his jacket for a cigarette and then suddenly dropped his hand. The lawyer did not smoke, and the man did not smoke in his presence. The man said, "I don't think he means to do right."

The lawyer took a deep breath, injecting his lungs with sea air as the hot sunlight baked his face. He fingered his naked chest and in ways looked like an undertaker attending himself. "Rupert doesn't do right," he pronounced drily, "he doesn't deserve to live."

The gulls shrieked, wanting more.

"You're starting to burn," the man said abruptly and immediately began helping the lawyer on with his shirt, which was silk, white on white, his three initials emblazoned on the breast pocket. The lawyer left the shirt unbuttoned and loose, and a bright breeze inflated the back of it. The man said, "What about the other guy?"

"Chase?"

"Chase."

The lawyer gave that some thought. "I respect the way he cares about his family."

"A second-hand family."

"Makes no difference. They live under his roof, they're family."

The man showed a poker face. "Dancewicz wants him. It's personal now."

The lawyer stared fiercely at a plastic Clorox bottle bobbing in the water. "Chase can take care of himself. He has good hands."

The gulls were squawking, nasty-eyed, flocking close, the bravest coming almost near enough to touch.

"You should've brought more bread," the lawyer said.

The telephone rang, and Ida Chase picked it up. The caller was Rupert Goetz, his voice strained, hollow. "I just want to know how you're doing," he said.

"All right," she said, keeping her voice polite.

"Are you alone?"

"Yes," she said. "I'll have Frank call you when he gets back." She heard him take a slow breath.

"Ida, are you happy?"

She did not want to get into that sort of conversation; yet she did not want to hang up on him. She said nothing.

"Ida . . . I think about you."

"We don't need this kind of discussion, Rupert."

"You sound bitter."

"Impatient, Rupert. I don't find this pleasant."

"I made mistakes," he said, ignoring the distancing effect produced more by her tone than her words. "I wanted to do what was best for us all, but it didn't work out that way. Everything went wrong."

"Frank trusted you."

"I'm not thinking about Frank now. I'm thinking about you and me. I never should have given you up, Ida."

"There's nothing to think about. You wanted something young, and you got it. You asked me if I'm happy. I'm happy with Frank, very much so. Which makes this whole conversation unnecessary."

"Ida." His voice almost didn't carry. "You're hitting me when I'm down. You never did that."

"What am I to say? I'm sorry? It doesn't work that way, Rupert."

A bit of strength entered his voice. "What are we now? Enemies?"

"You should try to understand something, Rupert. We're not anything."

He surprised her. He hung up on her.

Lee Gunderman sat with her forearms flat on the kitchen table, her hands together, her slim legs crossed under the table. "Nice of you to come over," she said. She had said that before, only minutes ago. She was up and down, airy and elusive one moment and hard-eyed and cold the next. Only her smile, wry and self-deprecating, was constant. "But then, I've always considered you my friend. You are, aren't you?"

Frank Chase said, "I hope so."

"Then why are you taking their part?"

"I'm not," Chase said quietly, sitting in a slight slouch. "I merely told his brother I'd talk with you, relay his promise."

"That grand policeman. I've met him, you know. The ugly business on your lawn." She lit a cigarette, one of Chase's. The pack lay between them. "I got the impression he didn't think much of me. I realize I come on strong, but that's my nature."

"I wouldn't worry about it."

She threw him a hard look. "What are you, Frank? Still a cop?" She took a quick puff. "And what am I in all this? A piece of shit?"

"Lee, you're free to do what you want."

"But you're ganging up on me—you, him, and that creep. Admit it."

Chase studied her. Her expression remained hard, but her eyes were moist, fragile. "I suppose it seems that way," he said.

Her voice turned crisp. "You're very likable, Frank. You have that quality. Women, I'm sure, trust you instantly. I know I did. And of course I flirted with you, to be naughty. But you didn't take the bait, a little insulting but entirely proper. For it was all in fun."

"I know that."

"You're so bloody gallant, Frank. No wonder Ida loves you."

Chase did not bat an eye. He toyed with the cigarette pack. Lee sighed as if from a deep tension that was starting to subside. She ran a hand over her hair.

"I'm sorry," she said. "I really didn't mean that the way it sounded."

"I took it as a compliment."

"You did right."

She walked him to the front door, opening it for him and then standing with her hands stuffed into the back pockets of her jeans, the sun shining in on her. She tilted her head.

"Karl says you sold a house on High Plain Road."

"Looks that way. First one in a while."

"Congratulations."

"Thank you." He stepped past the door.

"Frank." She followed him out, and they stood together on the wide front step next to flower pots full of dry earth, nothing

growing in them. "You didn't need to come here," she said. "I'd
already made up my mind not to go ahead with the complaint."

"Any particular reason?"

"Sure. I don't want to enhance my reputation as a whore. I'm
not one, you know."

He touched her. "I had figured that out for myself."

"You can kiss me if you want."

He kissed her cheek.

"I'd rather have a real one."

He kissed her on the mouth.

"Not bad," she said and accompanied him to the end of the
walk. The sun hot on their faces, they stood near an ornate
metal post bearing a mailbox and plastic tube for the Boston
Globe. "One other thing, Frank. Karl doesn't know anything
about what happened. I'd like to keep it that way."

Chase nodded, conscious of a passing car, a neighbor's. Lee's
stance was lazy, boyish. Sticking her hands back into her rear
pockets, she gave him a choice smile.

"Just so you don't get a big head. You kiss OK, Frank, but
nothing special."

They grinned at each other.

Chuckie Dearborn's wife, on her feet all day at Finn's, took
aspirin when she got home and went into the bedroom, where
she lowered the shades, kicked off her flat shoes, loosened her
uniform, and shed her pantyhose, which had runs in both legs.
She stretched out on the bed, on top of the spread, and drifted
in and out of sleep. One of her younger children opened the
door to peer in on her but otherwise did not disturb her, and
soon she heard them all fetching for themselves, letting her be,
which surprised her, though moments later, lightly dreaming,
there she was fixing supper for them all, handing out food the
older ones didn't like, which included Chuckie.

Something was bad with her husband, who bore bruises from
his brother over something he had done. She had seen the
bruises yesterday, along with the benumbed glint in his eye, as

though two-thirds of him were frozen. His silence had been suffocating, subduing even the children. Now, through her flimsy sleep, she heard the dull rumble of his voice and then his rough movements through the house, the thuds growing louder and nearer. He snapped open the door.

"You sick?"

She had one eye open. He was not a husband, merely a shadow, faceless because the bill of his baseball cap was yanked down to hide the bruises. She closed the eye and feigned sleep.

He slammed the door.

She slept as before, in drifts, and had difficulty distinguishing reality from dream when she heard another man's voice, one of her husband's few buddies, though she could not remember whether he was a fellow fireman or a laborer in Public Works —not that it mattered. She pulled a pillow over her head.

She did not hear him enter the room. Something else woke her, some inner warning, and she felt his presence well before she pushed aside the pillow and saw moonlight powdering the bottom half of her. He had raised the shade. He stood near the bed, the moonlight brightening the buttons on his denim shirt. He was not tall, and he stood awkwardly, his voice scarcely audible:

"Chuckie said it was all right."

She felt her face dissolve into a small groan that he probably didn't hear. He shifted his weight, embarrassed, his face wax-colored, and she tightened her shoulders, as if sealing herself inside her skin.

"This wasn't my idea."

He spoke hoarsely, his eyes flickering over her, and she said nothing. His appearance was nebulous. She was not certain he was there until he took a tentative step closer. She drew in her elbows and rearranged her bare legs, as if she were capable of crawling down into herself and staying there. He cleared his throat.

"I don't want to force you."

She tried to guess the hour to determine which of her children were in bed and which were possibly out of the house, but her mind mixed them up. The older ones became young again.

"I'll leave if you want," he said.

"That's what you better do," she said in a brittle tone colored by no emotion.

He hesitated. He clearly did not want to leave.

"Go," she said, as if speaking to a dog, and watched him back off.

She heard a car speed away.

She was off the bed, on her feet, searching for her shoes, when the pounding began. Great smashes, as if the house were falling apart.

Frank Chase, who had seen Lionel Dearborn earlier in the evening, saw him again, unexpectedly. It was nearly midnight, the front doorbell ringing. Chase opened the door and saw Dearborn on the step, his pitted face strained. Dearborn spoke rapidly and loud enough only for Chase to hear. Chase turned to Ida and murmured, "It's all right."

"You're sure?"

"Yes. I won't be long."

Dearborn drove swiftly through the deserted streets, his jaw set. He was holding himself tightly under control. He said, "I don't want him hurt, and I want it done quiet, so nobody knows. This is one cop to another."

"I'm not a cop," Chase said.

"You know what I mean."

Chase's smile was grim.

Dearborn said, "It's not that bad. All he's doing is busting up the place with a baseball bat." Dearborn passed a quick hand across his forehead. "Usually I can take care of him myself, but not when he's like this.

Chase said, "I'm not armed."

Dearborn gave him a hard look. "We take him with our hands. No weapons. He's my brother."

28.

THE KNIFE

Chuckie Dearborn lived in the town's Ballardvale section in a house set away from others and half hidden by scrub pine that was pale in the moonlight. An older boy stood like a sentry outside the front door, shivering as if it were the gut of winter and not the soggy middle of a summer night. The boy had telephoned his uncle, and now his uncle was approaching somebody he didn't know. His chin shot up, as if strangers were not allowed, but too much was beating up inside him for him to speak. He stared anxiously at his uncle.

"Sounds quiet," Lionel Dearborn said with a false casualness. "I guess he's quit busting things."

"He's got Mom," the boy said in a whisper, as if he did not want Frank Chase to hear.

"What d'you mean, *got her?*"

"He's holding her."

Lionel Dearborn strode past the boy into the house, Chase with him, and their gazes fell on furniture that was broken, splintered, strewn about. Chase's foot went down on a piece of glass, crunching it. Another boy stood near a door, a bit younger than the one outside. He said, "Who's he?"

"Just shut up," Lionel Dearborn said.

"Dad's got a knife."

Lionel Dearborn let his arms sway, as if concentrating his strength, fixing it all in his fists. His eyes shifted to Chase. "We can still take him," he said, and Chase rolled his eyes. Dearborn looked back at the boy. "Where?"

The boy pointed.

Lionel Dearborn and Chase entered a moonstruck bedroom that contained a broken bed, an upended vanity, a smashed mirror, and a hole in the wall from which pebbles of plaster were still dropping like detonating drips of water. The baseball bat lay on the floor. Chase's gaze slanted down to a wide-eyed child, a girl in bedclothes huddled in a corner. Then he looked at what was half sprawled in another corner, his eye for a while taking in only the woman's bare feet and white shins. Her husband held a hand over her head like a cap, a gesture that seemed loving. His other hand poised the blade of a butcher knife at her throat.

Both Chase and Lionel Dearborn were jerked to a standstill, their arms dangling to a stop. Lionel Dearborn took a breath and said, "Don't do it, Chuckie."

Chuckie Dearborn's eyes were scummed, as if he were blind, but his face had a fiery glow, as if he were banked high. His expression was venomous.

Lionel Dearborn said, "It's not her you want to hurt. It's me. Ain't that right?"

Chase whispered, "The child."

Lionel Dearborn turned toward her. "Honey. You go on out."

The child's face was blurred, a pale smudge. She gazed up at her uncle but did not budge. She was immobile with terror.

"Let her be," said Chuckie Dearborn, his voice a distant rumble, his wife's head limp under his hand, as if she did not care what happened. "Unless you think the kid's yours. Could be."

"Don't be dumb, Chuckie."

"Maybe they're all yours."

"Chuckie, put it down."

"Fuck you."

Lionel Dearborn sought his sister-in-law's eyes but couldn't make contact. Chuckie Dearborn's face suddenly spurted a smile, and slowly he wrenched himself up, raising his wife with him, keeping the knife edged against her throat. Chase braced himself, while Lionel Dearborn seemed to sag, the fight going out of him.

"You want her?" Chuckie Dearborn said with vicious laughter. "Take her!" He hurled her like a rag doll at his brother. Then the knife flashed, as if he meant to use it on himself.

Chase moved.

He struck Chuckie Dearborn twice, under the heart and then in the throat, the blows almost simultaneous. Chuckie Dearborn went down like a baby.

Chase sat in Lionel Dearborn's darkened car, waiting, three cigarettes already smoked when another car pulled up behind him and a woman climbed out. She was wearing a kerchief and a shapeless Aran sweater, and she passed by without seeing him, breaking into a trot toward the house. He had no way of knowing who she was but guessed she was Lionel Dearborn's wife, which relaxed him because he felt no longer needed. The family was closing ranks, sealing him out. Feeling a breeze, he closed his eyes. When he opened them Lionel Dearborn was standing outside the car looking in. Chase said, "How is everything?"

"I put cuffs on him. Only way I could talk to him."

"He's sick. What are you going to do with him?"

"That's my problem." Dearborn lowered his head. "The keys are in there. Why don't you drive yourself home. I'll pick up the car later."

Chase slid behind the wheel.

Dearborn said, "The knife didn't scare you. How come?"

"I could see it."

"That supposed to mean something?"

Chase shrugged.

"I owe you," Dearborn said.

"Yes," Chase said. "You owe me."

"I mean *really* owe you."

"That's what I mean too."

"You got something in mind?"

"Yes. I want to be a cop again."

Back in the winter of '68, the night wind howling, Rupert Goetz and Frank Chase, bundled in blue, slipped out of their cruiser and slowly approached the hardware store. "Somebody's in there," Goetz whispered, and Chase nodded, their breath floating between them. Chase studied the front of the store. Goetz was his senior partner, his mentor. Goetz said, "No night light. That's what tells me."

Chase blew on his bare hands. Down at the corner an emergency power company crew was drilling and digging—quilted men in helmets struggling with the street. Chase said, "There are a lot of lights out. I think you're working on a tip."

Goetz grinned. "You're learning."

"This isn't even our district. At least let's call for a backup. We'll get in trouble if we don't."

"Not when you're with me, Frank."

"Why be heroes?"

"Guns are in there. That's what they're after, a couple of coons off the reservation. It'll look good in our files, Frank. You want to make detective, don't you?"

"You sure as hell do."

Goetz adjusted his cap. "I'm going in. You take the back."

Chase unholstered his service revolver as the wind rocked him. Then he walked squarely on his heels over the sealed surfaces of the sidewalk that rose like a hump of frozen fluid into the alley, which was pitch-black. Chase kept close to a wall, and the wall gave way to a doorway he didn't know was there until too late.

The knife struck him so fast and entered so easily that it

carried no pain, but he knew it was bad, more than bad, and immediately felt out of touch with everyone and everything except himself, though he was only vaguely aware that he had fallen and was lying neatly on the ground. The ground seemed warm, as if he were drying it out. Faintly he heard gunfire, which he thought should be louder because he could clearly see the bursts, one right after the other, somebody shooting a whole load.

"Frankie, I'm sorry." The voice was shattered, but he knew it belonged to Goetz and felt safe. "I got him, Frankie. I got him good."

He seemed to sleep, eyes open.

He saw blurred figures, men with hard hats and lanterns, some superimposed and showing too many arms and legs, as if they were mythological. He opened his mouth.

"Frankie, don't talk. Where the hell's the ambulance?"

"Hey, you shouldn't move him."

"Don't tell me what to do!"

Chase felt himself being lifted and then carried, lanterns bobbing around him, other men running ahead, the doors of the cruiser opening. Other hospitals were closer, but Goetz drove him across city to Mass General, the siren wailing and the roof lights blazing.

"Frankie, don't die."

He spent more than a month in Mass General, reaching a crisis quickly and recuperating slowly. Goetz was frequently at his bedside, along with a particular nurse who had taken a fancy to him. When they were alone, she pressed his hand and told him how lucky he was and how well he was coming along. The Pakistani doctor on duty when he'd been rolled in told him the thickness of his clothes had aided his luck. Goetz said, "The sonofabitch used a stiletto on you."

"Is he dead?"

"You better believe it."

"We in trouble?"

"Frankie, we're fucking heroes."

When he was released from the hospital, he went not to his own little apartment to gather his strength but to Goetz's spacious one. Goetz insisted. Goetz was solicitous, contrite, brotherly. Ida Goetz, five months pregnant, tended to him.

"I don't want to be in your way," he said.

"Hush up," she said, serving him soup, later changing the dressing on his wound, which he could not see without the aid of a mirror. The ugly hole seemed too small for the damage it had done. He almost didn't want her to see it, but he enjoyed her touch, the smell of the alcohol she used on him, and the scent of the soap she used on herself. Looking over his shoulder, he smiled. Her black hair, severely cut, and her striking dark eyes gave her an Egyptian look.

"I see now why guys get crushes on their nurse."

"Works both ways," she said. "Who's the nurse that's been phoning you? Is it serious?"

"Her goal is to marry a doctor."

Ida patted his back. "Tell her you're going to make detective."

"Who says?"

"Rupert. Maybe not right now, but in time."

He glanced away.

"Did I say something wrong?"

His eyes went back to her in the instant. "No, never!" he said in a tone that told her too much, embarrassing them both.

The day that Rupert Goetz drove him back to his own apartment, Chase said, "Tell me something, Rupert. The tip you got —that came from the guy who owns the store, right? He knew the place was going to get hit. We were doing him a favor. Otherwise, what the hell were we doing in Dorchester?"

"You want me to answer that, Frank?"

"Yes."

"The guy's got friends. The friends are going to be good to me. What's good for me will be good for you. You can count on it."

Chase stared out the window. They were entering Marlborough street, the buildings drab in the cold sunlight. Goetz grinned and slapped Chase's knee.

"Ida's going to miss you."

Chase lay on his stomach in the predawn shadows in the bedroom, listening to the beginning chirps of birds and feeling the tension go out of him as Ida, sitting on him, massaged his neck and shoulders. Her weight on him was warm, her fingers cool. He said, "You shouldn't have waited up."

"Did you think I could sleep?" She kneaded the muscles between his shoulder blades. "You should be doing this to me."

"I will."

"Lie still." Her thumbs pressed into him as her weight slid forward a little. Her knees closed tighter against him. "Tell me more about it."

"I was mostly worried about the little girl. If her mother's throat was going to get cut, I didn't want her to see it happen."

Ida shuddered and with a husky voice said, "You were crazy to go there unarmed."

"It was a family affair."

"Not *your* family."

"I was an honorary member."

Ida was quiet. Her fingers traveled farther down on his back. He couldn't feel it, but he knew she was touching the small puckered scar he frequently forgot was there. Memories of an earlier time, a different bed, a less intimate touch welled up in him. In a distant way he smelled the alcohol and certainly the soap. He screwed his head around on the pillow. Ida, naked, seemed ghostly.

"What's the matter?"

"Thinking how lucky I am," he murmured.

"Frank, you were damned lucky. Please stay away from that Dearborn. You're not a cop any more."

"We need him."

"I need you," she said and climbed off him. She pulled the

covers up and found a place in his arms. In the room's dim quiet they drifted into sleep. The ring of the telephone jarred them out of it.

"My God," said Ida, springing up on an elbow. "Who can that be at this hour?"

"Let me get it," Chase said, swinging an arm out as though to stifle the phone as it rang again. "Must be Dearborn."

She watched him answer it and knew by his face that he was wrong about the caller.

Rupert Goetz said to Chase: "I want my family back."

29.

THE PISTOL

"You make me sound like a thief," Chase said, all the tension returning, muscles tightening. "As if I stole them from you. I didn't."

"Hang up," Ida urged him in a whisper, her body as tense as his, her legs tucked under her. "We don't need this."

Chase placed a hand on her thigh but kept the phone to his ear. He said, "Am I going to have trouble with you, Rupert?"

"Trouble?" Goetz's laugh was low and bitter. "You don't have trouble, Frank. I do."

"What kind of trouble?"

"We're straying from the subject. Family, Frank. That's the subject. I think we better renegotiate."

"You been drinking, Rupert?"

"Of course I've been drinking, but did you ever see me drunk? Never. And you never will, buddy."

"Do you know what time it is?"

"Frank, I don't worry about time any more. You reach a position like mine, you come and go as you please and do what you want. I'm a chief, Frank. I fart, and twenty guys yell 'excuse me.' That's what I've achieved. How about yourself?"

"Where are you?"

"Where am I? How the hell do I know?" He took time to cough. "Let me speak to my kid."

"Come on, Rupert. He's asleep. Do you really want me to wake him?"

Goetz hesitated. "What about Ida?"

"What about her?"

"She lying there beside you? She listening? Frank, I want you to do something for me. Tell her that I love her."

Chase grimaced, his hand slipping off Ida's thigh. She was staring at him with eyes as black as carbon, sitting on the bed with a propped arm. "No," Chase said into the phone. "I'm not going to tell her that."

Goetz's laugh this time was less bitter but more ironic. "Why not, Frank? Afraid?"

Chase disconnected.

"What won't you tell me?" Ida asked.

Chase reached for his cigarettes. "That he loves you."

"You were right," she said. "It wasn't worth repeating."

When he did not respond, she left the bed and slipped on a robe. Dawn was just breaking.

"I'll make coffee," she said.

Goetz hung the phone up hard and, kneading his forehead, walked toward the counter for coffee. He was in a cafeteria that years ago had been a Hayes Bickford and since had been under other managements, each progressively worse. The walls were greasy paneling and the floor a soiled checkerboard with missing squares. The counterman, who looked like someone Goetz might have arrested once, was joking with a derelict who might have spent the night at one of the tables. Now he was leaving in a shuffle.

"Where're you going?" the counterman shouted. The voice had a rusted quality, harsh on the ear. The derelict, deadpan, glanced back over the sag of his shoulder.

"London and Paris."

"No kidding!" The counterman's smile was quick and rubbery. "Hope the ticket's one-way."

Their humor at that ungodly hour astounded Goetz, also depressed him. And he did not like the looks of the eggs somebody was eating. Neither did he appreciate the smell of the place. He stood at the counter behind an aged Chinese, who was wearing raised heels and studying prices crayoned on a piece of cardboard. The heels gave the old man a little height, and the prices turned him away. The counterman, who earlier had given Goetz a knowing appraisal, now extended a smile. Goetz snapped a ten-dollar bill and dropped it on the counter.

"Black coffee, and give the change to the Chink. Tell him to go eat someplace decent."

"Sure you want to do that?" The counterman winked. "He could buy and sell us both."

"Not me he couldn't. Give it to him anyway, and give me my coffee in a paper cup, forget the cap."

The counterman busied himself. Goetz stood with his shoulders squared, trying to will away a headache. His tie was loose, and he tightened it. He had smirched his shirt but could not remember doing it.

"Here you go, friend."

Goetz took the coffee, blew on it, sipped a little, and then carried it out of the place to his car, parked in front. As soon as he drove off, the counterman pocketed the ten and went to the telephone. After about twenty rings he got an answer.

He said, "I got something might interest you."

"At noon I might be interested," the voice said. "Not at fucking six o'clock in the morning."

"I figured this you'd want to know now. Guess who's tanked up and giving his money away?"

Rupert Goetz attended a routine meeting and then worked at his desk, reading reports, initialing correspondence, returning telephone calls, consuming coffee. At times he stared blankly at a wall. At noon he had a sandwich delivered but didn't touch it. Instead he called in a rookie detective and chewed him out for bruising a suspect during interrogation.

"If you don't know how to hit, don't hit."

"I'm sorry," the young man said, unable to meet Goetz's

ice-blue eyes. Goetz's stomach settled. He reached for his sandwich.

"OK, take off."

An hour later he conferred with Lieutenant Donovan over current cases, including a number of rape-murders in Roxbury, a couple of them particularly brutal.

"How are we doing there?" asked Goetz, though he had already read the reports.

"Our guys aren't the right color," Donovan said with a shrug.

"Chase never had a problem there."

"Frank was special."

"Not that special."

Both men lapsed into silence. Donovan sat crosslegged directly in front of the desk, one foot stuck out. The black shoe was enormous, the toe scuffed. Regarding Goetz with concern, he said, "You have a bad night, Rupert?"

"Why?"

"You look like hell."

"That's funny," Goetz said. "I feel fine."

Donovan spoke slowly. "Anything I can do for you?"

Goetz gave him a weary grin. "I'm a big boy."

Twenty minutes to a half hour later Goetz cleared his desk and called it a day, leaving instructions that in an emergency he could be reached at home. He drove somewhat erratically in midafternoon traffic toward Charles River Park. Vigorously he rubbed his eyes, though his greater need was not for sleep but for Sherry. The urge to be with her had come as soon as he had finished with Donovan. Purposely he ran a red light, but his reflexes were good. He missed a speeding taxi with an inch or two to spare.

He stepped into a dim apartment, the curtains drawn, and immediately smelled pot, which didn't distress him. He was used to the aroma. Standing near the sofa, he slipped off his suitcoat and began unbuttoning his vest. Something was wrong.

He could feel it.

"You home?" he hollered, uncomfortably dry-lipped.

Sherry bounded toward him from the dark direction of the bedroom. A sweat-soaked T-shirt was all she wore. She rushed into his arms with a force that would have knocked a smaller man over. Her hair was wildly tangled, her smile ghastly, and her heart heaving so hard it scared him. The T-shirt, sticking to her skin, was not hers and not his. She breathed deeply into his ear.

"Don't say anything, luv. Please."

He spoke because he had to. "What the hell's going on?"

"I'm high as a kite," she said, rising on her toes and grinding into him. "Hug me."

She was warm and sloppy in his arms, and her hair flopped against his face. He went silent because of an acute feeling he could handle no increase of disorder in his life, and he gave in to the excitement of her fingers tearing at his shirt, the buttons snapping and popping. Then his attention was caught by another noise.

"Don't look," she said as the shape of a man stole by them to the door. He saw without looking, and he stood indifferently, as if the stranger lacked all semblance to reality. "Kiss me," Sherry said, her hands all over him while trying to drag him down to the floor, which he let her do. He kissed her as if to devour her face and slid a hand down into the heat of her. She tore at his pants, part of a four-hundred-dollar suit, the crotch ripping at the seam. "Fuck me," she said.

He did.

She lay on the rug near the sofa, stretched out on her side with an arm cushioning her head. She was more asleep than awake. The stereo was on low, Ray Price singing "For The Good Times," which Goetz listened to from across the room. He sat in a soft chair with his ruined pants in his lap and with only one stocking on. His knees, skinned bright red from the prolonged activity on the rug, looked ready to ignite. He held his gift to her in his right hand, the .22-caliber automatic pistol. It was aimed at her head.

"You don't think I'll do it."

She stirred imperceptibly. "I feel so good, Rupert, I don't give a shit."

The weapon was a weight he had been holding in position for three minutes. His eyes were a washy blue. Hers were closed.

"I've killed before," he said.

"I'm sure."

She raised an elbow, bent an arm behind her, and scratched her bottom. He squinted and sighed, watching her arm slump back into place, as if it had never moved. He felt like a ventriloquist holding a sexual conversation with a female mannequin.

"Look at me, Sherry."

"I don't want to."

"Look at me," he said in a penetrating tone and raised the weapon to his own head. She opened her eyes.

"I wish I had a camera."

His finger tightened on the trigger. "Are you daring me to do it?"

"No, Rupert, then you might do it."

She was quite alert now, and he, unexpectedly, was smiling. He seemed to be counting seconds, slowly, as if there were something else besides life and death, a third condition ready to leak through at any moment.

"No way," he said, lowering the weapon. "I've got more important things to do."

30.

THE ATTACK

Dance snatched up the paper bag. He left the Dodge Dart on Wildwood, cut through an abrupt strip of woods, and made his way to the back of Chase's house, the moonlight beating brightly on the grass. He used his free hand to swipe viciously at a sudden swarm of mosquitoes. Coming off a high, he was out of sorts and dropping into a state of orneriness that resembled courage, and he was a sight because of the bandage over his nose and the unhealed cuts in his cheek, the cuts reopened from shaving. Chase's wagon was in the drive, but it appeared that nobody was home. It was not yet bedtime, but the house was unlit, or seemed to be.

Moonlight lay on the garage floor like shards of glass and guided his way. He sidestepped a bicycle and pushed a lawn mower to one side. The door into the house was unlocked, and the house was quiet except for a distant drone. He slipped easily from one shadowy room to another, his movements instinctive. The drone grew louder but didn't bother him. He knew what it was, and he knew somebody was there. Sticking a hand into the paper bag, he walked quietly toward flickers of light.

The light and sound came from a television, rapid pictures and an exchange of gunfire on "Hawaii Five-O." David Goetz, wearing his baseball cap, sat on the floor in front of the set, his arms propped behind him. He knew all at once that someone was behind him, and he didn't move. Something told him not to. He watched a shadow fall over him and then saw the toes of a man's construction shoes.

"Take it easy, kid." Dance's voice was a whisper. His hand emerged empty from the bag. He smiled. "I didn't scare you, did I?"

Speechless, David stared up at the battered face and shook his head. Dance squatted beside him.

"I'm a good pal of your father's. Your stepfather, I mean. Where is he?"

David relaxed a little. "He's out."

"No kidding." Dance tucked the bag under one arm. "Your mother too?"

"They're up the street. You can see the house from here." David cocked his head. "I didn't hear you ring."

"How could you? You were watching television. Who's that there, McGarrett?"

David nodded a smile. "He's my favorite. He reminds me of my father. My real one."

"Don't look like him?"

"You know my father?"

"Sure, kid. I met him a long time ago." Dance's squat became uncomfortable, and he stretched out a leg and sat down. He drew two purplish capsules from his shirt pocket, jiggled them in his palm, and then ate them, chewing hard. He smiled at the boy. "You want to try one?"

"What are they?"

"They give you a bounce," he said, grinning when David shook his head. The grin frightened David, whose face became a fragile bubble under his cap. "Who do you look like kid. Your mother or father?"

"My mother, I guess."

"Who do you think I look like?"

David rubbed a hand across his mouth. "I don't know."

"I don't look too good, right?

"I guess you got hurt."

"You guess I got hurt, huh. Jesus, you're a smart kid." Dance pulled himself up. "Come on, let's go find your folks."

David shrank back, aware now that too much was wrong. "You don't need me."

"Sure I need you." Dance yanked him to his feet. "Didn't nobody tell you that?"

The boy fought, all of a sudden, pulling and scratching and trying to flee. His aim was to hide near a telephone: a number to call in an emergency. His stepfather had given it to him, had made him memorize it, had told him what to say. But he had no chance to do anything. Dance struck with an open hand, and he crashed against the television set.

They left the house as Dance had entered it, through the garage. David walked as if sightless, with Dance's hand on the back of his neck. Dance's other hand clutched the bag. They marched in the moonlight over the front lawn. They were near the street when Dance stopped short, jerking the boy still. A noise came out of dark shrubs, then a pair of eyes. A cat raced across their path, and Dance's arm whipped out. He fired through the bag, the sound cushioned by the silencer, and hit the cat in the middle, a lucky shot. The cat seemed to break in half. Dance had lost his grip on David, and he whirled around with a naked gun, the bag burning at his feet.

The boy was gone.

"Anybody for skinny-dipping?" Lee Gunderman said and saw her husband flinch. "For God's sake, Karl. I was only kidding. Well, half kidding."

The Gundermans' pool was large and the area around it contained by a chain-link fence, with an unnecessary number of gates, four, three of them padlocked. The dead-still water reflected the moon, a streak of lamplight, and the blue sizzle of an electric bug-killer high on a pole. Lee, on her third whiskey-sour, was the most relaxed of the four figures seated at the poolside table. Her husband was the most ill at ease. He said

to the Chases, "We should get together more often like this."
Lee laughed. "Say it like you mean it, Karl."

Gunderman's large face went blank. Frank and Ida Chase stirred uncomfortably, both still on their first drink. Ida said, "I don't think he'd have said it if he didn't mean it."

"Of course he means it," Lee said, fussing with the low front of her blouse, pulling it higher. "But you'd never know it by his voice. The only time he puts strength in it is when he's selling a house."

Chase lit a cigarette. Ida whispered, "You already have one going."

Lee said, "You should hear him sometime, depending upon the customer, when he speaks in a British accent you'd swear was real. Not bad for a guy born and brought up in South Boston. Of course he's all Andover now. Aren't you, dear?"

Gunderman was not listening. He was peering over his shoulder into the dark. "I thought I heard somebody rattle a gate," he said, turning back.

"Anyway," said Lee, cocking her head. "Karl thinks we should spend more time together, the four of us, since we are sort of like family. In a way."

"What way?" said Ida, but Lee went on as if Ida hadn't spoken.

"Actually we should have taken you two in tow from the start. Prepared you better for the town."

Ida said, "Smooth our rough edges."

Gunderman was suddenly on his feet. "I did hear something."

Then there was a pinging sound. Everybody heard it. It dimpled the deadness of the pool. Frank Chase, who should have reacted the fastest, took a slow drag on his cigarette.

Lee, drink in hand, stood up. "It must be one of the kids."

Karl Gunderman staggered back a step and half-pointed. "It's a guy with a gun."

Chase reacted.

He pitched the table over, knocked Ida off her chair, and yelled at the Gundermans, "Duck!" They didn't. Lee stood frozen in place, and her husband, swaying toward her, became her shield, a wide white-shirted target.

Dance's voice came out of the dark. "Chase!"

Chase's arm shot up, and he yanked Lee to the ground, next to Ida. Gunderman stayed standing, a soldier. Chase rasped, "Get down!"

There was another ping, this one explosively close. Tile shot up, chunks of it. Gunderman, with a hysterical little laugh, said, "He's still behind the fence. He can't find the right gate."

Chase sought Ida, fearing she was hurt, not a word out of her. She was all right. So was Lee, who gazed at him wild-eyed, grabbed at his sleeve, and murmured something about her husband.

"Chase!" Dance's voice again, this time curling out of the darkness, coming closer.

Chase said to Gunderman, "Where is he?"

Gunderman did not answer, for his eyes were now clamped shut. He stood firmly in place, powerful and pure, steel-like, mindless. Ida, emerging from shock, clutched Chase's hand. "Do you have your gun?"

He found himself smiling inanely while listening to a rattle, the right gate. "Would you believe it, no."

"Frank, kiss me. Just once and hard."

Chase couldn't find her mouth, nor she his. Lee was pulling at them both. Chase tugged at Gunderman, trying to knock him down. "Karl, you're going to get it."

Dance came through the gate, slowly, each step measured, his weapon raised. The blue bug light bathed his face and made his bandaged nose a mask. He called to Chase, "You're boxed."

Chase gripped the upended table, as if to charge with it, but it was too heavy to lift. He hollered, "Hold it! I have a gun."

Dance hesitated. Then he laughed. "You had a gun, you'd've used it."

Chase rose. He did it with resignation, Ida clutching unsuccessfully at his clothes. Lee screamed.

Moving closer, Dance laughed again. His weapon was aimed at Chase, but he was looking at Karl Gunderman. "Who the fuck are you?"

Those were the last words he spoke.

Sergeant Lionel Dearborn shot him through the back of the head.

31.

DECISIONS

"This private enough?"

"This is good," said Rupert Goetz, carrying a briefcase. "Can you lock the door?"

"It's not necessary."

"I'd feel better."

The man clicked the lock. His name was Charlie, and he was a broker and a boyhood friend of Goetz's, the same tenement block. Charlie ambled to a desk and sat behind it, tipping back. His crew cut was going gray, and his reading glasses rested halfway down his nose. The ring on his right hand was from Boston College. Goetz dropped the briefcase on the desk and arranged a chair in front of the desk. They were in a small rear office of a brokerage firm on State Street.

Goetz opened the briefcase and casually pushed it across the desk, with Charlie showing no surprise. They had talked earlier on the phone. Charlie tipped forward and with both hands adjusted his glasses. His facial features were large, especially his nose and chin. Taking his time, he counted the money in the briefcase. When he finished he shut the briefcase and worked the metal snaps shut, Goetz watching.

"Is it what I said?"

Charlie nodded, impressed, silent.

Goetz said, "I want it working quietly for my kid till he comes of age. That's well over seven years. The meantime, he doesn't have to know anything about it. It'll be a nice surprise."

Charlie nodded again.

"And you'll be like the executor or something. Leave me out of it."

"The bonds I mentioned will be best."

"You know about that stuff better than me." Goetz's mind seemed elsewhere, as if from sudden leaps in thought. Then his attention returned to Charlie. "As long as you arrange it right."

"I don't think you have to worry."

"That's why I came to you."

"You feeling all right, Rupert?"

"I'm feeling fine. Why?"

"You look a little under the weather."

"Never felt better. What are you doing?"

"Writing you a receipt."

"No receipt. You and I don't need one."

Charlie tore it up. "You want the statements to come to me."

"Right." Goetz's eyes were half closed. "I already told you, you handle everything."

"Yes, I can do that. Rupert, is anything the matter?"

"You're going to piss me off, you keep asking those kind of questions."

Charlie nudged the briefcase to one side. "Rupert, what really happened with Johnny Kale? Can I ask that?"

"Yeah," said Goetz, standing flatfooted. "He was a loser. Aren't we all."

The two men left the office. Charlie carried the briefcase.

Returning to headquarters, Goetz called Lieutenant Donovan into his office. Donovan had a Styrofoam cup of coffee in each hand and placed one of the cups on the desk. "I thought you might want that."

"I do."

Donovan seated himself, his back straight and his feet planted. His face was expressionless. Goetz sat sideways with his feet on the desk. Cautiously, using only one hand, he lifted the lid from his cup.

"Careful, it's hot."

"I can see that."

Goetz flipped the lid into the wastebasket, a tricky shot. He had done it hundreds of times and never missed any more. He stared at Donovan, who had lines in his face like a spider web.

"How's your daughter?" Goetz asked. Donovan had three daughters, but Goetz never asked about any of them except the youngest, an exceedingly bright woman who had gone to Paris on a scholarship and stayed there.

"I got a card from her the other day. She ate at a McDonald's on the Champs-Elysées."

"You say that nice. I didn't know you spoke French."

"A lot of things you don't know about me."

Goetz smiled cunningly. "You think I don't appreciate you."

"I didn't say that."

"Didn't have to." Goetz sipped his coffee. It was still steaming, still hot enough to burn. He pulled in his lips and regarded Donovan with a different kind of smile, more intimate. He said, "You're not far from retirement, are you?"

Donovan nodded.

"How'd you like to go out in a blaze of glory?" Goetz said.

Donovan waited.

"That Spitaleri kid. Still think you can get him?"

Donovan showed surprise. Then he smiled broadly. "Chief, I can nail him to a cross."

"Do it," Goetz said.

The lawyer sat in his desk chair next to the open window and sucked in sea air. The man in the jacket stood nearby with his hands in his pockets. The lawyer said, "We should've bet on that one. I'd have won."

"Dance was crazy," the man in the jacket said. "That always worried me."

"Now we don't have to worry."

The lawyer swiveled, his face cut by sharp slices of sunshine.
"I always worry. That's my strength."

"Your nephew says thank you."

"That's something else that worries me."

"I was surprised you let him come back."

The lawyer sighed. "My sister worries. She doesn't believe
anybody's all right unless she sees with her own eyes."

"You going to let him stay there long?"

"Couple days, that's all. You keep an eye on him, personally."

"What about our friend?"

"You keep an eye on him too."

"I can't be in two places the same time."

"Yes, you can," said the lawyer. "You get somebody to cut
you in half."

"ANDOVER COP KILLS HUB GUNMAN" was among
the headlines on the front page of the Boston *Globe,* late edi-
tion. Sergeant Lionel Dearborn had the paper but did not read
the story. He had not talked with reporters and did not intend
to. The police chief and Lieutenant Moynihan from the district
attorney's office were handling all interviews. Dearborn remained at his desk in the basement of the police station, occasionally glancing at his watch but never really reading the time.
Sporadically, almost imperceptibly, his hands trembled. Finally
he left the desk and headed for the stairs, stopping when he
heard the thump of somebody coming down them.

"Sergeant Dearborn?"

Dearborn glared at an aging man with a beard, whom he
recognized as a reporter from the *Herald American,* one of the
old pros. "You're not supposed to be down here," he said
roughly.

"Right, I know," the man said quickly, "but I've only got a
couple of questions. What about this Frank Chase guy? Why

was he a target?"

"Use your head," said Dearborn sourly. "He was a cop for ten years. Gives him enemies he probably doesn't even know about."

"Yeah, but that Dancewicz guy was a hitman."

"That what he was?" Dearborn consulted his watch. "Look out, I gotta go."

"Why'd you shoot him in the back of the head, sergeant?"

"I didn't have a choice," Dearborn said and shouldered by the reporter, nearly knocking him down.

It was hot, with the sun pounding the street. Dearborn trudged past Friendly's and on past the library, a bit of a climb, which reddened his face. A fast trot across the street against oncoming traffic reddened it more. He blundered into the way of a woman stepping out of the Andover Gift Shop and caught a whiff of her perfume, which was overly sweet. For a moment he feared he might be sick, and the next moment he was sure he would be. Then it passed.

When he entered Finn's, customers turned to gaze at him, all with deference. Some looked as though they wanted to come forward and give him a hero's handshake. Keeping his eyes straight ahead, he walked to the back, dropped into a booth, and waited for his sister-in-law to come to him. Clearing a table, she glanced at him as if he were just another customer. Finally she approached him.

"You want a menu?"

"No," he said and realized that the timbre of his voice was different, less commanding. She looked down at him impassively, as if she had mastered grief and pain. He said, "Can you sit down for a minute?"

"No," she said. "I have other customers."

"How's Chuckie?"

"You'll have to ask him," she said coldly. "We don't talk."

"What about the kids?"

"They're going to be OK, maybe. The question is, how am I going to be."

Dearborn groped for an answer but had none. He wanted to touch her hand, for there had once been tenderness between them, though he knew that most of the tenderness had come from her.

"You look tired," he said.

"Yes, I am."

When he reached for her hand, she turned sharply away.

32.

LAST SUPPER

A long thin hand touched Karl Gunderman's arm, catching him unawares, and he seemed to shiver and stiffen all at once, as if he had been stabbed with a blade of ice. Then his head swiveled. His face, looming large, was too waxy, too white.

"Karl you work too hard."

"It's all I know how to do."

"You don't get enough sun."

His wife now had a hand on each of his arms, gripping him, as though she had the strength to pick him up and carry him somewhere. His face sagged to one side from encroaching fatigue, but his shoulders stayed straight. He had on a neat striped tie she had chosen for him at the Andover Shop, though the colors didn't quite go with the suit he was wearing.

She said, "I'm going to work for you."

He gave her a vague uncomprehending smile.

"I'm going to involve myself in the business. I think I should. I certainly have the energy."

He nodded, standing slightly pigeon-toed, still in her grasp. She raised her quick angular face to his. Her mouth quivered.

"I could have lost you, Karl."

"I could have lost you."

"No. You stood in front of me. You protected me."

"I still don't remember anything I did."

"I do, Karl. I do." She stood on raised toes to kiss his cheek, and the kiss embarrassed him, as though he didn't deserve it.

He said, "I talked to Frank."

She let her hands drift from his arms, sensing he wanted to move them. She waited.

"I told him he shouldn't stay in this town. I told him I didn't care if he did, but personally I felt he shouldn't."

"You did right."

"I told him he could have his job for as long as he wanted, but I said I wanted him to know my feelings."

"What did he say?"

"He thanked me."

"I thank you too." She passionately tried to grip his arms again, but he stayed free. He took a breath, as if something were sucking at his heart.

"I told him something else, and I'm telling you. I told him he scares me. I told him he scares me more than anyone I've known."

"They're different from us, Karl. You were right all along. They're not our kind of people."

"He understood. I'm sure he understood."

"I don't care if he did or not," Lee said heatedly, and Gunderman looked at her with a mix of curiosity and concern.

"I do," he said firmly. "For my peace of mind."

Frank Chase stood on the front lawn, where the neighbors next door could see him. He felt their eyes and even their fears. It was going to rain, and he could feel that too, which made him wonder whether he was getting arthritis, a cop's disease. Stepping to his left, away from the failing sunlight, he took himself out of range of the neighbors, nice people, though Ida had had more to do with them than he. He tightened his tie. He had on a business suit, the sort he wore when selling houses.

Somebody touched him.

He did not flinch. The touch was too familiar. Ida had come out of the house and approached him without his seeing or hearing her. He had a moment of hazy vision and did not see her properly.

"Where's David?" he asked.

"Watching us from a window. Don't look."

"I've put him through a lot."

"He's a beautiful kid, Frank."

"More than beautiful," Chase said in a strong whisper. He moistened his mouth. "But we'll be wrenching him up again. I know that's not good."

"He might be tougher than you think."

"I hope so. I'm not too good with kids."

"Frank, he loves you."

"I love him."

"Tell him so. He's like a lot of people. He needs to be reassured."

They were touching. Ida's hand was hot in his. The dark eyes watched him. She had a few hard lines in her face, and Chase felt responsible for them, though he had a few of his own, put there as if by a knife.

"Are you expecting a customer?" she asked.

"No."

"Are you afraid we won't be able to sell it?"

"That won't be a problem."

"What's the matter, then?"

He looked at her carefully. "Will you miss it?"

"We've had lousy luck here, but, yes, I'll miss it. A little. Won't you?"

"Hard to tell." He attempted a smile. "I won't miss the pool. I prefer to swim in real water."

She winked. "I'll swim anywhere with you."

"Are you sure?"

"I'm flexible, Frank, and I'm not hard to please. I don't think you ever believed that." His eyes watered, which embarrassed him, but she would not let him look away. She said, "All we need do is live decently. We can do that, can't we?"

"I want to."

"Who's going to stop us?"

"No one," he said. She let him glance away. He watched a robin pulling at the lawn, no cat around to disturb it. He said, "In ways I'm still a cop."

"What does that have to do with anything?"

"Cops are funny people, maybe even a little bent."

"You're not bent, Frank. Never think that."

"I'm not straight either."

"Who is? Is the mayor of Boston straight? The president of the United States? As far as I'm concerned, you stand taller."

"You put me in big company. Only a mother would do that."

Her eyes penetrated his. "No, Frank. A wife."

She walked with him across the lawn to the ranch wagon. He had an appointment to keep, no expectations. He did not want to be disappointed. Ida arched her feet for a kiss, and he gave her a deep one. They held their embrace, neighbors watching from a window. She spoke into his shirt.

"I love you, Frank."

"I don't think it's any secret the way I feel about you. It never was. Maybe that was the problem."

"No problem now." She lifted her face and slipped her hands over his backside. Her eyes turned somber for a moment. "Where are you meeting him?"

"Behind the library."

"Why there?"

"I don't think he wants anybody to see us."

"Will it take long?"

"It shouldn't."

"I want you to take David and me out to eat afterwards. Someplace nice. OK?"

"Andover Inn?"

"Perfect."

"We may not have cause to celebrate."

"It's not a celebration, Frank. Just a regrouping."

He climbed into the wagon. She closed the door after him, softly, and then stepped back, her arms crossed.

"Good luck," she said.

Lionel Dearborn had a book in his hand. He approached the ranch wagon and said, "Don't get out." He stood by the open window of the wagon and looked in at Chase, who appeared infinitely calm but was absolutely tense.

"What's the book?"

Dearborn did not answer. Instead he moved one step back, as if he wanted to stay out of Chase's range and have nothing more to do with him, which Chase sensed with a stir of sadness. Dearborn said, "Topford. Ever hear of the town?"

Chase nodded. "About fifteen miles from here. Pleasant place."

"That's right. And a three-man department, one vacancy. Take it now and you could be chief in a year."

Chase raised his eyebrows. "I'd think you'd be interested in that for yourself."

"I like Andover." Dearborn's tone was cold, almost nasty. "It's my town."

Chase shifted his gaze to the brick back of the library, ivy crawling up it. "How do I apply?"

"In person. Fast." Dearborn stood quite still, a weariness showing in his face. "I'll be truthful with you. The pay sucks. That a factor?"

"No."

"Good."

Chase looked at him. "Thanks."

Dearborn nodded halfheartedly. Chase extended a hand out the window, and after a hesitation Dearborn stepped forward and gripped it. They exchanged a very small smile.

"Good luck," Dearborn said.

"I guess you heard what happened to your nephew."

The lawyer did not bother to respond. He stood rigidly by the open window, his hands clenched and his back ramrod-straight. His face was set rather like a dead man's, with the bones ready to burst the skin.

"I'm sorry," the man in the jacket said, more apologetic than sympathetic. He too stood tensely, a gloss of sweat on his upper lip. He added, "It wasn't my fault."

"No one said it was." The lawyer's voice was low, with no inflections. His head swayed a little, as if he had a crimp in his neck. "It's going to rain. I can feel it in every bone."

"Wasn't good the way they grabbed him. Right in front of your sister."

"I don't want to hear."

The man in the jacket shifted his weight and planted his hands in his pockets. "What should I do?"

The lawyer looked at him somewhat nearsightedly. "What I said."

The man nodded.

"Use who you want," the lawyer said with a distant air, as if part of him were no longer accessible.

"It could cause talk, taking out a cop that high up."

"Then make it look like he did it himself. I have to tell you everything?"

The man shook his head. One of his eyes seemed bad, perhaps from a cold. He said, "Just so I know, what about the other guy, Chase."

"Forget Chase. He did right." The lawyer's head straightened, and his voice was dismissive. "My wife and I are going to spend some time on the islands. Call me there when it's done.

Rupert Goetz, sitting alone in the crowded Newbury Steakhouse, ordered a tenderloin. His gesture was expansive, and his elbow brushed a fork to the floor. His eyes held the waitress, as if no one else should have her attention. Her hair was black, with no hint of gray, and he pictured her brushing it with a motion like Ida's. He said, "What are you doing afterwards?"

She viewed him without surprise. "I live with somebody."

"I do too."

"Then you see the problem."

"No," he said.

She smiled. She did not want to be rude. She edged away, which he scarcely noticed, as if he were going into a dream. He was oblivious to other patrons, soft-edged shadows seemingly seated far away, though some were close enough to touch. After a while, he closed his eyes to think. The lids fluttered. He remembered once giving his son a hard slap for a little mistake. He regretted the hit.

When he opened his eyes he saw the waitress approaching him with a plate in one hand and a fork in the other, as if she meant to feed him. Her expression seemed playful, like Ida's whenever she had wanted to tease him. His mouth stretched to its limits in a smile. He was aware of her face but not of the rest of her. The face, becoming more and more like Ida's, floated in and out of his line of vision.

"Enjoy," she said.

He spread a napkin over his lap and flexed his arms. In his mind he was loving Ida, holding on to her, absorbing her, which was like absorbing himself. She bore his odor and much of his sweat. She reached around and slapped his bare bottom, as one would a newborn.

His laugh was attention-getting.

People watched from other tables, the bold and bloody bites of a man who liked his meat rare, practically raw. He sat loose and easy in his three-piece suit, unarmed, a man having his last supper.